The First Time Again

Barbara Meyers

The First Time Again was originally published by Samhain Publishing, Ltd., May 2013 and edited by Christa Desir

This edition published by Barbara Meyers, LLC, and edited by Alison Nissen

Cover by Steven Novak, Novak Illustration

Print ISBN: 978-1-951286-13-2

Digital ISBN: ISBN: 978-1-951286-40-8

1. Contemporary Romance – Fiction. 2. North Carolina (U.S.) – Fiction.

3. Family Relationships – Fiction.

THE FIRST TIME AGAIN

4. Small Town – Fiction.

5. Sports – Fiction. I. Title.

Chapter One

♥

Hayley Lynn Christopher

and

Raymond Matthew Braddock

Were united in Holy Matrimony

At Good Shepard Chapel

Perrish, Florida

On the Twenty-fifth of June, Two thousand—

Trey Christopher dropped the cream-colored card embossed with swirling pink roses back on the passenger seat. He'd stopped for a fast-food meal on the road, but why he'd thought it'd be a good idea to sort through the pile of mail while he ate, he had no idea.

He stared at the half-eaten grilled chicken sandwich in his hand and realized he no longer had any appetite.

He shoved it back in the paper bag it came in and set it aside. Maybe he'd be hungry later, though he doubted it. Out of the corner of his eye he glanced at Hayley's wedding announcement once more before burying it under a stack of magazines and bills.

He put the car in gear and headed back onto the highway. He had another couple of hours of driving, three at the most before he reached his grandparents' place outside Ednaville, North Carolina. He'd hoped to arrive before nightfall, but it didn't look like that was going to happen. He didn't want to negotiate the curving lane to their place in the dark, but he'd have no choice.

Damn. He'd lost Hayley for good, and it bothered him more than he thought it would. They'd been divorced for over two years. Things had not been good between them for at least two before that.

He'd made a half-hearted attempt to get Hayley back when he got out of rehab last summer. She'd laughed in his face, which, he knew was no better than he deserved. He'd treated her horribly and he couldn't blame her if she didn't want to sign on with him again. Hayley had adored him, and he'd taken her love and trampled on it without realizing what he was throwing away until it was too late.

He glanced in the rearview mirror and turned up the sound system another notch. Too bad he couldn't drown out his own thoughts.

Hayley had moved on without him. She'd adopted her stepsister's little boy and married Ray who treated her the way she deserved to be treated. With love and respect.

Ray was probably gaga over her, which is how it was supposed to be. Hayley had flat out told him she'd never felt for anyone the way she felt about Ray. Her implied *not even you* had sat there for several seconds before she purposely changed the subject.

No one's gaga over you Trey reminded himself. He'd gone from being a happily married, professional quarterback on a Super Bowl winning team to an unemployed, divorced has-been with a substance abuse problem and a bum knee.

Pity Party. Table for One. The words from his drug counselor at Mooring Pines popped into his head. Brad had warned him not to get too down on himself. Part of the process of a recovering addict was not only to ask forgiveness from those he'd hurt, but also to learn to forgive himself.

Easier said than done. No one could be harder on Trey than he was on himself. He'd let so many people down.

Hayley, at least, forgave him. The last time he'd talked to her she'd even *thanked* him. The divorce forced her to grow up, she said, and helped her figure out who she was and what she wanted. She'd learned not to settle for anything less.

Money was pretty much all he had left from his former life.

Money would pay to renovate his grandparents' farmhouse left to him after his grandmother's death last year.

He sniffed remembering the funeral. Before that he hadn't been home in ages, and he'd only been out of rehab for a couple of months. He was still feeling his way along in a world where he didn't view everything through an alcohol and painkiller induced stupor.

His mother had hugged him for a long time, and he'd stupidly clung to her as if he were a small child instead of a 6'3" former athlete. His father hadn't been quite as friendly, nor had Trey expected him to be. The old man had made a lot of sacrifices to get Trey into an SEC school to give him a shot at a pro career.

All you can do is try. Brad's voice again, warning him not to expect too much. Healing takes time. How many times had Trey heard that? A hundred? A thousand?

It could take his dad a month to forgive him. Or a year. Or ten years. No matter how long it took, Trey would keep trying. *One day at a time.*

He turned the stereo up another notch until the car vibrated from the bass pouring through the speakers.

Trey's mood turned from sour to foul by the time he reached the outskirts of Ednaville, population two thousand, nine hundred seventy-three. He'd fought his way through a thunderstorm fifty miles back, his knee ached like a sonofabitch, and he had to pee. Badly. As in a half hour ago. He'd decided he could hold it until he got to the house. *Bad idea.*

He ignored the sign posted just inside the city limits. He figured the local cops, of which he was pretty sure there were still at least two, would be home, possibly in bed by now. He wondered if old Charlie Langston was still on the job. A typical easygoing country boy, Charlie'd been ancient when Trey was growing up here, but he could be counted on to break up the occasional teen drinking party. He'd escort the unfortunate offender home and have "a word" with their parents. That's all it took for him to keep the peace. He rarely made an actual arrest or handed out citations for any infraction.

Good old Charlie, Trey thought fondly. He himself had been one of those less than fortunate teenagers who'd been escorted home in an inebriated state. His parents grounded him for a month each time. His father gave him the silent treatment for at least a week. His mother baked him chocolate chip cookies and rubbed his back in sympathy every time she walked by.

Trey smiled thinking of his softie of a mom.

Red and blue lights swirled in his rearview mirror and rapidly became bigger and brighter. A siren sounded a couple of times in warning with that "bwap bwap" sound.

Trey pulled off onto the soft shoulder of the road. His low beams illuminated the "Leaving Ednaville City Limits" sign fifty feet away. He swore as he reached across to the glovebox to find his registration. His bladder reminded him that it was full. Very, very full.

He opened the car door. The cop car had stopped behind him with its high beams on and the colored lights still rotating. He reached into his back pocket for his wallet and started to walk toward the patrol vehicle when the door popped open, and a cop Trey didn't recognize got out. He held out a hand in warning. "Whoa, now. Stop right there. Put your hands out where I can see them."

The cop had his other hand on the butt of his sidearm. Trey complied. "I was just going to get my wallet," he said. "Figured you'd want to see my driver's license."

"Uh huh. Now turn slowly and place your hands down flat on the hood there." He gestured toward the cruiser.

"What?"

The cop raised his voice as if he were addressing a rather slow child or a senior citizen with a hearing deficiency. "I said, 'turn slowly and place your hands—l'"

"I heard you," Trey said. "I just couldn't believe you said it. Is this an episode of COPS?"

"No, sir. Just do as you've been instructed. I should warn you; I am equipped with a taser as well as other means to bring you under control if you do not voluntarily abide by my commands."

"You've got to be kidding me." Trey stared at the cop who was decked out in what looked like a legitimate Henderson County police uniform complete with a cap which bore the county logo instead of the City of Ednaville official seal.

"Sir? Do I need to call for backup? Or are you going to place your hands flat on the hood of the vehicle like I asked?"

"Backup? You have backup here? When did Ednaville join the twenty-first century?"

"Sir. Place your hands flat on the hood of the vehicle. Now," the cop barked.

"All right, all right. Don't get your boxers in a knot."

Trey did as he'd been told feeling ten kinds of foolish doing it. The only saving grace was there no one would see it. "My wallet's in my back right pocket," he informed the cop who slowly made his way closer. "My license is in the front."

"We'll get to that. Legs apart."

"Are you fucking kidding me?" Trey turned to look at the guy over his shoulder. "You're going to *search* me before you give me a damn speeding ticket?"

"Sir. Please do as you're told. We don't want any trouble here."

"Then why are you making it? How about if you forget you even saw me doing sixty in a thirty-five? Better yet, how about you take out my wallet, check my driver's license. Maybe there's some way we can reach an agreement and make this all go away. How does that sound?"

"Are you attempting to bribe a police officer, sir?"

"I never actually said—"

Trey suddenly found himself facedown on the hood of the police car. The cop grabbed his left wrist first, then his right, forcing them back behind him. "What the?" He heard a metallic clasping noise. "Are you fucking *kidding* me? You're handcuffing me?" Trey sputtered in outrage. Even knowing it would be better to shut his mouth and cooperate, he knew he wasn't going to do it.

"Do you do this to all your traffic stops?" He asked snidely. "Especially the cute young things who can't read a speed limit sign? What do they do? 'Oh, officer, I'm so sorry.' They bat their eyelashes at you while you throw the cuffs on them? Huh? Do they spread their legs first time they're told, so the big, strong cop can subdue them?"

"Spread your legs," the cop grated out.

"Fuck you."

The cop kicked Trey's left foot and then his right one, effectively separating them. Trey grunted in surprise as his right knee, forced to move without warning, sent an extra strong pain message to his unmedicated brain receptors.

"Asshole," Trey murmured into the hood of his car.

"Officer Spoley, to you. Do you have anything on your person or in your pockets I need to know about? Drugs, paraphernalia, needles, anything that's likely to injure me?"

Just my fists. Although they weren't much use at the moment. "No," he answered dully. God, he needed to pee. Being bent over the hood of the car wasn't helping matters. He'd have stopped before if it hadn't poured rain and if his knee didn't object every time he got out of the car.

After an uncomfortably thorough pat-down, Trey felt his wallet being removed from his pocket. "Well, well, well. If it isn't the high and mighty Trey Christopher. Or should I say burnt out, over the hill, drug addict, Trey

Christopher. Ednaville's golden boy. Come back home all rusted out."

"Can I stand up, now?" Trey asked. Officer Spoley still had his palm firmly planted between Trey's shoulder blades effectively keeping him in place.

"Certainly." Spoley stepped back. "I don't imagine you're a flight risk. Not with that busted knee of yours."

Spoley gave Trey a smug little smile which made Trey almost certain Spoley knew who he was *before* he'd kicked his legs apart. His knee began an entirely new round of throbbing, but at least it distracted him slightly from his insistent bladder. He needed to get out of here, get to the house and ice the knee or else he'd barely be able to walk tomorrow.

"You got something specific against me, Officer Spoley?" The cop's name niggled at his memory. Trey felt certain he should know what kind of history he had with the guy, but at the moment he couldn't place him.

"I might. Then again, I might not. But I'll share something with you my daddy used to say: Be nice to the people you meet on your way up the ladder. You might be meeting them on your way back down."

"Look, just write me the ticket and spare me the sermons, would you?"

"Have you consumed any alcohol this evening, sir?"

"No."

Spoley stepped closer and sniffed the air. He was a couple inches shorter than Trey which put his nose on a level slightly below Trey's mouth. "I'll have to ask you to take a breathalyzer exam, sir."

Below the handcuffs, Trey flexed his fists. "Yeah. Sure. Whatever."

"Wait here," Spoley instructed. From the trunk of his vehicle he removed a portable breathalyzer unit.

He offered a large straw-like mechanism to Trey. Trey got a bad feeling. He tilted his head back. "I haven't been drinking. I'm not taking a breathalyzer test."

"That's your right, Mr. Christopher. However, in the eyes of the law, refusal to take a roadside sobriety test carries with it the same penalty as taking a test which shows you over the legal limit for blood alcohol levels."

"I'll take my chances."

Spoley stared him down for a few seconds and then shrugged as if it didn't make any difference to him. But

Trey got the distinct impression that for some reason it did.

"If you wouldn't mind taking a seat next to your car," Spoley indicated the shoulder. "I have some paperwork to do."

"Hey, look." Trey tried for a friendly tone and even he could tell he hadn't quite made it. "Can you take the cuffs off? We both know I'm not going anywhere. Hell, take my keys and hang onto my wallet while you're at it as insurance."

Spoley nodded once as if he knew he'd gone above and beyond the call of duty for a routine traffic stop. Trey turned around and Spoley released the cuffs. Trey rubbed at his wrists and glanced around at the surroundings he could see from the car lights. There were no houses nearby. Not one car had passed them since they'd stopped. Beyond the pool of light around their cars it was pitch black. "You mind if I go over there and take a leak?" He indicated a small clump of bushes about twenty-five feet away. "I gotta pee like a sonofabitch."

Spoley looked at him as if considering his request and the possible ramifications of his answer before he said, "Sure. Go ahead."

"Thanks, man."

Trey limped behind the bushes and unzipped his fly, nearly groaning in relief. He peed for what felt like five minutes before zipping up and making his way back to the cars. He leaned against the driver's side of the hood and did his best to keep the majority of his weight off his bad knee. What came next, he wondered? A cane? A walker? Most mornings he felt like an old man before he even got out of bed.

He waited for Spoley to finish. And waited. And waited. And waited.

The guy enjoyed messing with him a little too much. Trey renewed his silent vow to pay Spoley back at the first opportunity.

Just as Trey decided to approach the patrol car, because seriously, how long would it take even the most incompetent cop to write a speeding ticket—Spoley opened his door and got out. He strode toward Trey with a spring in his step.

"Here's your license and registration, Mr. Christopher." He handed the documents back to Trey and Trey shoved them in his front pocket, anxious to get going. He stifled a yawn.

"These are your citations," Spoley said.

"Citations? How many tickets did you write? I only went over the speed limit once."

"Yes, sir." Spoley smiled a creepily pleasant smile as if he hadn't been the cop from hell a short while ago.

"This is your traffic citation." He handed the multiple page document to Trey.

"This is for driving under suspicion of being under the influence and refusing the breathalyzer."

"I haven't been drinking. I don't drink. I haven't had a drink in over a year."

"This one is for attempting to bribe a police officer." Spoley used a conversational tone as he glanced back over the next document as if checking for accuracy before handing it to Trey.

"Bribing a police officer? You've got to be kidding me."

Spoley gazed at him steadily, daring him to say more. Trey shut his mouth, something he knew he should have done much, much earlier.

"And this one, as you can see, is for violating county ordinance #513849-B."

"Yeah? What kind of trumped-up charge is that?"

"Indecent exposure, of course." Spoley touched the brim of his hat and strutted back to his car. He got in, killed all the lights but the high beams, made a U-turn and disappeared into the darkness of a side street.

Trey crawled back into the Cayenne's driver's seat, easing himself down, babying his knee. Screw it, he though Spoley had a chip on his shoulder, but Trey had something Spoley probably didn't have Money. Lots of it. A decent attorney ought to get him out of everything but the speeding ticket.

Unfortunately, even after he negotiated the winding country road, located the house, and parked in the driveway, the bad feeling didn't go away. By then he had a pretty good idea who Officer Justin Spoley was, and why he might still hold a grudge.

Chapter Two

♥

Trey reluctantly woke at dawn the next morning knowing he wouldn't get any more sleep. From his grandparents' bed he stared up at the plaster ceiling. The walls were covered in ancient cabbage rose wallpaper, which his grandmother had probably picked it out in 1955. He'd already added to his list of things to change.

Experimentally Trey shifted slightly to see how bad things were. Right knee throbbing. Constant twinge in right shoulder. He turned his head to glance at the nightstand. Which over the counter pain medication should he chose? Naproxen sodium worked well and was supposed to last all day, but it didn't. Not for him, anyway. He could take more than the suggested dosage of ibuprofen and he could take it more often.

He reached over and uncapped the bottle, tumbled four tablets into his hand and swallowed them with a gulp of water from the bottle he'd set next to them last night. He'd have to give them a few minutes to work.

He stuffed the extra pillow under his head and listened to the sounds of the birds waking up. Filmy lace curtains, possibly as ancient as the wallpaper let the grayish light filter through from outside. Trey knew by the time he got up and made his way to the kitchen, the mountains in the distance would be obscured by fog which would burn off by late morning.

He scrubbed his hands over his face and yawned. Carefully, he flexed his left knee hearing the joints in his cartilage crack and pop from ankle to hip. He lowered the leg and stretched his arms over his head trying to work out the kinks. He'd learned to be careful, to go slowly, especially first thing in the morning. His body had taken a beating from years on the field. He'd paid for all the success he'd had in his career by feeling this way each and every morning.

His right shoulder protested as he carefully rotated it to warm up the muscles. Probably should ice it once he got out of bed and got moving.

Last but not least he carefully bent his right leg. Slowly, slowly, slowly, feeling it resist as he did. Damn it hurt. But he was almost getting used to it. Funny what you could accept when you had no choice. He'd never have the range of motion in this leg he'd once had. He knew that. He also knew he had to get back into physical therapy to give himself the best possible outcome after the last surgery. Another on his list of things to do.

Eventually, he sat up and swung his legs over the side of the bed. Levering himself up with one hand on the nightstand and leading with his left leg he got himself upright and limped to the bathroom down the hall.

More ancientness greeted him in the form of a claw-footed tub, a pedestal sink and a toilet missing lots of its original enamel coating. Luckily, the plumbing, though hardly modern, worked. He peed and washed up, splashing lots of cold water in his face and making a mess of the small space.

He looked down at the puddle he'd created on the curling linoleum. He threw a towel on it and used his left foot to move it around to mop up the water. Another thing to add to his list. Find a cleaning service.

Dragging his right leg along with him, he made his way to the kitchen. The best room in the house. He paused at the arched opening to look at it. Time stood still in his grandmother's kitchen. Nothing had changed in years except the appliances she'd been forced to replace when the old ones wore out.

The round oak table surrounded by a variety of mismatched chairs took up most of the open floor space. The cabinets, he recalled, had gone through a few incarnations of color over the years, but were now covered in an off-white shade. Ecru, maybe. Or eggshell.

Some sort of reddish linoleum covered the long countertop, sealed along the edges with a strip of silver metal.

Above the cracked porcelain sink, double windows offered an unobstructed view of the back of the house including his grandmother's now neglected garden. Some of her annuals were still going strong, poking their blooming heads through the overgrowth of weeds.

Another thing for the list. A gardener or a professional landscaper. Maybe both.

Trey limped across the scarred wood floor to the coffeemaker. This, at least, he could handle. By trial and error, he'd learned how to make coffee after years of having someone else do it for him. His mother. His wife. A waitress. Room service. His housekeeper, Miriam.

He thought of her fondly. She'd been uber efficient and as far as he knew, nonjudgmental. She'd called him Meester Trey and performed even the smallest task promptly. Not once had she complained of his less than stellar behavior, not about the mess he'd make of the bathroom or the broken bric a brac he knocked over in one of his under-the-influence moments. She never said a word about the procession of women he'd paraded through the house after Hayley left.

Miriam had stayed on until he'd decided he couldn't possibly remain in the big house outside Jacksonville. He couldn't stay in Jacksonville period. Too many memories. Too many temptations. Too easy to slide back into the kind of life he'd worked hard to get himself out of.

He'd given Miriam a glowing letter of recommendation and a year's severance pay. She might be the one person from his past life who didn't completely hate him.

Trey began to unpack the big shopping bag he'd brought in and left on the counter last night. A few of the basics. He'd go into Henderson later and go grocery shopping. He also had to find an attorney. Another item for his list. Probably that should go at the top. Everything else could wait.

He pulled out the bag of Arabian Mocha Sunani and held it to his nose breathing in the faint scent through the white bag with his favorite coffee shop's logo front and center. He opened the bag and sniffed again at the beans. Intoxicating. He rummaged through the shopping bag for the grinder he'd packed. Or thought he'd packed. He didn't find it.

Great. Just great. How was he was supposed to start his morning without coffee? He thought of hurling the bag of beans across the room to vent his frustration. He wanted to punch something or beat the hell out of something. He couldn't even get a decent cup of coffee in his own kitchen.

He tried one of the meditation techniques they'd taught him in rehab. Bracing both hands on the counter, head bowed, he took in a deep breath over a count of four, held it for a count of seven, let it out for a count of five. Again. Then again. One more time for good measure. He lifted his head. He still wanted to hit something. Maybe he'd install a punching bag in every room for moments such as these.

Okay. No Arabian Mocha Sunani for him this morning. *It's not the end of the world. Just one of life's little frustrations.* Maybe Grandma J had left some Folgers or Maxwell House in one of the cupboards. He began opening cabinet doors. His mother had cleaned out the refrigerator and gotten rid of any perishables. But there were a few canned goods and boxes of things like rice and pasta in the cupboards. He saw a larger can at the back of one of the shelves.

"Aha." A discount chain store brand of ground decaf coffee. Karma, he decided. For all those cups of gourmet coffee he'd been served in the past and hadn't fully appreciated.

Cheap decaf was better than nothing. Maybe he could add some cinnamon from Grandma J's spice rack to liven it up.

While the coffee brewed, he wrapped an ice pack around his knee and strapped another one to his shoulder. The tee shirt and cotton pajama bottoms insulated his skin from direct contact with the ice packs. He rummaged in the kitchen drawers until he found a small notepad and a hodgepodge of pens, paperclips, rubber bands and other miscellany.

When the coffee finished, he took a mug of it out to the back porch not quite prepared for the nip in the air. He'd become so used to the heat and humidity in northern Florida this time of year it hadn't occurred to him he'd need a robe or a jacket. He opened the door to the mudroom off the porch. Hooks along the wall were lined with jackets and hats and scarves. Various boots and shoes were arranged along the baseboard underneath. Some were Grandma J's and some were Grandpa Mike's. In a bin nearby were gardening gloves mixed in with a few hand tools, old pots and packets of seeds.

Trey spied Grandpa Mike's plaid jacket and got it off the hook. It was a little snug across the shoulders, but it'd do. The shoes all looked too small for him.

He settled himself in one of the chairs on the porch with his coffee and notepad on the table nearby. He took a sip of the coffee. It was drinkable. That's about all he could say for it. Steam rose out of the cup mimicking the swirls of gray that obscured the mountain view.

Trey began to write.

1. Find an attorney

2. Buy a coffee grinder

3. Grocery store

4. Cleaning service

5. Landscaper/gardener

He sipped some more coffee, knowing he had more to add to the list, more things he'd prefer not to do. As part of his new self-discipline, he also knew he'd do them anyway.

1. Physical therapist

He needed someone good and he sure as hell hoped he could find someone in the county seat of Henderson, a decent-sized town about ten miles from Ednaville. Since there was a small hospital there, it stood to figure, there'd be most other medical services available as well.

1. Therapist

As much as he'd resisted therapy, he had to admit it had helped him get through that initial year of sobriety. Brad never seemed to tire of throwing whatever Trey said back in his face and forcing him to figure out how to deal with his own problems and *issues*. Trey knew he needed someone like Brad to keep him accountable.

Trey put the pen down and let his gaze wander over his property. The old barn needed some shoring up and a paint job. Probably a new roof as well. The outbuildings included a few close to falling down. He'd probably let them or tear them down himself.

He hadn't really figured out what he was going to do now that he was here. He didn't fancy himself much of a farmer. He doubted he'd want to be tied down to livestock around the place, although that's what Grandpa Mike did. Farmed. Raised cows and pigs and goats. Grandma J gardened and sold a lot of what she grew, vegetables and such. Apples from the orchard. Homemade jellies.

He'd inherited his grandparents' home and their land by virtue of being their only grandchild, his mother the only one of their three offspring to bear a child. His Aunt Mamie was considerably older than his mom. She'd married late in life, maybe too late. She and Uncle Orrie never had any kids. Uncle Kurt, well, what could one say about Uncle Kurt, the forgotten middle child in between the two sisters?

Although it wasn't something the family ever mentioned, Uncle Kurt being gay was the equivalent of the elephant in the living room everyone tiptoed around. He lived in Asheville and owned—no surprise to Trey at least—a couple of successful art galleries. If he were part of a committed relationship, he'd never admitted to it, at least not while his parents were alive. Vaguely, Trey wondered if things would be different now that Grandma J was gone?

Trey went back into the kitchen, shrugged out of the jacket, and poured more coffee. Taking it with him he got the shower going and stood under the hot spray for a long time musing about changes he could make to the house. A bathroom that would suit his needs with a big Jacuzzi tub and a shower stall with jets everywhere and a bench in the middle so he wouldn't have to stand up the whole time. He groaned at the thought, even though the ice pack and now the warm water helped ease the stiffness in his knee.

He wanted to preserve the architectural integrity of the old farmhouse. He'd have to find a good contractor to help him figure out how to do that and still get all the modern updates he had in mind.

Two hours later he parked on Main Street in Henderson and got out of the car. His stomach growled, the lone granola bar he'd eaten after his shower a distant memory. He could get some breakfast at the diner on the corner of Main and Spring Street.

He stopped outside the plate glass window to feed quarters into the newspaper machine for a copy of the Henderson Times. Maybe there'd be ads for lawyers and therapists in it.

Martha's Home Cookin' did a brisk business for a Thursday morning, but there were a few empty tables and one booth. Trey couldn't help but notice the speculative glances sent his way when he walked through the door, and the brief lull in conversation before it surged again and ratcheted up a notch or two. He heard his name whispered once or twice—the curse of being a former local with a former claim to fame. No way could he hide in his hometown. He'd gone to junior high and high school in Henderson as did every kid who resided in Ednaville. He didn't expect to reconnect with anyone he'd known in his formative years because he'd made no effort to keep in touch with them. He hadn't attended his ten-year high school reunion and since college even his visits to his parents had been brief and none-too-plentiful.

The best he supposed he could hope for was to be accepted or possibly ignored by the locals. After his encounter with Officer Spoley last night, he didn't hold out too much hope for either, but the townspeople would have to make the best of it. And so, he supposed, would he.

Since a sign near the entrance told him to seat himself, he chose the booth because he could angle his body in the corner near the front window and stretch his leg out beneath the table without it being too noticeable.

Within seconds a waitress appeared, coffee pot in hand. "Coffee?" She reached for one of the mugs already on the table.

Trey glanced up at her and nodded. "Thanks."

She set a plastic coated menu next to him. "Specials are on the board over there." She tilted her head in the direction of a dry erase board on the far wall. "Get you some juice or something?"

"Sure. A large orange juice. And a glass of water if you don't mind."

"I don't mind at all," she assured him with a smile.

Flirting, Trey, thought. Or trying to. She appeared to be close to his own age. Blondish-brown hair pulled up in a ponytail. Hazel eyes. A few extra pounds here and there, but nothing off-putting. But he wasn't going to encourage her. Or anyone else for that matter.

He opened the menu, the words blurring before his eyes for a minute before he focused on them.

Truth was, Trey wasn't so sure of himself with women anymore. Or with anyone for that matter. Without the crutch of alcohol to smooth the way, to make him the life of the party, to lower his inhibitions so he could relax and pretend to be himself, he had no idea how to proceed.

He'd never had a problem giving up drinking during training or during the season. He'd been in control, never thought of himself as addicted. But after the first knee surgery, when he'd been afraid he'd never play again, he'd been all too ready to make himself oblivious of that frightful reality.

The fact that he'd come back after the first surgery, had played decently for most of that season was, in his mind at least, a minor miracle. But he'd gotten sacked in the last quarter of the last game. If they'd won, the Jacks would have been in the division play-offs. Instead, he'd been escorted off the field on a stretcher, forcing himself to hold back the howls of pain until he made it to the ambulance.

The Jacks lost. He never played again. He had another surgery. Complications set in. Physical therapy had been excruciating. His patience and his temper wore thin. Doctors didn't think twice about writing prescriptions for him, and there were enough of them who didn't know what medications he'd already been prescribed by one of their colleagues.

Before he knew it, he was hooked. He quickly discovered that washing painkillers down with a glass of Jack Daniels added to their effect. Pretty soon he wasn't feeling anything. Not the depression over the fact that his pro football career was over. Not resentment of Hayley when she tried to intervene, to get him some help. Not any feeling at all for the parade of women he screwed and dumped.

Until he got where he needed to be he wasn't about to start up with women again, not even one woman. Not when what he'd probably do is screw up again, cause hurt without meaning to. Nope. Not happening.

The waitress set down glasses of juice and of ice water. "Anything look good?"

Another come on. Trey didn't look up from the menu. He sure as hell didn't want to encourage her by making eye contact. "I'll have the Mountain Man Special," he told her. "Eggs over medium. Bacon crisp." He chanced a glance up at her. "Can I get biscuits and gravy instead of toast?"

"Sure thing. You want grits, too?"

"That'd be great, thanks." He closed the menu and set it at the edge of the table, aware of her lingering next to him longer than it took her to write down his order.

He pulled the newspaper toward him and finally she took herself off.

He doctored the coffee and took a sip. It wasn't Arabian Mocha Sunani, but neither was it expired discount store decaf, either. It was passable.

He opened the paper and leafed through it quickly checking the ads for local professionals. On page six he found two ads for attorneys. One of the names caught his attention. Ryan T. Reagle. As kids they'd called him Reagle Beagle. Trey smiled to see Ryan still used that nickname. Ryan T. Reagle. Legal Beagle.

That's who I need, Trey decided. He remembered Ryan as a serious kid, a good student. He'd desperately wanted to play sports. He'd tried them all. Unfortunately, poor eyesight coupled with a complete lack of coordination and limbs that grew so fast he couldn't keep up with them prevented that.

In high school, if Trey recalled correctly, Ryan had found the track team. His long legs and thin frame were built for jumping hurdles and running marathons. He bet if he looked in his yearbook, he'd find Ryan had lettered in track all four years.

Trey made note of the address near the courthouse just a few blocks away. He'd stop in Ryan's office after breakfast and see if he was available. If not, he'd take the first appointment.

Must be my lucky day, he thought as he pulled out a special healthcare section. He leafed through it and found listings of the physical therapists as well as the other kind of therapist listed by specialty. He didn't recognize any of their names and he'd much prefer to see someone who had no connection to him at all.

"Here you go, sugar." Trey set the paper aside as the waitress set plates before him. "Want me to warm that up for you?"

Trey flickered a glance her way and said, "Sure."

She refilled his coffee cup. Again, she hesitated, but when he picked up his utensils she stepped away.

He glanced around the restaurant in time to see one or two patrons sending speculative looks in his direction. Not hostile, necessarily. Curious maybe. Interested even.

He piled everything except the grits onto one plate and mixed it all together. He'd loved doing this as a kid and now there was no one to stop him. Not that he hadn't been taught manners, but he couldn't see what difference it could possibly make to anyone if he liked to chop up his bacon and shove it into the eggs until they ran all over the plate and into the hashbrowns. Who would care if he added biscuits and gravy to that mess? No one, that's who. Since he now had only himself to please, that's exactly what he planned to do.

He read the rest of the paper while he ate. The waitress stopped by one more time, but he declined her offer of another refill.

He threw a generous tip on the table and went to the counter to pay. She was there, too, and took his money. "You don't remember me, do you?"

He looked at her full-on then, since it didn't seem like he could avoid it. What could he say? "No, can't say that I do."

"Terry Miller. We went to high school together. You were a year ahead of me. I sat behind you in World History my sophomore year."

"Did you?" Trey racked his brain for a memory, any memory of a younger version of this woman and came up blank.

"Yeah, well, you never noticed me back then, either."

Trey fought the urge to apologize. He didn't owe this woman anything other than civility and the tip he'd left on the table. He couldn't help it if she knew who he was and expected the same in return.

She handed him his change. He smiled at her. "Great to meet you, Terry. I'll probably see you again."

He decided to walk to Ryan's office. He needed to use his leg, keep the muscles moving, even if it pained him to do so.

The law office of Ryan T. Reagle was a step above what Trey expected for a small-town lawyer, decorated in muted tones of gray with burgundy accents. An opaque window on a far wall slid open as soon as he closed the door. A chubby redhead smiled in his direction and asked if she could help him.

"I don't have an appointment, but I was wondering if Ryan's available?"

"Does he know what it's regarding?"

"No, but it's a legal matter."

"What's your name? I'll see if he can see you."

When Trey gave her his name she showed no indication of recognizing it. He remained standing after she slid the frosted panel closed. A minute later she held the door to the inner sanctum open for him. "End of the hall, turn left," she told him.

The hallway wasn't very long and featured dark gray carpeting with burgundy and cream striped wallpaper covering the walls below a chair rail. The top half of the walls were painted the same cream as the stripe in the wallpaper.

He tapped on the open door to Ryan's office, but the other man was already on his feet and coming around his desk. Ryan hadn't changed much. He was still tall, thin and bookish. He offered his hand. "Trey Christopher, as I live and breathe. Back in town for less than twenty-four hours and in trouble with the law already." He grinned when Trey's mouth dropped open and then indicated the chairs in front of his desk. He went back to the other side and dropped into a burgundy leather swivel chair. The furnishings were cherry, the upholstered pieces carrying through the same color scheme as the outer office. "Come on, have you forgotten how small towns operate? Word of mouth. Gossip on the street. Better and more accurate information than that newspaper will give you."

Confounded, Trey could only stare at Ryan. "Are you saying—"

"That I know Justin Spoley pulled you over last night and threw a whole bunch of citations at you? Sure. As soon as he logged it in, it became public record. Clerks over at the courthouse are all abuzz with it."

"Damn. I hope that doesn't mean my mom and dad already know he cited me for indecent exposure."

"They may not know the particulars, but I'd be willing to bet by now your dad knows you got pulled over for speeding inside the Ednaville city limits."

"Great. That's just great." Trey let himself stew in that information for a minute."

"So. Is this a social call? Or are you looking for a lawyer? Because I make it my business to stop assholes like Spoley from overstepping their legal boundaries."

"You know him?"

"Hell, yes. You remember him. Or the name at least. He played defense for Forest City. Senior year? Last game of the season? A shot at the state championship on the line? Justin intercepted one of your passes—"

"—and started running with it." Trey could see it all, the field, the other players. For a moment he felt his own dismay knowing it was his last shot at quarterbacking a high school championship. He could almost feel the way adrenaline shot through him. He had to *do* something.

"You took off after him and to this day, I'll never know how you caught up with him."

"He made a fatal mistake. He looked back to see who was there," Trey put in with a grin.

Ryan nodded, his eyes alight with the memory. "He tripped. Fumbled. You recovered."

Trey nodded. He'd scooped up the ball and reversed direction. Somehow, he'd managed to elude the rest of Forest City's defense. His team had rallied around him, blocking for him as he zigzagged his way up the field to score just as the final seconds ticked away.

Henderson had gone on to win the state championship that year instead of Forest City. Was it even possible that Justin Spoley had never gotten over it?

"I remembered him after he let me go," Trey admitted.

Ryan grinned again. "You had no idea who he was? Oh, man, that must have pissed him off."

"You're not saying Justin Spoley had it in for me last night because of a high school football game?"

"It's not a secret. Over the years he's told different versions of the story, but yeah, I'd say he's held a grudge against you since that game. His belief is you got the break he was supposed to have. The scouts saw you make that play and subsequently overlooked him. You got the offers from the best schools, he got the ones from the second tier. You went on to play pro. He sat the bench in college. You married a gorgeous cheerleader, went to the Super Bowl a couple of times. He's stuck here making traffic stops. He pulls you over, identifies himself and you had no idea who he was. No wonder he gave you a citation for every charge he could think of."

"It was *high school* for Pete's sake. I can't believe he hasn't gotten over it and moved on."

Ryan opened his middle desk drawer and withdrew a small cloth. "We could sit here and analyze Spoley's victim mentality and discuss his motive for carrying around this kind of baggage for ten years, but it'd be a waste of time. Not to mention boring." Drawing off his wire rimmed glasses he polished first one lens and then the other before replacing them and dropping the cloth back into the drawer.

"You want to tell me what happened last night and we'll go from there?" He drew a blank legal pad toward him and picked up a pen.

Trey related the events of the previous evening. Ryan made notes and asked a few questions.

"I'll cop to the speeding ticket. Everything else is bogus."

"Technically, maybe not bogus, but also not provable. Refusing the breathalyzer could be a problem given your past, uh, very public history."

"I haven't had a drink in over a year," Trey grated out. "I wasn't drinking last night."

"It does seem extreme. He could have started with a roadside sobriety test rather than a breathalyzer. Made you walk a straight line, close your eyes, touch your nose. He didn't, though. Didn't suggest it. You're sure about that?"

"I'm sure."

"Attempted bribery? Hard to make that one stick, either. It's your word against his, if it even comes to that."

"I never actually offered him a bribe. What about the other one?"

"The indecent exposure. Did Spoley follow you behind the bushes?"

"No!" Trey exploded, outraged. "He was busy writing tickets."

"His word against yours. You asked if you could go take a leak. There's no evidence you actually did." Ryan grinned. "Unless you left any other, uh, evidence behind."

"You're enjoying this a little too much, you know that?"

"Aw, come on. When I was a kid I wanted to be you and now I'm defending you. I'd be lying if I said it doesn't make me a little happy to have you as a client."

"Believe me, Ryan, you do not want to be me. No one does. Not even me most of the time. So, can you make most of this go away or not?"

"I think so. Except, as you said, the speeding ticket, which you're willing to cop to anyway. The sobriety test might be a little sticky. Depends on the judge. Let me have Nikki make copies of those citations and get some more information and we'll go from there."

By the time he left Ryan's office, there was almost a spring in his step. A very careful spring, that is. Not only did he feel like he had reconnected with, okay, if not exactly an old friend, an old acquaintance. One who didn't hold a grudge for anything or take delight in his fall from grace. Ryan's cousin worked for the orthopedist who'd taken over old Doc Fleming's practice. He promised to call and get the names of the best PT's around. Ryan's wife had a friend who did housecleaning part-time. Trey had drawn the line at asking for referrals to a local psychotherapist. He'd track one down on his own.

Chapter Three

♥

"Ryan Reagle gave me your name and number. I'm looking for someone to help me out around my house. If you're available, give me a call."

Baylee Westring scribbled down the number. Thank God, she thought. She needed another job. Any job. At this point, she'd clean caves for Al Quaida's crew just to make a buck.

She started her ancient Toyota and shot Vivian Longstreet's Victorian mansion a dirty look as she pulled away from the curb. The old bat collected miniature figurines of dancing cats. They covered every available doily-covered surface on every piece of antique furniture in the oversized house. Vivian expected each and every figurine to be lifted and dusted along with the surface beneath and then replaced in exactly the same place. Impossible. She followed along behind Baylee each week, fussing and tsking and clucking her tongue rearranging the endless collection to her satisfaction.

It was only one day a week but Baylee approached each Wednesday with dread and loathing nonetheless. She'd raised her hourly rate in the hope that Vivian would fire her and find someone else to clean her clutter under her critical eye. Though Vivian had tried to haggle with her, Baylee had stood her ground, insisting her time was worth twenty dollars an hour instead of the fifteen she'd been charging.

Unfortunately, Vivian had given in making Baylee wish she'd doubled her rate instead. Vivian was the last remaining Longstreet and she'd inherited all of her family's considerable wealth. Baylee had no intention of being underpaid for even this sort of menial work as her thirtieth birthday loomed.

At a stop sign she hit the redial key before continuing to maneuver the little car through Henderson.

"T.C. Talk to me."

Baylee took the phone away from her ear and stared at it for a moment. Who answered their phone that way?

"Hello? Anybody there?"

She recognized the same voice as the one from her voice mail. She shouldn't be thrown by it. "I'm uh, that is, um, you left me a message."

"Going to have to be more specific darlin'. I've left about a dozen messages already today."

He sounded distracted but not annoyed. Like he was humoring her.

She cleared her throat and attempted to be more professional. "You need help around your house?"

"Right. When can you start?"

"Oh, um."

Baylee pulled into the parking lot of a convenience store. This conversation which should have been simple felt anything but. "Well, don't you want to like, meet me, interview me, call my references?"

"Nope. Ryan's wife wouldn't recommend you if she thought you were going to screw me over."

"You know Jenny?"

"No. I haven't had the pleasure."

"Then how did—"

"When can you start?"

Well, excuse me! Just what she needed. Another overbearing client. She hoped he had money because she planned to charge him top dollar, sight unseen, just because of his attitude.

"I'm free tomorrow."

"Great. What time?"

"I don't know. How's nine?"

"How's eight?"

Baylee sighed and didn't bother to cover it. "Fine."

"I'm outside Ednaville. 2371 Sycamore Road. See you then."

He disconnected. Baylee sat for a minute staring at the brightly displayed signs in the store window touting discounts on beer and cigarettes before she scanned her cell phone's contact list and hit auto dial.

"Jenny, who the hell is T.C.?" she asked as soon as her best friend picked up.

"Huh? What? Seth put that down. Don't you dare. You little monster. Come here."

"Jenny?"

"Sorry. Seth is testing parental boundaries again. Give me that." A childish howl filled Baylee's ear and she held the phone away until silence abruptly reigned.

"Jenny? What'd you do to him? Tape his mouth shut?"

"No, but that's a good idea. I put him in his crib and shut the door."

"Aww, Jenny."

"He's almost two; therefore, he gets two minutes. That's how much time you've got to tell me what you're talking about."

"Some guy called today about having me work for him. He said he got his number from you. He calls himself T.C."

"That doesn't ring any bells."

"Oh. I forgot. He did say he'd never met you."

"Do you mind if I point out you're not making any sense at all?"

"Never mind. Go get Sethie. Give him a kiss from his Aunt Baylee."

"I would, but I don't want to reinforce his negative behavior."

"Talk to you later."

Baylee disconnected. The mystery of T.C. could wait until tomorrow morning. At eight o'clock. Maybe she'd purposely arrive late just to see how he reacted. Maybe he wouldn't hire her. As badly as she needed the money, she had an unsettling feeling about this guy.

She put the car in gear and took her time heading home simply because she was in absolutely no hurry to get there. Once upon a time she'd had a lovely two-bedroom two-bath townhouse to call home. Since her first year in college she'd worked for the biggest privately owned bank in Asheville. After graduation, with a degree in finance and a minor in business, she'd worked her way up to assistant vice-president for operations. In recognition of her longevity, hard work and promotion, she'd been given stock options. The bank was solid with a proven track record. She'd borrowed money to buy her options figuring First Bank of Asheville would be gobbled up by one of the big banks soon enough and the value of her stock would double, possibly even triple. The economy was going gangbusters. There was no way she could lose.

Except she had. First to fail was her marriage which had been a disaster from the beginning although both she and Scott had been unwilling to admit it and were incapable of being honest with each other. Correction. She had been honest. For a long time Scott had not been. Then the economic downturn began. The value of North Carolina real estate plummeted as it did all across the country. Like many community banks, First Bank hadn't been prepared for such a drastic change. In less than a year it went from being the bank it had always been to being closed down by the FDIC. The bank's stock was worthless and Baylee had a significant uncollateralized loan she couldn't repay. Especially after she lost her job. The townhouse she and Scott owned lost more than half its value. Scott had moved out and she couldn't afford the mortgage payments on her own even if it had made financial sense to keep paying them. She'd walked away from the townhouse as foreclosure loomed. She'd been trying to ward off declaring bankruptcy.

She'd applied for other jobs, of course, including those in banking, but it seemed she was either over- or under-qualified or otherwise not suited for the few jobs available locally. Somehow, she'd scrape together the necessary funds to relocate if she found a position elsewhere. She'd scrambled to do anything and everything she could to survive until the economy improved. She'd worked in Bart Browne's CPA office during tax season, but that had ended a month ago. After she housesat for one of his clients she'd picked up a few jobs here and there. Until she found something more permanent, she'd turned herself into a personal assistant for a few locals and did cleaning for a few others. In the meantime, she'd moved back home.

She parked in front of the white clapboard structure and surveyed it critically. It hadn't been in the best part of town when she'd been growing up, just a middle-class working neighborhood. But this section of Henderson had deteriorated in the past twenty years and the house had not held up well. The porch sagged, the cement steps were crumbling, and the paint peeled noticeably in several sections. Her childhood home needed some TLC. Don't we all she thought derisively as she opened the car door. Fat chance the house or any of its occupants would be the recipients of any tender, loving care any time soon.

I miss my mommy. Baylee had this thought often and smiled sadly. Cancer had taken Diane Westring over two years ago right before the rest of Baylee's world imploded. While alive, her mother had been the heart of the family. She kept the modest house clean and comfortable and everything and everyone in it running like clockwork.

No problem had ever been too big for her mother to handle. She'd taken in her own mother who suffered from dementia and cared for her until she'd passed away when Baylee was in college. When Baylee's older sister

Lisa's brief marriage fell apart, Diane insisted Lisa and the twins move in. She'd cared for the boys while Lisa somehow made it through nursing school. Baylee's father Mike had never hidden his disappointment at not having a son. Diane went along with his wish to become foster parents to a young boy whom they eventually adopted.

Baylee's childhood bedroom was now occupied by the twelve-year-old twins, Jonah and Joshua. When he wasn't being held in a juvenile detention center, her adopted brother, Matty had inherited Grandma's former bedroom. Baylee hadn't exactly been welcomed home with open arms and had no choice but to sacrifice her privacy when she'd been relegated to a daybed in what had originally been a small parlor at the back of the over-crowded house.

Lisa's no-frills compact pulled in behind her. The back doors opened almost before it stopped and a twin tumbled out of each side. Baylee exited her vehicle and closed the door.

"Hey, you guys."

"Hi, Baylee," they both responded as they raced each other to the porch, Joshua breaking stride only long enough to yank on her ponytail, one of his more irritating habits she'd been unable to break.

"Ow!" she reached up to comfort her stinging scalp with her fingertips. There had to be a way to booby trap her hair, she often thought. A small mousetrap would do the trick if she could figure out how to disguise it to catch her nephew unaware. She was pretty sure if he triggered it once he'd never yank on her hair again.

"No TV, no video games, no phone," Lisa called after them. "You're both grounded."

Jonah gave Josh a shove so he could be the first through the door. The screen slammed behind them in protest. "How many times have I told you not to slam that door!" Lisa shouted in frustration.

Baylee gave her sister a good onceover. Four years older than Baylee, she looked at least ten. Single motherhood to two rambunctious adolescent boys had taken a toll on her. She was rail thin, her over-processed blond hair dry and lackluster. Hello Kitty scrubs lent her an air of comic tragedy. To Baylee she looked the way she always looked. Exhausted.

"You guys are home early," Baylee ventured when Lisa stopped next to her.

Lisa looked grim. "Because your nephews can't keep their pants on."

"Excuse me?"

"I got a call from Principal Willis. On the way back from a class trip to the Biltmore, those two were mooning drivers from the back window of the bus. They've been suspended for three days."

Baylee stifled the laughter bubbling in the back of her throat. Had Lisa forgotten she'd pulled the same sort of stunts at their age? She'd been wild to the point of being uncontrollable as a teenager. Karma had come back to haunt her.

Baylee, on the other hand, had been the good girl. She studied hard and behaved herself. *And look where it got me.* Divorced and broke. Except for the children and the exhaustion, she and Lisa could be twins.

They headed toward the house together and started up the steps when a non-descript white sedan parked at the curb. Baylee paused to glance at the driver, a sinking feeling in the pit of her stomach.

At the opened door Lisa looked around to see what had snared Baylee's attention. She gazed at the man exiting the driver's seat. "Damn."

Silently, Baylee agreed as the man approached. He wore an open-collared short-sleeved white shirt and black slacks along with a badge and ID at his belt.

"Afternoon, ladies," he greeted them pleasantly enough.

"Officer Frost." Baylee replied.

"Mateo around?" His gaze took in the house behind her as if he could somehow see inside and answer his own question without their help.

"I doubt it," Lisa replied. She glanced at her watch. "He should be getting out of school about now."

"The school says he missed first period today," the man replied.

Baylee heard Lisa's audible sigh of resignation. "I don't know if he's here or not, but you might as well come in. Maybe Dad knows."

Jack Frost—yes, that was his real name, Baylee reminded herself—

followed them in. His physical presence seemed to fill up the living room shrinking everything else into insignificance.

The twins were in the kitchen. Baylee could hear the sounds of them putting together a snack, but there was no sign of her father.

"Daddy?" Lisa called.

She went down the hall to his bedroom. Baylee set her purse down and turned to Officer Frost. "You're welcome to have a seat." She indicated the worn sofa, matching chair, or her father's recliner.

"I'm fine," he replied, his piercing gaze making her uncomfortable even though she'd done nothing wrong and had nothing to hide.

Lisa was knocking on bedroom doors and calling to her father and Matty before opening them. She came back empty-handed. "Dad's not here. Neither is Matty."

"Mind if I take a look in Matty's room?" Frost asked.

Lisa's gaze collided with Baylee's.

"I'll go with you," Baylee said. She walked down the hallway with him behind her. She opened the door to Matty's room and stepped inside. Frost did likewise, taking a walking tour of the small space. There wasn't much to see. A twin bed with a rumpled plaid comforter, a matching dresser and bookshelf took up most of the space. The closet door hung ajar. Frost opened it a bit wider and glanced in. Nothing to see there except for Matty's clothes, shoes, and basket of dirty laundry. A few personal items were scattered around. A car magazine. Some loose change. A fast food wrapper and empty cardboard cup.

Matty was messy like a lot of teenage boys, but he wasn't slovenly. Diane wouldn't have stood for it. He'd retained at least some of what she'd instilled in him, Baylee thought sadly. But she'd be hurt if she'd lived to see his frequent brushes with the law. Which hadn't started until after her death.

"Okay," Jack Frost said. He indicated his inspection was over and followed Baylee back to the living room. Lisa had escaped to the kitchen with her sons. The murmurs of their conversation were barely audible.

"You know an unexcused school absence is a violation of his probation."

"I know."

"I need to speak to your father."

"I know."

"And to Matty."

"Yes."

They'd been through this routine before, Baylee just about had it memorized. She wasn't Matty's guardian. She had no control over him which made her powerless. Her father, though legally responsible for Matty, had been unable to deal with his disappointment when Matty first started getting into trouble after Diane's death. He drank before then, too, but since the loss of his wife, he found solace in a bottle and seemed to have given up on their adopted son.

"How have you been?" Frost asked.

He'd relaxed his stance somehow and looked slightly less official in his capacity as Matty's probation officer.

"Me?" Baylee asked in surprise.

"Yes. You." He almost smiled. She didn't think she'd ever seen him smile before.

"I'm fine."

"Are you?" He did smile. He had a nice smile even though he looked like he could break somebody's neck if he wanted to.

"Yes. I am."

"How are things going around here in general?"

They're falling apart, Baylee wanted to say but didn't. Her father drank. Matty acted out. She feared the twins were beginning to follow in his footsteps. Lisa wasn't strong enough to handle them by herself. And Baylee had no say in any of it. In fact, there were days when she felt invisible.

Baylee told him the truth. "We're doing the best we can."

From his shirt pocket he withdrew his business card and handed it to her. "I'm sure you have one of these, but take this in case you don't. My private cell number is on the back. Call me if there's anything I can help with. Or, if you just want to call. For any reason."

Baylee stared at him. Was he flirting with her? Her twisted radar where men were concerned made it hard to tell. She accepted the card. "Thank you."

"Don't forget to have both your father and Matty get in touch with me."

"I will. Goodbye."

She closed the door behind him and turned the card over to see the handwritten phone number. She dropped the card in her purse trying to think why she would ever need to call him.

Chapter Four

♥

Mateo Westring eased the front door open and quietly locked it behind him. He tiptoed down the hallway to his bedroom, listening for a moment in case anyone in the house was still awake. He closed the bedroom door and breathed a sigh of relief.

The alarm clock on the nightstand read eleven-thirty-eight p.m. in red numbers. Way past his nine o'clock curfew.

He shrugged out of his clothes and went into the bathroom wearing boxers and a tee shirt. He brushed his teeth, scrubbed his face and got into bed. He set his alarm for six a.m. He'd try to make it to school on time tomorrow.

As he did every night he went over his plans, current and future in his head. He had lucked out connecting with Mamacita again just when she needed someone to help her. Even if it messed him up with his probation officer, he needed to be there for her. But he doubted good old Jack Frost would approve since it violated his curfew. Mateo figured what Jack Frost didn't know wouldn't hurt him. What was the worst thing that could happen? They'd tack on some more community service time for his probation violation? He wouldn't mind if they did. He liked spending time at the county animal shelter. Dogs and cats were undemanding company. He didn't mind cleaning up after them. They loved any bit of attention that came their way. He sure as hell could identify with that.

Ever since his adoptive mom died, he'd been floating alone in the world. Because of the age difference he barely knew his older sisters. His father became a drunk after Diane's death. Once upon a time, he thought the sun rose and set with his adoptive dad and he thought the feeling was mutual. But in his current state, Dan Westring was not capable of being the kind of father Matty needed. His dad looked right through him now, when he was sober enough to even notice he was around.

Lisa had trouble handling her two boys by herself. Matty had screwed up big-time there, because Jonah and Josh would have been like cool little brothers.

He didn't know how to reach out to Baylee. She had enough problems of her own and no time for his. What with losing her job and her house and her ex-husband turning out to be a fruit. Matty could have told her that the first time he met the guy even though he'd been a kid at the time.

He turned over and punched his pillow, allowing sleep to overtake him. All his problems would still be there in the morning waiting for him to figure them out.

Chapter Five

♥

"Hi, Mom."

"Trey!" His mother's delight transmitted through the phone. "I was going to call you later, see if you got in okay."

"Yep, I'm here."

"You should have let me stock up for you. Did you get to the store?"

"I'm heading there, now, as a matter of fact."

"You're coming for dinner, though, right?"

"I don't know, Mom. How's Dad?"

"He's fine. You'll come."

Trey ruminated for minute. He wanted to see his mom. Wanted her comfort and acceptance. But that meant he'd also be sitting at the table with his father. *You can only do what you can do.* Brad's advice again. Avoiding people or unpleasant situations wouldn't make them go away. The bad feelings they brought up wouldn't go away either. His father would have to get used to having Trey around because for the foreseeable future he wasn't going anywhere.

"I'm roasting a chicken," his mother wheedled. "Mashed potatoes. Gravy. Baby peas."

"Are you making biscuits?"

Lynn Christopher laughed. They both knew his agreement was a foregone conclusion. "Of course."

"Want to know what's for dessert?" she teased.

"Chocolate chip cookies?"

"It's a surprise. We'll see you at six."

"I'll be there." Trey disconnected. If his mom knew about him getting pulled over last night, nothing in her manner just now gave it away. More likely his dad would hear something at the hardware store today and he'd be the one to break it to her. Or one of her friends might get wind of it and tattle.

"Great." Trey muttered under his breath as he maneuvered through the traffic in Henderson. "Just great."

In this small town environment there were few secrets. Reputations were built on good deeds or bad. There never seemed to be any in-between. Parents were judged by their children's behavior from infancy on. Andy Christopher had enjoyed the admiration of his peers while Trey had been the hometown hero on his way up. But he'd also shared their disappointment when Trey's downward spiral began and possibly a certain degree of shame when he'd hit rock bottom.

Trey would like to be somewhere in the middle. The highs and lows were for the birds. He'd like to get through every day and just not screw it up too badly, not do damage to himself or hurt anyone else. Make it to bed at night without regret. Get up the next morning and repeat.

One day at a time. Rehab drilled that phrase into the heads of everyone who went through it. Really, Trey thought, is there any other way to live? All he had was the present moment. He had control of the choices he made leading up to it, but once he was there, he couldn't undo it.

Recovery had taught him to be more reflective, something he'd never had time or interest in before. But the sleepless nights, the endless cravings, the actual withdrawal from painkillers and booze gave him lots and lots of time to contemplate. His physical mobility had been drastically limited due to his knee. As an inpatient he'd been forced to keep a journal. Reluctant at first, he found rambling on paper helped clear his head and deal with his emotions. Even after his release, he'd kept at it. He'd learned to meditate, as well. He wasn't exactly enlightened but he was more at peace with himself than he'd ever been. He'd never be able to explain this kind of stuff to his dad who was a no-nonsense kind of guy. He didn't believe in psychological mumbo jumbo. He expected men to pull themselves up by their bootstraps and deal with whatever came their way. How many times had he told Trey to suck it up, rub dirt on it, walk it off, be a man?

In Henderson Trey ambled through the local version of the giant super store everyone loved to hate. He hadn't thought about obtaining things like milk and cereal, meat and fresh produce, for a long time. Miriam did the food shopping. Or, he supposed, Hayley did when necessary.

Now he was on his own and he'd have to fend for himself. He supposed he could learn to cook simple meals

How hard could it be His mom did it all the time. She wasn't a gourmet by any means, but everything created in her kitchen tasted good and left her men satisfied. He sincerely hoped she'd made chocolate chip cookies and she'd send some home with him after dinner.

He stocked up without regard to nutritional value. If it looked good, he bought it, making sure to get staples like salt and flour and sugar.

By the time he got home and put the groceries away he had some time before he needed to leave for his parents. Time to meditate, clear his head, center his thoughts.

He found his grandparents back porch the perfect place to do this. He couldn't manage to sit cross-legged on a mat, nor did he think it was necessary to achieve what he wanted. He sat at the table in one of the cushioned chairs and used another for a footrest. He'd loaded the kind of soothing music he liked onto his I-pod, the kind without words, filled with chants and sitars.

He got comfortable, closed his eyes and let his mind wander.

He woke an hour later, and knew he was going to be late. He yanked the earbuds out of his ears, got himself together, located his keys and called his mom.

No excuses. "I'm sorry, Mom. I'm on my way."

"That's fine, sweetie," she assured him. "We'll see you when you get here."

His mom was used to holding meals, heating leftovers, and men eating on the run. She'd somehow managed to keep him and his father fed that way from the time he was in the peewee league right up until the last game of his senior year in high school. There was always a practice, a game, a camp, somewhere to chauffeur him. If his dad couldn't do it, she did. And she always managed to feed him before, after or on the way.

He pulled to a stop in his parents' driveway, spewing gravel. Their arthritic golden retriever, Bo, hauled himself up from where he'd been lounging on a rug on the front porch and offered a hoarse bark.

"Hey, Bo," Trey greeted, pausing to rub him behind the ears. He wondered how much longer the dog would last. He'd always thought of Bo as his replacement because his parents had gotten him when Trey left for college.

He opened the screen door and *home* greeted him. Nothing much had changed since his visit last year for his grandmother's funeral. He strode through the living room with its comfortable furniture, to the kitchen where his mother was at the stove dishing up food.

She turned and her face lit up. She set down the spoon and the bowl and hugged him.

His mom was all soft rounded curves. He dwarfed her, but she didn't seem to mind. When they separated, she smiled up at him. "How's my boy?"

"I'm good, Mom. It's good to be home."

His father stomped in from the mud room off the kitchen. They eyed each other for a moment. Trey stuck out his hand. "Dad. How are you doing?"

Did he imagine it or did his dad take his hand reluctantly? He knew there'd be no hugs. There never were. Dad was tough. Cold. Hard. Where his mom was soft his dad was all sharp angles. Maybe that's why they were still together. Each made up for what the other one lacked. Not just physically, but in personality. His mom's warmth somehow balanced his father's sternness.

But shook hands they did. "Glad you could finally make it," Andy said. Trey didn't apologize. His mom was okay with it, and she was the one cooking dinner, wasn't she?

"Me too," he answered. He turned back to his mother. "Can I help? Want me to put those on the table? He nodded toward the bowls and platters.

"Yes. Here. You take these."

"Andy, if you wouldn't mind." She thrust the platter of sliced chicken at his dad who seemed about to object. If Trey remembered right, his father wasn't usually expected to help with dinner preparation or clean up afterward. But he took the platter and followed Trey to the table in silence.

"I poured iced tea for everyone," she informed Trey as she set a basket of biscuits next to him. "But if you'd like something else..."

"Tea's fine, Mom. Everything looks good."

"Well, then." She reached for his hand. Trey reached for his father's. For as long as he could remember they'd always done this when the three of them were at the table about to share a meal together. They joined hands and his mother offered a simple blessing and thanks for food and family. Andy clasped his fingers around Trey's whether he wanted to or not. He might be the tough one, but Trey had no illusions as to who was in charge around this house. Their tactics might differ, but Lynn had a way of bringing Andy around to her way of thinking that still amazed him. She also knew how to soothe his temper and make him see reason when the situation called for it.

As they passed bowls and Trey filled his plate he wondered if she'd had to do that today, so his father would agree to sit at the same table with him for a family meal.

His mother hadn't held any of his transgressions against him, even though he knew he'd hurt her with his careless behavior. She ached not for herself, but for him. She'd told him one of the hardest things was to see how much damage he'd done to himself, watching his life fall apart when she'd been powerless to stop it. But he'd never doubted her love.

The thing about moms, he guessed, was they loved their kids no matter what.

He supposed his father still loved him too, but he wasn't a soft touch when it came to forgiving and forgetting. Trey didn't know what else to do except get in his father's face on a regular basis, get him used to having his son around again, and see if they couldn't find some of the common footing they'd lost these past couple of years.

"Heard you got pulled over last night," his father began once they'd started eating.

Here we go.

His mother's fork clattered to her plate. "Oh, Trey, you didn't."

"Speeding, Mom. It was no big deal."

"Thought they cited you for DUI, too," his dad put in. "And a couple other charges."

"All bogus, Dad. A bunch of bullsh—" He glanced at his mom. "B.S. This cop Spoley. Has a hard—er, is overly zealous. Probably has a quota or something."

"Trey you weren't—you weren't—" Trey saw the distress in his mother's eyes. He hated that expression, hated to be the one who caused it. "No, Mom. I wasn't drinking. I don't drink. I don't take anything for pain except over the counter stuff. This cop just wanted to give me a hard time is all."

He shot a look at his father. "You don't have to believe everything you hear about me, Dad."

His father fixed him with a stare out of blue eyes the same shade as his own. "Seems like most times what I hear about you is true whether I want to believe it or not."

"Yeah, well, that was the past. Maybe next time you could come and ask me before you listen to the crowd down at the store." His father owned Henderson Hardware where the local tradesmen gathered each morning for coffee and bits of local gossip. Most of what they gossiped about was based in fact, sometime a truer version than got printed in the *Henderson Herald*.

Trey would have to toe the line now that he was home. Not that he didn't plan to anyway. Trey Christopher. Upstanding Citizen. That was the plan. Maybe that's why he'd come back. Because here, with his parents, extended family and the locals watching, he'd known he wouldn't be able to get away with much. They'd make him accountable for everything he did. Maybe he never should have left in the first place.

"Justin's Spoley's had it in for you since that last championship game," Andy allowed. "Man, that was some game, wasn't it? Everyone thought we'd lost it after you threw that interception. But you charged down the field after Spoley and recovered his fumble. I don't think I've ever been so—" The light in Andy's eyes dimmed when he looked at Trey. He cleared his throat and spoke to his plate of food. "Hard to believe he could hold a grudge that long. Your best bet is to steer clear of him while you're here."

"I'm not going anywhere, Dad," Trey said. "Ryan Reagle told me the same thing about Spoley."

"Did you show him the card from Hayley?" Andy asked Lynn.

"No."

Trey glanced from his father to his mother, noticing the signal she was sending with her eyes, the tightness around her mouth.

"What was it? The wedding announcement?" he asked, striving for a neutral tone and honestly believing he achieved it.

"You knew?" His mother asked, not bothering to hide her surprise.

"She sent me one. We're still friends, Mom. Even if we're not married to each other any more."

Andy snorted from his end of the table. Trey switched his attention to his father. "What?"

"Friends. I'd think you're the last person Hayley'd want to be friends with."

"I've talked to her a couple of times. She doesn't hate me anymore."

"That doesn't make her your friend." Andy forked up another bite of gravy-drenched chicken. "Not after what you did to her."

"It's in the past, Dad. We all know I screwed up, okay? I can't go back and undo it. Believe me, I tried. I squared things with Hayley as best I could."

"That girl was the best thing ever happened to you."

Trey could see Andy didn't want to let it go. "I know, Dad."

"Andrew." His mother's tone held a note of warning. The same voice she'd used with Trey when he was a kid and stepped over the line and included his middle name. Rarely did she call Andy 'Andrew.' When she did, there was trouble ahead.

Andy fixed her with a perplexed look. "What? Why shouldn't I be able to say what I think at my own table in my own house with my own son? Why shouldn't you?" He set his fork deliberately on his plate and rested clenched fists on the edge of the table. "You think he doesn't know what it did to us? Sitting on the sidelines helpless while he threw his whole damn life down the drain? You think he doesn't need to know you cried yourself to sleep night after night worrying about him?"

"Andy!" His mother stared at her husband as if he'd grown two heads.

"What!" he shouted back. "Hayley was like a daughter to us. We loved that girl like she was our own and everybody at this table knows it. Including him." He jerked his thumb in Trey's direction.

"Okay, Dad, okay. I get it."

His father turned on him, his eyes ablaze. "No, son. I don't think you do. What scares me the most is I don't think you ever will."

"Looks like Justin Spoley's got company when it comes to holding grudges." Trey pushed back from the table. "Mom, thanks for dinner. Dad." He nodded in Andy's direction. "Thanks for the insights."

He could hear his mother calling after him as he strode through the house and pushed through the door. He didn't go back. He couldn't. He flew out of the driveway spraying up more gravel than he had pulling in. His temper pulsed beneath a thin layer of self-control.

Breathe.

He made himself do it. Counting. Inhaling. Exhaling. Until he reached his house. It didn't do much to still the wild beat of his heart, but it cleared his mind. Slightly. Enough to remember he hadn't had even one chocolate chip cookie. He'd also left behind the foil-covered plate of them his mother planned to send home with him.

Chapter Six

❤

Baylee's father stumbled in after ten, which meant he'd spent most of the afternoon and evening on a bar stool. Although she knew better than to confront him when he was under the influence, lately there was never a good time to approach him about anything. Matty still hadn't come home and technically, at least, Matty was her father's responsibility.

While her father rooted around in the refrigerator for sandwich makings, Baylee said, "Jack Frost stopped by this afternoon. Matty cut first period today which is a violation of his probation."

Dan Westring straightened and gazed at her through bleary eyes. He chewed on a slice of salami he'd managed to extract from the package in his hand. In the light of the refrigerator, he looked old and tired and sad. And drunk.

Sadness crept up on Baylee without warning. Her family was drowning and she didn't know what to do to save any of them. Not even herself.

He swallowed and put another piece of salami into his mouth while he stared at Baylee. She wondered if what she'd said had penetrated the fog in his brain. "Daddy, we have to do something. You have to do something. Matty can't keep getting in trouble like this."

Dan Westring swayed and staggered a couple of steps to the counter. The refrigerator door swung shut behind him leaving them in the dim glow of the light over the stove. He dropped the package of salami on the counter and clung to the edges of the solid surface for support. "Kid don't listen to me," he slurred.

He stared at the scarred speckled Formica as if it could offer up some answers.

"Dad, you need to stop drinking. Maybe if you did—"

"You blaming this on me? Whadda you know? You never had no kids to raise." He shook a finger at Baylee. "I'm a failure. That what you're saying? You think I don't know that? I'm a loser. So are my kids." His tone softened. "Nothin' but a bunch of losers." He left the lunchmeat on the counter and brushed past Baylee. "Get outta my way."

Baylee stayed where she was while he shuffled down the hallway. The door to his bedroom closed but the words he'd spoken reverberated in her head. *Losers. Losers. Losers.*

She heard Matty come in after eleven, but she was done confronting anyone in this house about anything. Hours later she finally fell asleep but getting up when her alarm beeped the next morning was a struggle.

She knew where Sycamore Road was, of course. Her grandparents' best friends, Mike and Josephine Pritchard had lived on Sycamore Road. They were both dead now, though, as were her own grandparents. But during her youth she had occasionally visited the Pritchards with them.

She wouldn't apologize for being late. Best to let *T.C.* know who was in charge. It had taken her awhile, but she was learning. She wasn't going to be a doormat for anyone. Not anymore. And certainly not for some over-bearing guy who sounded like he was used to ruling the world and getting his own way.

2371 turned out to be the Pritchard's house. It didn't look much different from the way it did when they lived there. Josephine, whom everyone called "J" had passed within the last year, so Baylee wasn't surprised to see not much about the property had changed since then. Except there was a black Porsche Cayenne parked near the back porch. Turbo, she noted as she drove past and parked a few feet away. *Money.*

Yippee! Her heart did a little pitter-pat. She could name her own price.

She got out, mentally debating about using the front door or the back. Formal or informal? Which way to go? Locals used the back. But no way to tell if the occupant of the house was local or not. Although it seemed unlikely based on his choice of car. The nearby back porch facing the driveway helped make her decision.

She hesitated for a moment before she climbed the three stairs to the porch to gaze at her surroundings. She'd always liked the Pritchard's place. It was nestled in the midst of some gently rolling hills with the Blue Ridge range as a backdrop. The house set far enough back from the road to offer privacy, but not anonymity. The old barn was empty now as was the feed lot and the chicken coop. A few other outbuildings were ready to tumble down, taking the rusting fences surrounding them along.

Trees dotted the yard and the pastures beyond. Birds chirped and flitted in the branches and a couple of squirrels gallivanted underneath a big oak closest to the house.

Near the porch there were flower beds badly in need of weeding. A twining rose climbed up a trellis. There was the old swing at the end of the porch. Baylee could remember sitting there contentedly, swinging and daydreaming to the rhythmic squeak of the chain against the hook while the adults gathered around the wicker table and chairs to chat and drink glass after glass of sweet tea.

A pang of longing for those simpler times hit her. She hadn't known then how many mistakes awaited her, how many difficult lessons she had to learn. But learn from them she would. Her new motto was a slightly amended version of "Been there; done that." To which she had added "not doing it again."

She stepped up to the porch toward the door before she realized she wasn't alone. She turned to see a man seated at the table. He used one of the other chairs as a footstool, an ice pack balanced on the knee of the outstretched right leg, his left bent at the knee.

His arms were across his chest, his thumbs tucked underneath his armpits, his head down. There was a mug on the table, but the man didn't move.

Baylee wondered if this could possibly be the mysterious T.C. He looked young, thirtyish, with burnished blond, gold-tipped hair and from what she could see from his seated position, tall and in good shape.

She cleared her throat and took a step toward him. When she got no reaction, she poked his upper arm. Beneath the long-sleeved jersey he wore, her finger met solid muscle. "Excuse—"

His head snapped up and a pair of stunning blue eyes lasered right through her. She sucked in a breath and stumbled back unable to look away.

T.C. *Trey Christopher*.

Why hadn't she figured it out before? The Pritchards were Trey Christopher's maternal grandparents. In fact, he'd been at their house on a few of those occasions when she'd visited as a child. He always seemed to have a pack of other boys with him and she'd learned early on to avoid them because they'd do nothing but tease and torment her if she invaded their territory. Which seemed to be everywhere except the back porch where the adults lurked.

She had more memories of him than just those from childhood, one in particular, which had plagued her all through high school and beyond. Now here he was. Here she was. His presence was having the same impact on her as it had that other time. She scrambled to get hold of herself. She was an adult woman of almost twenty-nine not a naïve teenager of fifteen.

"Sorry," he said. "I didn't mean to startle you." He grinned which turned his already handsome features into to-die-for good looks. She did nothing but stare even though she knew he was making a joke, since she had been the one who had startled him.

"You okay?" he asked. "You look like you've seen a ghost."

I did. The ghost that's haunted me for fourteen years.

"Want to do this another time?"

No. Been there. Done that. Not doing it again.

She got hold of herself. Finally. "No, it's fine. I'm fine."

He studied her for a few seconds. "I'm Trey, by the way. And you are?"

"Baylee. Baylee Westring."

He chewed on the inside of his lip as if contemplating something while he continued to peruse her from head to toe. She'd come dressed to work in a faded pink tee shirt, ancient jeans and sneakers. Over which she wore a hoodie she'd bought on sale at Wally World for five dollars last spring. Her hair was pulled back in a ponytail to keep it out of her way. And zero make-up. As the cleaning lady she didn't have to impress anyone, and she liked to be as comfortable as possible while she worked.

As if remembering his manners, Trey straightened in his chair and pulled his feet off the other one. He helped the right one along with both hands supporting his thigh after setting the ice pack on the table. "Please. Have a seat." He indicated she was welcome to take any one of the four chairs. She opted for the one opposite him instead of the one next to him where his foot had just been.

She sat and he looked at her for a long moment before he spoke. "Have we met? You look awfully familiar for some reason."

Baylee pushed her glasses up on her nose. Since he was fishing she decided to join him. "Maybe from high school."

"Nope. That's not it. Seems like somewhere more recent."

Your grandmother's funeral last year, maybe? Not that she had any intention of enlightening him to their past history if he couldn't remember it. She'd seen him at the funeral, at a distance. They hadn't spoken or touched. But she'd been haunted by *that* memory for months afterward. What, she'd wondered at the time, was it going to take to get him out of her head for good?

Certainly not this. Why was she still here? Why had she sat down as if she was seriously going to consider coming to work for him in what evidently was now his house. He'd be nearby all the time. She couldn't possibly.

Apparently, he was waiting on an answer and she finally grasped the thread of the conversation. "I don't know."

He shrugged as if it weren't important.

"Can you start today?"

"I'm not sure."

He cocked his head to one side. "Not sure because...?"

I'm not sure of anything at the moment. "Not sure if I want to work here. For you."

He seemed to understand. "Ah, I see. My reputation precedes me. Tell me, other than Ryan Reagle, is there anyone in this county who doesn't hate my guts?"

"I didn't mean—"

"No, no. I get it. I'm the town hero, the golden boy who made it to the big time and threw it all away. I failed the town, I failed my team. I failed everybody including myself, and now I can't catch a goddamn break. I get it, okay? I'll clean my own damn house. Sorry I wasted your time."

Trey scooted back to brace his hands on the chair arms and shoved himself up to stand. He limped across the porch and opened the screen door and let it slam shut behind him.

Baylee tried to sort out her feelings. She had no idea what he was talking about, but she knew for a fact there were quite a few locals who didn't think too highly of him and would be quite happy to make sure he knew it. Yes, he'd been a high school hero, a local football legend who'd made it to the pros. He'd had some good seasons with the Jacksonville Jacks with at least one Super Bowl ring, possibly two to show for it. She knew he'd been injured and he'd sort of gone downhill after that, but she hadn't followed his fall from fame all that closely. She'd had too many of her own problems to worry about at the time. Trey Christopher had been on a far back burner until she'd seen him again last year. Even then, she hadn't given him any serious thought. As far as she was concerned, he was unreachable, so far outside her normal sphere of acquaintances, she doubted she'd ever see him again.

She might hold a grudge against him. She might have some less than stellar memories of their one high school encounter. But he needed someone to clean his house and she needed the work. Was she going to be stupid and stubborn and walk away from a job because of some ancient history he didn't even remember?

The answer? No. She wasn't. She'd charge him top dollar and she'd do her best to keep a reasonable distance from him. But there was no good reason to walk away from this gig.

Irritated, she adjusted the glasses on her nose again. The frames were slightly bent and the prescription was four years old. If she took this job she might be able to afford another supply of contact lenses.

Decision made, she got up and tapped on the screen door's wood frame. "Hello? Trey?"

Silence greeted her. Carefully she eased the door open and closed it gently behind her. The kitchen hadn't changed much since the last time she'd set foot in it, except for appliance upgrades. She spotted dirty dishes in the sink and crumbs on the counter.

She crossed the kitchen and listened. From the bathroom near the back bedroom she could hear a shower running. Fine. She'd start in here and when Trey came out of the bathroom, they'd settle things between them. Like her hourly rate, for instance.

Trey turned the shower off and stood with his palms flat against the tile under the showerhead staring at the water swirling down the drain. He'd always done things big, he supposed, so when he failed, he failed hugely. Publicly. He'd take his licks, especially since he and the rest of the world knew he deserved them. Karma. He struggled for a Zen moment, to put everything in balance, keep it in perspective. Honestly, he hadn't thought he'd have to *beg* someone to clean his house. Not in this rural area and in the current economic climate.

Baylee Westring had turned him down, but he could find someone else. What was so great about her anyway? She certainly wasn't blessed with the gift of sparkling conversational skills. Frankly, she came across as a bit of a space cadet the way she'd stumbled through their brief meeting.

His initial impression was she looked like she had a bit too much on the ball to be cleaning houses. Even dressed as she was, she *looked* if not exactly sophisticated, then smart and capable in some indefinable way.

He'd already been thinking maybe she could do more than clean house. Maybe she could be like his personal assistant or something. Keep track of stuff for him the way Hayley used to. Although Hayley so much more than an assistant. He hadn't realized how much he'd counted on her, how much she did to keep things running smoothly for him, until he'd lost her.

Enough self-pity for the day, he warned himself. While he used to spend hours wallowing in it, he'd cut it back to five minutes per day. Usually in the morning after his shower. Once he got it over with, he refused to waste any more time beating himself up for things he couldn't change.

"Onward and upward," he muttered to himself as he stepped out of the shower with the towel wrapped around his waist. "Or at least forward."

He opened the bathroom door allowing the cloud of steam to escape out into the hall. Usually, he'd turn right to step into the bedroom next to the bathroom. But he heard water running and dishes clinking from the direction of the kitchen and turned the other way.

At the end of the hallway, he leaned against the wall and took in the scene. Baylee stood at the sink rinsing dishes and loading them into the dishwasher, her back to him. She did odd little dance steps while staying in one place and hummed along to an unseen music source. Near the door were a bucket and a canvas bag with rags and cleaning supplies. A broom and a mop leaned against the wall next to them.

Trey didn't know why the entire scene amused him. Or why stayed after she'd made it clear she didn't want anything to do with him. Not even if she was getting paid for it. He crossed his arms over his chest and waited for her to notice him.

After a couple more minutes she closed the dishwasher. She turned and jumped when she saw him. She put one hand to her chest and yanked the ear buds out of her ears. She didn't comment on him startling her which intrigued him. Instead, she stared at him.

"What are you doing?" he asked, not bothering to hide his amusement.

"I—um—cleaning." She gestured with one hand at the now empty sink.

"I don't recall hiring you." Trey couldn't figure out why he had such a strong desire to toy with her, to try and keep her off balance. He only knew he enjoyed it.

"Oh, well, then, um—never mind, I guess." She gestured at the sink. "No charge for doing the dishes."

"How much do you charge anyway?"

"It depends on what I'm expected to do."

Behind the wire-framed glasses, she had sort of light brown eyes almost the color of amber, he noted. "Cleaning house for starters. What's the going rate?"

"Twenty-five dollars an hour."

Trey snorted. He couldn't help it. Maybe in a city. But he knew good and well that no one, not in Henderson and certainly not in Ednaville would pay twenty-five an hour for housecleaning. Hell, he imagined most of the people around here cleaned their own houses or lived in their own filth. Maybe in an area closer to Cashiers or Highlands, or Asheville even, *maybe* she could find some sap to pay her twenty-five an hour. Maybe.

"Twenty-five an hour seems a little steep."

"You can afford it."

"I can. The question is, are you worth it?"

"I'm worth more, actually. But I'm running a one-day special."

Hutzpah, Trey thought. She was blatantly trying to take advantage of him and he should be bothered by it, but for some reason he wasn't. He figured twenty-five dollars an hour was probably a small price to pay to have her clean his house and entertain him in the process. God knew he could use some diversion from his own dismal thoughts.

"For twenty-five an hour this place better be spotless when you get done with it."

"It will be."

"And I'll need you to sign a confidentiality agreement."

He could see in her eyes his statement amused her, though she schooled her features to remain neutral. "No problem."

"Carry on, then."

As soon as he disappeared down the hallway and she heard a door close, Baylee took a deep breath trying to still her wildly beating heart and soothe her frazzled nerve endings.

Trey Christopher was a hunk, plain and simple. He looked good enough to eat standing there with his hair wet while the towel around his waist threatened to slip down another notch. He hadn't shaved and he had that sexy two- or three-day beard stubble sported by many male celebrities. Even though he was no longer a professional athlete, he obviously worked out. A lot. He had those well-defined muscles in his upper body guys get with weight training and those abs of his had to be due to crunches. A whole lot of crunches.

He'd been a charming hunk in high school, too, but his behavior when he'd had too much to drink had been a definite turn-off for her. She knew better than to be fooled twice by any attention Trey Christopher sent her way, didn't she?

Of course, she did.

Chapter Seven

♥

"**C**an you cook?"

Baylee jumped when she heard Trey's voice. One of the pitfalls of working with ear buds stuck in her ears all the time. Anyone could sneak up on her without her noticing. She also tended to sing song lyrics out loud and she'd been known to throw together an impromptu dance routine on occasion.

She yanked the buds out of her ears and stared at him. Every nerve ending she possessed went on red alert being this close to him. She could see the tiny lines radiating out from his eyes. He was only a couple years older than her, but the squint lines around his eyes were sexier than hell.

Oh, was he built. Like the football player he'd been his whole life, well, up until a couple of years ago, he had that broad athlete's chest that tapered to his waist and long muscled legs currently encased in faded denim. His forearms, below the sleeves of a faded, soft-looking blue tee shirt were corded with muscle and flecked with golden brown hairs.

Baylee realized her mouth hung open and she promptly shut it, covering the shock of his presence with irritation. "I'd appreciate it if you wouldn't sneak up on me when I'm working."

"Fine. Next time I'll send a spitball your way as warning."

She gave him what she hoped was a withering stare, but it didn't seem to faze him one bit.

"So. Can you cook or not?"

"Why?"

"Because I'm hungry. You're here. I'm paying you."

"You're paying me to clean," she corrected.

"Yes, but since I'm paying you by the hour, it shouldn't matter to you whether you're cleaning or cooking. *If* you can cook, that is."

Baylee rolled her eyes. What self-respecting North Carolina country girl didn't know how to cook? Or garden? Or can vegetables? Or pluck feathers off a freshly slaughtered chicken? "You'd be surprised what I know how to do."

Trey's eyebrows rose. He gave her a speculative look. Uh-oh. Did he think she was flirting with him? Did he think she was throwing out a double entendre or something? Insinuating some kind of sexual intent? As if.

"I'm sure you're a woman of many talents, but how are you with eggs and bacon?"

"In addition to cleaning up after you, you want a short order cook as well?"

"Forget it. This is more trouble than it's worth."

He turned and did his limp/walk across the kitchen. Baylee watched him for a minute debating. He had a great ass. Really, what difference did it make if she spent her time cooking or cleaning? Twenty-five an hour was twenty-five an hour. The longer she stayed, the more money he'd have to fork over when she left. One of the things she did enjoy about her current work situation was quick cash.

He took a carton of eggs and a package of bacon out of the refrigerator and set them on the counter.

He reached into a bottom cabinet near the stove and pulled out a cast iron skillet. He turned to set it on a burner and yelped in pain. The pan fell from his grasp, bounced off his foot and landed on the freshly mopped linoleum. Baylee expected him to grab his foot, but instead he grabbed his right shoulder with his opposite hand and swore a blue streak while staring at the welt on his foot.

Baylee bit her lip, caught between laughter and sympathy. Clearly, he was in pain, but the earlier scene was right out of *The Three Stooges*. She picked up the skillet. Gently she nudged him away from the stove. "Move over, Curly, before you permanently disable yourself. Are you all right?"

Trey mumbled something she didn't catch. He hobbled to the refrigerator and yanked an ice pack out of the freezer. He pulled out a chair and sat. After propping his foot on the seat of the adjacent chair, he settled the ice pack on it. "Sorry about the language," he said.

Baylee laid strips of bacon in the skillet and turned the heat up underneath it. "What do you want besides bacon and eggs?" she inquired over her shoulder.

When he didn't immediately answer she glanced at him and after a second or two he yanked his gaze up from wherever it had been.

Had he been checking her out? No way. If Trey thought she was going to be his temporary convenience and come running just because he crooked his little finger at her, he could forget it.

He continued to use the fingers of his left hand to massage his right shoulder. "Toast? Grits. Coffee. Juice."

"Got it." It really was like being a short order cook. She turned back to the stove where the bacon began to sizzle. She lowered the heat.

"I'll make the coffee," he volunteered.

She glanced at him again over her shoulder. "You know how to make coffee?"

"It's one of many things I do rather well."

"I'm sure you're a man of many talents."

"I'd let you do it, but you'd probably mess it up."

"Probably," she agreed. She didn't know why, but the fact he thought he was better at brewing coffee than she was amused her. "How do you want your eggs? And how many do you want?"

"Three. Over easy if you can manage it."

She gave him another look through veiled lashes. "I'll give it a shot." She'd been cooking over easy eggs practically her whole life. "Where do you keep the grits?"

He directed her to an upper cabinet as he got to his feet. He replaced the ice pack in the freezer and stepped to the counter near the sink. He emptied the grounds from his earlier coffee into the garbage and rinsed the carafe and the filter. Then he went through the ritual of adding water to the machine and grinding the beans.

Baylee turned to watch. He dumped the ground coffee into the filter. "You grind your own beans?"

"A decent cup of coffee is one of my few remaining vices."

"Ah," she said as if she understood what he meant, though of course, she did not. She went back to her own efforts, laying the bacon on a plate covered with a paper towel, popping bread into the toaster, stirring the grits and cracking the eggs.

The coffee was done brewing about the time everything else was ready. Trey had retrieved a carton of orange juice, butter and jam from the refrigerator. He'd poured a mug of the delicious-smelling coffee into a mug and took the seat he'd occupied earlier, again propping his right leg on the adjacent chair.

Baylee set the eggs, bacon, grits, and toast in front of him.

"Hey, I'm sorry. You should have made some for yourself."

"I ate already." A container of yogurt nearly three hours ago. Her stomach growled giving away the lie. Trey pretended not to hear it. "How about some coffee?"

"Um, I should probably get back to work," Baylee hedged.

Trey pointed to the chair across from him. "Sit."

"Excuse me. I'm not a trained hound you can just order around."

He got up and poured another mug full of coffee and set it at the place he'd indicated. Sorry. Please sit."

The aroma of the coffee, something exotic and spicy and rich, wafted in her direction. She opened the refrigerator for the small carton of cream she'd noticed earlier.

She took the seat Trey had indicated and added cream to the mug until it was a warm golden-brown color. She lifted it, sniffed, and took a sip. "Mmm."

Her gaze met his over the rim of the mug. He looked both pleased and amused by her reaction. "Told you."

He started eating, chopping the bacon into crispy bits and mixing it with the eggs until it was a runny brownish, yellow and white mess. Baylee sipped her coffee and tried not to stare, which was hard to do since he was right across the table from her, directly in her line of vision. He was so damn easy to look at.

She let herself drift back in time, remembering the party Jenny had dragged her to the summer before their sophomore year of high school. A gathering of mostly graduating seniors, of which Trey had been one. The annual senior drunk was the unofficial term for this particular get-together. Jenny's cousin Bart was in Trey's class and he didn't seem to care if Jenny and Baylee tagged along with him.

Even now, Baylee couldn't quite figure out how Trey had singled her out from the group of half-drunk teenagers gathered around the bonfire, or how he'd hooked his arm around her neck in a possessive gesture. They'd both been drinking, of course. As usual, Trey was the life of the party, joking and laughing and cutting up. Mister Popularity. He called her darlin' and nuzzled her neck. She could remember the feel of all those guy muscles when he pulled her closer still, whispered in her ear.

Usually, a girl like her would be beneath Trey Christopher's notice. But that night, by some miracle she'd snagged his interest. She'd wondered ever since if it was just a matter of being in the right place at the right time. Or was it because she'd worn contacts instead of her glasses. Maybe she'd simply been convenient and willing and slightly drunk for the first time in her life. Drunk enough not to object to Trey getting what her grandmother would call "too familiar" with her.

She'd worshipped him from afar her entire freshman year, catching glimpses of him in the hallway or the cafeteria. Following his every move at every football game of the season. He always seemed to have a girlfriend of the month, one of the cheerleaders or the drum majorette or some hottie from the marching band dance line. He loved them and left them with a remarkable regularity, never noticing their broken hearts and longing looks.

But that warm spring night, when he had his arm around *her,* she had just enough beer buzzing through her system to feel like she'd landed in a fairy tale with the prince of her dreams.

He maneuvered her away from the thinning crowd of kids and climbed to the hayloft. Once there, Trey pulled her down with him. He'd been all knowing hands, sexy whispers and practiced kisses. She thought she'd caught fire, the way everything he did made her so hot. Her skin burned and her blood simmered. Surely she'd burst into flame. Though she'd only been fifteen, he made her body ache in ways it never had before or since.

Somehow, he got her out of most of her clothes. His hands never seem to still and, caught up in the newness and excitement of being with a boy, along with having her normal inhibitions lowered courtesy of the beer buzz, she barely protested.

Trey's skin was hot and slick beneath her fingertips. His shirt was unbuttoned and untucked which gave her access to his entire upper body. All those boy muscles thrilled her. The scent of him intoxicated her. The hair on his chest tickled her fingers. She didn't recall panicking when she heard the slide of his zipper. Not even when she felt the brush of him, foreign and completely male, against her thigh, or when he positioned himself between her legs, like a heat-seeking missile searching for access to its target.

She was lost, lost, swept away in the never experienced sensation. But suddenly, like a broken reel of an old movie, everything stopped. With a sigh, Trey wilted above her, his weight crushing her as he sank down on top of her. Something was wrong. It took Baylee's inebriated brain a moment to realize what it was. Trey was not moving. At all. She was lying on a pile of straw in a dusty hayloft with her clothes undone or twisted around her and the dead weight of Trey Christopher on top of her.

"Trey?" she whispered.

He didn't answer. He was breathing, though. Had he fallen asleep? Was she that boring? She shoved at him enough to get out from under him. Embarrassment burned her cheeks. She tugged her clothes back on or back into place, whichever was required, trying not to look at Trey who was sprawled on his side, half buried in the hay, like he hadn't a care in the world. His shirt was half off his shoulders, his fly was still unzipped and he was sort of spilling out of it, but not in an attractive way. She looked away, embarrassed for him and disgusted with herself.

She'd left him there, as she half-stumbled, half-fell down the ladder from the loft. She found Jenny and Bart, both of whom were ready to leave. To this day, Jenny was the only person who knew what had happened in the loft.

Trey graduated with his class two days later. Afterward he'd gone on a week-long class trip to the Bahamas. She never saw him or heard from him again until last year at his grandmother's funeral.

Baylee jumped when she realized Trey had snapped his fingers not once but twice in front of her face. "What?" she said irritably, trying to hide the blush rising in her cheeks.

"I said would you like more coffee? In fact, I said it twice. Are you prone to seizures or something?"

"Of course not!" she snapped.

He gave her an assessing stare. "Well, you were definitely out of it."

He got up and retrieved the carafe from the counter and brought it back to the table to refill his mug. He lifted the carafe in her direction. She nodded and he topped hers off before taking his seat again.

He'd finished eating and pushed the dirty dishes to the side. "Let's talk."

Baylee added some more cream to her coffee. She composed herself, banishing the nightmarish memory to the furthest recesses of her mind, refusing to think about the impact it had on her subsequent choices in life, and held Trey's gaze.

"Do you think you could work two days a week?"

Baylee couldn't help it. Her eyes bugged out and she set her mug down harder than she meant to on the scarred oak. "Two days? Are you that much of a slob?"

Trey grinned and emitted a slight chuckle. "I was wondering if your duties extend beyond housecleaning." He inclined his head in acknowledgment of the empty dishes next to him. "And cooking."

"That depends. What did you have in mind?"

"Laundry, for one thing. Grocery shopping. Maybe the occasional errand." He glanced toward the screen door. "I'd like to get my grandmother's flower garden back in shape. At least pull the weeds. Until I get some P.T., I'm sort of useless because of my knee."

"And your shoulder," Baylee pointed out. She took another sip of coffee. "What'd you do to it anyway?"

"Threw one too many passes. Got sacked one too many times. Played one too many games." Trey shrugged. He reached up and dug his fingers into the shoulder muscle one more time then gave an exaggerated shrug and stretched and rotated his head to loosen his neck muscles.

"Sometimes it hits me if I move the wrong way or pick up something from the wrong angle."

"Maybe you need a massage," Baylee suggested.

His eyes lit up. "Are you offering?"

She hesitated. "Not for the happy ending you're probably expecting. Plus, my rates go up."

"A happy ending for me these days is pain relief. Period. Even if it's temporary."

Baylee shrugged. She got up from her chair and came to stand behind him. "Want to show me where it hurts?"

Trey dug his fingers into the shoulder again. Baylee noticed the gold flecked hairs along the back of his hand. "Right. There." She put her fingers where his were and he dropped his hand.

"Okay." She dug in with her thumbs. Trey groaned.

"Did I get it?" she asked, pleased with his reaction in spite of herself.

"Oh, yeah. Right there. Harder."

"I don't want to hurt you." Still, she dug into the knot of muscle as hard as she could first with both thumbs and then with her knuckles.

"You can't hurt me," Trey grunted.

Wanna bet?

Chapter Eight

♥

Baylee wriggled around on the lumpy daybed mattress until she could reach the shelf above her head. She found what she wanted immediately and pulled it down with one hand. She pushed the curtains aside and lay back on the pillow. A shake of the snow globe sent the lavender-tinted glitter swirling. Gently she wound the silver key on the side and listened to the childish voices singing "It's a Small World."

When the glitter settled, she shook the globe again, entranced by Snow White's gabled castle and the tiny figures gathered in the settling snow around it. She liked to pretend she was there, in the fortress of such a magical castle where nothing could hurt her. She'd live a fairy tale life complete with a charming prince and a happily ever after at the end.

The thought always made her smile although lately the only part of any fairy tale she lived most days was Cinderella's drudgery.

She'd acquired the snow globe during a family vacation to Disney World. Baylee had a blurry memory of a long car ride during a particularly hot summer and a couple of nights in a no-frills motel room. Her parents shared one queen bed and she and Lisa were in the other. Meals were unexpected treats from fast food joints.

Her parents must have scrimped and saved to make the trip because it was the only time they ever vacationed as a family. But when they arrived at the Magic Kingdom, when Baylee got her first glimpse of the castle, she'd been absolutely mesmerized. She'd stared at the panes of glass in the window, the turrets and towers, as they approached en masse. She'd been disappointed to discover there was little to the interior, at least little that was accessible to her. But maybe that was best, she'd decided, for she could use her imagination to fill in what it looked like inside. Plush cushions, a fireplace, a purple bedroom with a canopy bed. A home fit for the princess she would be some day.

Even now, the thought made Baylee smile. She might be far from being a princess, but that didn't mean she couldn't dream. She couldn't wait to escape not only this house but this town with its gossiping tongues and pointing fingers.

Yes, she'd leave the past and her disappointments behind and Trey Christopher was going to help her do it. Her smile widened. The job with him was going to bump her finances considerably.

There was no better place to escape to she'd decided. Orlando, Florida or bust.

Chapter Nine

♥

Two mornings later Trey leaned against the door of the dining room and sipped his coffee. The last thing he wanted to do was sit behind his makeshift desk and go through everything he'd allowed to accumulate on top of it. He didn't see as how he had much choice. Maybe he'd start by going through his voice mails and text messages. Then the FedEx envelopes. He should probably institute some sort of filing system for his investment reports, contracts, bills, and miscellaneous mail. His lip curled in distaste.

During his marriage, Hayley did those things. He no longer had a wife. What he needed was an assistant.

Tires crunched on gravel. Coffee cup in hand he went out to the porch to watch Baylee exit her car and load up her cleaning supplies. She hesitated only a moment when she spied him there watching her.

"Good morning."

"Good morning." He opened the screen door for her and followed her in, a smile on his face. He'd just found his assistant.

Forty-five minutes later, replete with two helpings of French toast and sausage along with orange juice, Trey settled back in the kitchen chair and studied Baylee from across the table. He'd insisted she take a break after she made breakfast and cleaned up. She sipped her coffee and held his gaze.

"Would you be available to work for me full-time?"

She set down her cup. "Full-time? You don't need a full-time cleaning person."

"No. I had something else in mind."

She raised her eyebrows, waiting.

"I need an assistant."

Baylee frowned. "To do what?"

Trey waved in the direction of the dining room. "You dusted around the mess on the dining room table the other day. I need help getting it organized and keeping it that way."

Baylee sipped some more coffee. "What makes you think I'm qualified to do that?"

"You used to work in a bank."

Baylee glanced away for a second and then back at him. "I never told you that."

"Was it a secret?"

"No. I didn't think you'd snoop into my background."

"I didn't snoop. Ryan mentioned it."

"Oh."

"Are you interested or not?"

Baylee propped her chin in her hand and regarded him. Something was going on behind her eyes. Some sort of calculation, Trey thought.

"I'm interested in hearing your proposal."

"I'll pay your hourly rate for forty hours a week, but I'm the boss. You clean, you cook, you shop, you organize and anything else within reason I ask you to do."

"Who gets to decide what's within reason?"

"You do. If I ask you to do something you object to, say so. We'll work it out."

Again, he saw her calculating. Numbers? How to take advantage of him? He wished he knew.

"What if you don't have enough work to keep me busy for forty hours?"

"I'll pay you for forty hours. There might be weeks when it's more or less. You can keep track of your hours and tell me if it balances out to more than that in a month. If you're caught up, you can take off no matter what time it is."

"You're overpaying for this kind of job, you know that, right?"

"I was already overpaying for you to do nothing but clean."

Baylee grinned. Trey liked her smile. He liked that she was smart enough to be amused by the fact that he knew and allowed her to take advantage of him when she'd negotiated her hourly rate.

"How much notice do you want if I decide to quit?"

"You haven't said you'd take the job and you're already planning to quit?"

"I don't plan to stick around here forever cleaning houses and running errands. I've plastered my resume all over the Southeast. It's just a matter of time before I find something comparable to what I was doing before. Will two weeks notice be enough?"

"Sure."

"Great. Should we start now?"

Baylee managed to contain her glee until she left Trey's house. Organizing him wasn't as hard as he apparently thought it was. Working in bank operations, she'd had to be organized in order to have vital information at her fingertips if an emergency called for it. Overseeing a couple of months of paperwork for one former pro athlete paled in comparison to keeping track of the amount a large bank holding company generated.

She didn't think she was being overly optimistic when she'd told Trey she'd find another banking position soon. Even though she'd barely had any nibbles, the economy would turn around sometime. When it did, she'd be ready.

While she worked, she added and subtracted figures having to do with her own financial situation. Trey's overly generous salary offer was several thousand dollars below what she'd once made at the bank. Initially she'd had her suspicions about what exactly Trey wanted her to do for that kind of money, but as best she could determine, he had no ulterior motives or interest in her beyond her housekeeping and personal assistant skills.

She wished she didn't find him attractive. Shouldn't her experience with him in the hayloft at that high school party have turned her off of him forever? Yes, definitely. But it apparently it hadn't. Supposedly Trey had given up drinking and his dependence on prescription drugs. He wasn't that seventeen-year-old boy any longer.

Besides, Baylee made sure to hide her attraction to him under layers of indifference, professionalism, humor, and mild sarcasm. He'd never find it there.

Meanwhile, Baylee knew almost to the penny how much she owed on her two credit cards, both of which were nearly maxed to their limits. She had to use them until things improved, until she made some money, until she found a real job. She could barely make the minimum payments each month and the interest always outstripped what she managed to pay toward them. She couldn't wait to use her first few paychecks to pay both off. After that she swore she'd hide them in a drawer beneath her underwear and take them out only in case of an emergency.

The tires on her car were going bald and she needed an oil change badly. Maybe she would splurge on a haircut in a salon instead of relying on Lisa to trim her ends every couple of months. More contact lenses. Maybe some new glasses. Her list went on and on. She could hardly wait to get home and write it all down and run the numbers on a calculator instead of in her head.

As a boss, Trey was an odd combination of demanding and lackadaisical. He wasn't concerned with how she organized him, but he wanted to be able to find everything. She'd explained what she was doing as she did it.

Before they'd even begun, he produced a confidentiality agreement and told her to take as much time as she needed to look it over before she signed it. When he'd mentioned it the other day, she'd been amused, but she could see he was dead serious about it. If she violated Trey's privacy, the agreement guaranteed he'd make her regret it. She read through it, made a copy for herself, and signed it.

Chapter Ten

♥

Trey stared at the unappetizing meal he'd removed from the microwave. He stabbed at the rice and vegetables and chicken, ungluing them from each other and mixing them together.

It was food, he reminded himself. He was hungry and taste wasn't high on his list of priorities. He took a bottle of sweet tea from the fridge, picked up the plate of food and settled himself at the table on the back porch.

While he ate, he viewed what was now his domain and tried to ignore the tendrils of loneliness that crept up on him, especially in the evenings. Technically he'd been alone for well over a year, ever since his divorce from Hayley became final. But he'd had a lot to do. He'd sold his house in Jacksonville, oversaw disposing of most of the contents. He'd had a lot of physical and psychological therapy, especially after the last knee surgery. He'd had what felt like a ton of loose ends to tie up from his former life and he hadn't thought too much about what the future would hold. If he had he might have started drinking and popping pills again.

No, he told himself. He was never going down that road again. He'd find something to do, to occupy his spare time, or he'd find someone to spend it with. Maybe he should take a cooking class.

He shoveled forkfuls of food into his mouth, chewed and swallowed until the plate was empty. He leaned back in the chair and sipped the tea, letting the surroundings soothe him, the cool evening air surround him, the mountains in the distance comfort him.

This was home for better or worse. He had no desire to be anywhere else. *If you can make it here, you can make it anywhere.* The lines from the classic song about New York City played through his head. If the world only knew how much tougher it was going to be for him to re-conquer Henderson, North Carolina. Maybe he should stop looking at it as a fight and simply accept what was.

He glanced at his journal. He might write in it later but for now he wanted to replay the events of the day in his head brood a little.

He'd gotten off easy in court this morning, and he knew it. If the powers that be in Henderson County wanted to make his life difficult, he'd handed them a golden opportunity when he'd sped through Ednaville and been stopped by Officer Justin Spoley.

Judge Artemus O'Toole had been a fixture in the Henderson County Courthouse for thirty years. He attended the same church as Trey's parents, his wife bought homemade jam from Grandma J every year and he played pinochle with Andy Christopher and several other locals at the lodge.

Over a pair of half-glasses he'd peered at Trey who stood before him with Ryan at his side. The judge clucked and tsked and shuffled the pages in front of him.

"Is Officer Spoley available this morning?" he asked, glancing first at his clerk and then at the bailiff. The bailiff motioned to the gallery area behind them. Trey wasn't surprised when Justin Spoley stepped forward in full uniform and greeted the judge.

"This is quite a list of citations you've leveled in Mr. Christopher's direction, Officer."

"Yes, sir."

Judge O'Toole cleared his throat and picked up one of the pages. "Indecent exposure. Mr. Christopher exposed himself to you, is that correct, Officer?"

"Uh, no, sir."

"You witnessed him engaging in some sort of depravity within the Ednaville City Limits?"

Spoley coughed. "No, sir. Not exactly sir."

"You got videotape or pictures of Mr. Christopher indecently exposing himself? Witnesses? Complaints?"

"No, sir."

"Charge dismissed."

He stared at Spoley who was wise enough to keep his mouth shut.

Trey slid a glance Ryan's way, but Ryan remained professional and showed no outward sign of emotion.

"Now, then." Judge O'Toole picked up another page. "Attempted bribery of a police officer. Mr. Christopher offered you money? In return for what exactly, Officer Spoley?"

"To not write him a citation for speeding."

"How much did he offer you?"

"He didn't mention a specific amount, but he suggested we could reach an agreement."

"What sort of agreement?" O'Toole asked.

"He didn't specify, sir."

"He didn't specifically offer you any monetary reward?"

"No sir, but that's what he implied."

"Or it's what you assumed. Did you in fact take any money from Mr. Christopher?"

"No, sir."

"Charge dismissed." He banged his gavel again. He glanced at his clerk, and she nodded.

"Driving under the influence." He swung his gaze to Trey. "Mr. Christopher were you intoxicated when Officer Spoley stopped you for speeding?"

"No, sir."

"Were you under the influence of any illegal drugs or substances when you were stopped?"

"No, sir."

"Yet you refused to allow Officer Spoley to administer the portable breathalyzer."

"Yes, sir."

O'Toole stared hard at Trey for a moment. "Well within your right to do so." He turned his attention back to Spoley. "Officer Spoley did you have any reason to believe Mr. Christopher was intoxicated when you made the stop?"

Spoley didn't reply immediately. O'Toole continued. "Was he driving erratically? Did he not seem in control of his mental capacities when you spoke to him?"

"No, sir."

"He did not seem in control of his mental capacities when you spoke to him?"

"No, sir, he wasn't driving erratically."

"But he was in control of his mental capacities?"

"He appeared to be, sir."

"Why did you ask him to take a breathalyzer test?"

"I wanted to be sure, sir."

"Officer Spoley, how long have you been a police officer?"

"Ten years, sir."

"Are you telling me you're unable to ascertain whether a motorist is in control of his mental capacities once you've spoken to him and asked him to step out of his vehicle?"

"No, sir. I mean yes, sir."

"Do you administer a breathalyzer to all your traffic stops to make sure they aren't under the influence?"

"No, sir."

"Why did you attempt it with Mr. Christopher?"

"I was aware of his history. Sir."

Judge O'Toole seemed to ruminate on Spoley's answer. His gaze moved from Spoley to Trey to Ryan and back.

"I'm sure you've had other citizens who've had a past history with driving under the influence. Do you immediately attempt to administer a breathalyzer test to all of them?"

Spoley hesitated. "No, sir."

"This smacks of some kind of profiling on your part, Officer Spoley. In the eyes of the law all citizens are innocent until proven guilty and they are all to be treated the same. You've left the county vulnerable to legal action by Mr. Christopher, should his counsel advise him to pursue such action.

"Charge dismissed." He banged his gavel and glared at Spoley.

Trey had a hard time controlling the smug grin tugging at the corners of his mouth, but he managed to contain it.

"Now as to the citation for speeding," the judge continued, lifting another page and staring at it. He looked at Trey. "Mr. Christopher, how do you plead?"

"Guilty, Your Honor."

"Excellent. Two hundred dollar fine and fifty hours of community service."

"Fifty hours of community—"

"Thank you, Judge." Ryan's normally calm tone rose authoritatively over Trey's objection.

"I'm not done. You'll do your service at the county animal shelter. Have it completed in ninety days." He gave Trey a thoughtful look before he turned his attention to Spoley. "Officer Spoley, I suggest you exercise better judgment in your future traffic stops and keep your personal feelings out of your citation book." He pounded his gavel one more time. "Ten minute recess."

The judge disappeared through a side door behind the clerk's desk. Ryan steered Trey to the clerk for paperwork. While they waited for her to complete it, Trey glanced around the nearly deserted courtroom. Beyond the railing that separated the room were rows of old-fashioned wood benches where Baylee had taken a seat near the aisle to wait for him. But now she stood talking to Justin Spoley.

Trey couldn't hear what they were saying, only the murmur of their voices. Still, it annoyed him that Baylee would even speak to a man who obviously had it in for him. Not that she owed him anything, he reminded himself. She cleaned his house and organized his office. He paid her to do it. The end.

Yet her familiarity with Spoley rankled. It figured they'd be acquainted, Trey also acknowledged. They'd grown up in the same area and were close in age. No surprise that their paths might have crossed before today.

He had to turn his attention back to the clerk. She handed him a copy of the judge's determination on the various citations and a number to call to set up his community service at the animal shelter.

When he and Ryan turned to leave, only Baylee was waiting, her bag over her shoulder, car keys in her hand. "Hi, Ry," she said to Ryan. They hugged briefly. "How's my godson?"

"Wearing us out," Ryan informed her. "Who knew parenting was so exhausting?"

"Ha. You and Jenny love every minute of it."

"True. We're just too tired to realize how much fun we're having."

She switched her attention to Trey. "All set? I only caught the end. You have to pay a fine and do community service?"

"He got off easy because he has such a good lawyer," Ryan said, ribbing Trey.

"You know that guy, Spoley?" Trey asked Baylee.

A look Trey couldn't readily interpret passed between her and Ryan. "We're acquainted."

Ryan glanced at his watch as they exited the courtroom. "I've got to get back to the office." He and Trey shook hands and agreed to touch base later in the week.

"How about an early lunch?" Trey asked Baylee. He had a physical therapy appointment at eleven-thirty, which gave them about an hour to kill. "Is food all you ever think about?" Baylee asked as they headed for the elevator.

"Not all," Trey returned cheerfully. "But it is one of my basic needs."

"Are you buying?"

"Of course. Let's get something straight. When you're on the clock working for me, I pay your expenses. In any case, I wouldn't invite you to lunch and expect you to pay for it."

"Trey Christopher, chivalrous gentlemen," Baylee teased. "Who would have thought?"

"Not too many people up until now," Trey assured her. "I'm a work in progress."

"Aren't we all," Baylee murmured.

They rode down the elevator in silence and made their way outside. Baylee clicked the Cayenne's remote and they got in. Trey insisted she use it for shopping or errands on his behalf or to chauffer him to his doctor and p.t. appointments, because he was often extremely uncomfortable afterwards.

Trey thought some more about the interaction he'd witnessed between her and Spoley and about the look that had passed between her and Ryan. Something was going on there, but they hadn't seen the need to enlighten him.

He supposed, if he had the time and the energy, he could formulate a conspiracy theory where all three of them had a secret connection and were out to get him, but his imagination wasn't that good.

After they were seated at a booth at the Mountainside Diner and had placed their orders, they discussed Trey's upcoming trip to New York for meetings with the ESPN executives.

"You could come with me," he suggested. "If you want."

"Really?" Baylee looked delighted by the idea. "I've always wanted to go to New York City. I want to see Central Park and the museums and a Broadway play, and—"

"Whoa. Hold on, there. It's only for a couple of days. You won't have time to do all that."

"Oh." He'd deflated Baylee's enthusiasm as quickly as he'd caused it.

He tried to backtrack. "I mean, you can do some of those things. Just probably not all of them this trip."

"Do you need me to go to your meetings with you?"

"No. Probably not. You can be a tourist during the day. Maybe join us for dinner, though. It wouldn't hurt for you to meet the others because you'll probably be dealing with them on the phone and through e-mail."

Baylee brightened when he indicated there would be more trips in the future. Maybe next time, he'd tack on a few extra days and take her to a play and wander a museum with her. Come fall he'd be spending a lot of weekends in either New York or Atlanta.

They went on to discuss the travel and hotel arrangements which Baylee would need to coordinate with the executive producer's assistant.

After lunch she drove him to his physical therapy appointment. "Can I ask you something?" Trey began once she had parked in front of the facility. "Feel free to tell me it's none of my business."

"I'll be happy to." A smile twitched at the corner of Baylee's mouth.

"That cop Spoley—"

Baylee's expression changed to a slight frown.

Trey forged ahead. "Something going on between you two?"

"No."

Trey fixed her with a look. "That's it? 'No.' You were talking to him in the courtroom."

"He was talking to me," Baylee corrected.

Trey crossed his arms over his chest and made no move to exit the vehicle. He stared out the window trying to figure out why Baylee having a conversation with Justin Spoley bugged him so much.

She sighed and he turned to look at her. "He's got a thing for me, okay? I don't know why. Every time he asks me out, I turn him down. That's it."

"Why don't you go out with him?"

"I don't like him. There's something about him, I don't know, he turns me off."

"He hasn't gotten the message, though."

"Apparently not."

"Is that what he did earlier? In the courtroom? He asked you out?"

The smile appeared at the corners of her mouth again. "I guess it's too late for me to tell you this is none of your business."

"It isn't. But I want to know."

"Yes. He asked me out. Again. I turned him down. Again. Happy now?"

Trey grinned. "Definitely. Spoley's a jerk."

"Aren't most men?"

"Probably. But if you're going to date a jerk, at least date one who's trying to change his ways."

"Ha. I'll let you know when I find one."

Trey winked at her as he opened his car door. "Darlin', I'm right here."

Trey hated to admit it, but he'd been wiped out after his appointment. He'd found an excellent physical therapist, but she was brutal. He'd taken some ibuprofen and in spite of his discomfort, he'd managed to conk out. When he woke, Baylee was gone. She'd put away the groceries she'd shopped for during his appointment and straightened the kitchen. His mail was sorted, she'd left checks for his signature and arranged his e-mail messages in order of importance.

He was unaccountably bummed. He would have liked for her to still be there to share a lousy frozen dinner with him, watch TV, play cards or talk to him. Hell, she didn't have to do any of that. He'd have been happy if she'd just *been there*. But he had no right to ask or expect her to stay.

He went inside to pour himself a cup of coffee and set his plate in the sink. Upon returning to the porch he picked up his journal and his pen. Once he set his thoughts down, he'd meditate and maybe take a long, hot shower. Maybe he could erase the thoughts of Baylee and Spoley together before he went to sleep.

Chapter Eleven

♥

Matty stepped inside Mamacita's front door and let the warmth of the small house envelope him. Even though his memories of being here as a small child were faint, he always experienced that same sense of welcome and comfort as soon as he closed the door behind him.

How often had his biological mother dumped him with Mamacita when he was a baby? He remembered her handing him over to Mamacita without a backward glance or a second thought about the tears on his face. Mamacita would envelope him against her ample bosom so different from his mother's skinny, bony frame. She dried his tears and rubbed his back.

Many times he'd been told his mother had been sick, but he knew the truth. His addicted mother cared more about drugs than she did about him. He supposed that counted as a sickness. One day she handed him over to Mamacita and she didn't come back. Matty didn't remember missing his mother. He'd have happily stayed with Mamacita forever if he could. But it wasn't to be.

A woman in a business suit carrying a briefcase came. She spoke in officious tones while Mamacita held him close. She followed the woman to her car and buckled Matty into a child seat in the back. Matty cried and fought the restraints, wanting to get back into Mamacita's arms. She was crying too, even while she tried to soothe him. Even now he could recall how sad she'd looked which had only made him cry and kick harder.

He'd worn himself out and fallen asleep, and when he woke up, he was somewhere else. He had blurry memories of that time and of the few foster families he'd been placed with before he'd arrived at the home of Dan and Diane Westring. There he'd stayed. They adopted him. They might even have loved him, Matty thought. But Diane died and Dan crawled further into his bottles of booze. Somehow Matty had arrived back at the only place he'd ever felt loved.

He wasn't even sure how he'd found it. He'd taken off on his bicycle one afternoon out of sheer lonely desperation. Dan was quietly drinking in front of the television. Lisa was yelling at the twins about sneaking out of the house the previous night. Baylee wasn't around. No one noticed when he slipped out the front door.

The bicycle was a yellow mountain bike he'd got for his twelfth birthday. He was too big for it now, but it was the only transportation he had. He'd started riding with no particular destination in mind. He'd ridden through one of the tonier sections of Henderson where the big houses, some of which had been converted into bed and breakfast inns, lined the street. He kept riding until he crossed the railroad tracks.

Like he'd turned a page from what had started out as a fairy tale and became a horror story, the landscape changed dramatically. Many of the houses were in disrepair. Porches sagged and boards covered windows. A few of the occupants stared at him with a lack of curiosity in their gazes as if nothing could surprise them anymore.

Henderson wasn't such a big place that he hadn't known this section of it existed, but he never had cause to come here. He didn't today either, but something drew him on. He passed yards filled with weeds, dirt and trash, abandoned houses and old cars that would never see road time again.

He turned down one of the streets at random and skidded to a halt before a house unlike all the others. Although it was old and in need of paint, the porch was swept and the front yard clean of debris. Instead of grass, there were flowers rioting everywhere, including climbing up a trellis to one side of the porch. Two ancient metal lawn chairs covered with cushions flanked the front door. A small picket fence, also in need of paint surrounded the perimeter of the yard. An old Toyota pick-up was parked in a narrow drive next to the house.

A sense of déjà vu washed over Matty, but he couldn't think why. He glanced down the street in each direction. The sense of familiarity became stronger. He leaned his bike against the fence and looked closer at the flowers and the porch. There were two windows facing the street. In the lower right corner of one of them was a faded decal. Matty stared at the graphic design of a turquoise hand depicted there. It was peeling up on the bottom but he saw the few letters left. "SA" and "HAV." Safe Haven.

A program the county had used at one time to give children a place to go if they felt they were in danger. He'd seen a few of the old stickers around town. Diane had explained to him what they were. But that was before she'd died. He hadn't found a safe haven since.

While he stood staring the screen door opened and a man several years older than he was came out. He was of mixed race like Matty, of average height, with coal black curly hair and dark brown eyes. He wore an army green tee shirt and fatigues. "Can I help you?"

Like everything else, something about the man seemed familiar to Matty, but he didn't know why or how to explain his presence. They stared at each other while Matty tried to formulate a response, but the man asked him a second question before he could. "Do I know you?"

"I don't know."

The man stepped off the porch and came closer never taking his gaze from Matty. "What's your name, son?"

"Matty. Mateo. Westring."

"Matty?" The man's face broke into a huge grin. He reached across the fence and squeezed Matty's shoulder. "Oh, boy will Mamacita ever be glad to see you. Come on in."

He turned but Matty didn't follow. "Mamacita?" he repeated.

The man stopped and turned back. "She's my grandmother. She took care of you whenever your mother couldn't. Loved you like you were one of her own. Like to broke her heart when she had to give you up."

Matty stared at him as he went on.

"You don't remember me, either I guess. Desmond." He stuck out a hand and Matty automatically shook it. "She already had custody of me. State didn't think she could handle a toddler. Come on, now. She'll never forgive me if you don't come let her have a look at you."

Like in a dream, Matty followed Desmond up the walk and through the front door into the tiny living room that like everything else felt familiar. He breathed in a combination of old furniture and home cooking. "She's back in the kitchen," Desmond told Matty.

"Mama? I got somebody here to see you."

"Who that?"

A rotund woman with graying hair tucked up in a loose bun turned from the stove where she'd been stirring a fragrant pot. Oxygen lines trailed over her stout bosom from a tank on wheels next to her. She stared at Matty through the thick lenses of her glasses, her gaze going from him to Desmond and back.

"That's not? It can't be. Lord, Des, don't you fool with an old woman. Matty?"

Matty nodded. "Yes, ma'am."

The woman toddled toward Matty her arms outstretched until she enveloped him in a hug murmuring words he couldn't understand. He had to bend down to her because he was almost as tall as Desmond, but he didn't mind. She smelled like flowers and whatever she'd used to season the pot on the stove and underneath it all was something Matty must have recognized from long ago. Did caring have a scent all its own?

The hours melted away that first afternoon in Mamacita's kitchen. She and Desmond reminisced and, in their memories, Matty retrieved missing pieces of himself. They'd pressed Matty to stay and eat. Desmond helped her dish up the food from the stove. After Mamacita's recital of a blessing over the meal which included her thankfulness for having Matty once again under her roof, Matty ate like he'd been starving. The rich red sauce included beans and chunks of meet over rice jumbled with bits of colorful peppers and onions. Along with it was some sort of fat, floury tortilla-like bread with a chewy, yet tender texture.

They chatted during the meal, Matty carefully editing each mention of his adoptive family.

Mamacita's expression clouded with sorrow when he told her about the loss of his adoptive mother. She covered his hand with hers. "I know she was a good woman. She raised a fine son."

Matty blushed. He'd done some things neither Mamacita nor Diane would have been proud of.

After a simple dessert of fresh sliced strawberries and peaches over angel food cake, Matty thanked Mamacita. She hugged him hard. "You come back and see me soon."

Desmond walked him to the porch. "I've been home on leave the past couple of weeks. I'm headed back to the base tomorrow for the last six months of my second tour. I don't know if I'll re-up after that." He glanced back to the house and motioned Matty to follow him down the steps.

"Mama thinks she doesn't need any help, but I don't like her being alone. She gets disoriented sometimes and she's fallen twice. She still has a few friends and neighbors around, and the county sends out a nurse once a week to check on her, but that's it."

"What's wrong with her? Why does she need oxygen?" Matty asked. "Diabetes. Congestive heart failure." Desmond raised a hand and let it drop. "Old age. I was hoping to keep her out of a nursing home until my tour's up at the end of the year."

"I can come by and make sure she's okay, see if she needs anything," Matty offered. "After school and on the weekends.

"You'd do that?"

"Sure," Matty said already looking forward to spending more time in the small house where acceptance and approval greeted him as soon as he crossed the threshold.

"Wow, man. I'd really appreciate it." He gave Matty a man-hug and clapped him on the shoulder. "You ever need me, Mama's got my contact information next to the calendar in the kitchen. You got a cell phone?"

Matty knew he was one of the few kids his age who didn't. "Un unh."

"Call me from Mama's landline, then."

"Okay. I will." Matty got on his bike, waved to Desmond, and pedaled home.

It didn't seem like anyone had missed him that first evening, so Matty kept coming back after school and on the weekends. He did whatever needed doing while he was there. Mama seemed happy to have his company and help and he knew Des was glad his grandmother spent less time unsupervised.

Jack Frost would track him down sooner or later, Matty knew. The man never gave up. He took his job seriously and, Matty had to admit, he acted like he cared. But Matty wasn't convinced that wasn't just an act on his part. He'd seen the looks his probation officer sent Baylee's way a time or two. She was oblivious, but Matty wouldn't put it past him to use Matty's behavior as an excuse to hit on her.

Whatever, Matty, thought as he fell asleep. What could Jack Frost do? Matty had mostly been behaving himself except for breaking his curfew several nights a week and cutting his first class a couple of times when he'd overslept. He'd be thrilled if more community service was added to his sentence. Then he'd have somewhere to spend the rest of his free time. Anywhere but in this house where everyone ignored his existence.

Chapter Twelve

♥

Apple Jack's had been a local watering hole for as long as Trey could remember. There were a few other smaller hole-in-the-wall type drinking establishments dotted around Henderson, but Apple Jack's was the most established, set in a rambling structure that had once housed a cider press at the south end of the main highway which unevenly bisected the town.

The menu featured standard bar-and-grill fare and the jukebox blared when there wasn't a local band featured on the small stage overlooking an equally small dance floor.

The clack of balls from the pool tables punctuated the clink of ice against glasses and on a Friday night such as this, the high-pitched chatter of the locals ready to blow off steam for the weekend.

At Ryan's invitation, Trey had joined him for a game or two of pool. They hadn't been there long, Ryan nursing a beer and Trey a soft drink, when he noticed Baylee seated at the crowded bar with Justin Spoley. *How could she?* Even as he thought it, he realized he was way out of line. Baylee had lived in Henderson her whole life. She had a history with the locals much different from his. Plus, she had no loyalty whatsoever to him except that which extended between employer and employee.

Still, he couldn't help resenting how chummy she seemed with a man he thought of as his arch enemy and he comforted himself with the thought that he wouldn't be human if it didn't rankle just a little bit.

"Trey. Your turn."

It took a moment for Ryan's words to penetrate. Trey'd been pretending nonchalance he didn't feel, leaning against one of the supporting pillars his arms crossed over his chest while he glowered at the pair with their heads together at the bar. Baylee hadn't even noticed he was there.

"What's with those two, anyway?" he muttered to Ryan who'd come to stand next to him and followed his gaze.

"Baylee and Dusty?"

Trey turned to look at him. "Dusty? I thought his name was Justin."

Ryan grinned and took a sip of his beer. "Identical twins. Dustin and Justin." He inclined his head in their direction. "That's the twin. He and Baylee have been friends since college."

Trey turned his back on the bar, took a sip of his soda and picked up his stick. He walked around the table studying the damage Ryan had done on his last turn. He lined up a shot, sent the cue ball spiraling toward the solid blue ball and watched it drop into a corner pocket.

He didn't like this possessive feeling he had toward Baylee. He didn't know where it came from or why. She wasn't his type. He wasn't even interested. Why should he care who her friends were, who she spoke to or drank with? Except he did. He glowered again as he looked in her direction to see her smiling at Dustin Spoley who had just tugged on a lock of her hair. Which he couldn't help but notice she wore down, the bountiful curls and waves softly framing her face. If she'd lose the glasses she'd be even more attractive, Trey thought.

"Is she dating him?" Trey asked as Ryan moved forward to line up his shot.

Ryan glanced at them over his shoulder. "They're just friends as far as I know."

Once again Trey purposely turned his back on the bar area. Out of sight, out of mind, he told himself. He wasn't particularly looking forward to another Friday night of being home alone. When he and Ryan were done here, however, he had nothing else to do and nowhere else to go.

Surprisingly, he didn't have the urge to drink, either. He'd avoided establishments like Apple Jack's for more than a year. Alcoholics were never cured of their addiction, but they could recover from it. For the rest of their lives. Once upon a time, Trey would have been the life of the party in a place like this, buying drinks for the entire crowd. He'd be the one chatting up Baylee, or any other woman he chose to, although he hadn't noticed any of the other women really, except for her.

He would drink until he couldn't see straight and chances were he'd either pass out or fall down. One way or another, he'd make a fool of himself and hope one of his drinking buddies would be kind enough to arrange transportation home. He had enough blurry memories of embarrassing moments like those to last a lifetime. Enough recriminations from women with whom he'd stepped over the line. He preferred his hard-won sobriety thank you very much.

More locals crowded into the bar and Trey found himself face-to-face with two of his cousins. Brandon and Cooper Rawlings were his Aunt Cathy's sons. Aunt Cathy being his dad's eldest sister. The three of them had been lumped together during the summers of their childhood at one house or the other and often with Grandma J and Grandpa Mike.

His cousins clapped him on the back, and they fell into their old routine of conversation. Both his cousins worked in the family apple orchard business. They'd married local girls and each had a couple of kids. Trey's comfort level increased knowing he had at least one friend and a few family members who didn't hold his past against him.

Trey managed to snag the harried waitress and order beers for the two of them, one more for Ryan and a cola for himself. They teamed up for another game of pool. Coop had just taken his second shot when the waitress returned with their drinks. She handed Trey back his twenty along with his Coke. "Gentlemen at the bar bought your drinks."

"Oh, yeah? Who's that?"

She shrugged. "I don't know. He's at the end. Blue shirt."

Trey sampled his beverage and immediately spit it out. It spewed all over the worn wooden planks of the floor. Ryan and Brandon jumped back to avoid being splashed. "Hell, cuz, what's with you?" Brad asked, carefully holding his mug of beer out of harm's way.

Trey didn't answer immediately. He set his glass, which was liberally laced with spiced rum on a nearby ledge while he scanned the crowd around the bar. The other three followed his gaze. Ryan had set his beer down as well and took up a position next to Trey. "Spoley," he muttered at the exact moment Trey spied him.

Justin Spoley's gaze bored into Trey. He lifted his glass in a mocking toast. Trey saw red. He took a step in Spoley's direction, but Ryan's grip on his elbow stopped him. "Don't. It's exactly what he wants." Ryan's authoritative tone surprised him. Trey willed the rage he felt back in check. He looked at Ryan. Brandon and Coop hovered close by. "What's going on? What happened?"

Trey nodded in Spoley's direction. "You know that guy?"

"Spoley?" Coop asked.

"He's an asshole," Brandon supplied. "Pulled me over for doing forty in a thirty-five last year."

"Jerk," Coop agreed. "Ticketed Julie for a rolling stop. Probably would have let her off with a warning except she let loose on him for pulling her over in the first place and making her late to pick up Annie from dance class." Trey took note of Coop's pride in his wife's ability to stand up for herself.

Brandon picked up Trey's drink and sniffed it. "Asshole," he confirmed. "He still got it in for you for winning that championship game in high school?"

Trey shrugged.

"He needs to get over it."

Trey turned his back on Spoley. "Come on. Let's finish this game." He wanted to get the hell out of Apple Jack's, but he'd be damned if he'd give Spoley the satisfaction. If he asked them to, he knew Brandon and Coop would join him in teaching Justin Spoley a lesson for the stunt he'd pulled, but he also knew he wouldn't ask. He'd deal with Spoley in his own way and in his own time.

It occurred to him that he hadn't noticed either Baylee or Dustin Spoley during his most recent scan of the bar area. They must have left at some point and Trey hadn't noticed. He was glad Baylee hadn't witnessed what had happened with his drink. He was afraid she didn't have a very high opinion of him and for some reason he didn't want to drop any lower in her estimation.

Ryan and Brandon had to head home once they finished their game and Coop clapped Trey on the back. "Come on over for supper. Julie's got a big pot of chili on the stove and I'm pretty sure there's an apple pie in our future."

Trey vaguely remembered attending Cooper and Julie's wedding with Hayley a few years ago. What he couldn't remember was the reception. But that was when he'd still been with Hayley, still been on top of his game. Chances were good his behavior hadn't ruined the event for everyone else. "I'd like that."

Julie had put on a few pounds since Trey had last seen her, but she was attractive in that young housewife kind of way. Coop was obviously crazy about her and their two children.

Five-year-old Annie and three-year-old Aaron clamored for their father's attention as soon as he walked in the door with Trey behind him.

Coop ladled chili into bowls and recruited Trey to pour iced tea into three glasses while Julie settled the children in booster seats with meals of their own.

Julie never seemed to sit still enough to enjoy her own meal, but she somehow kept track of the thread of conversation even with constant interruptions because of the children's needs. Cooper relayed the incident in the bar earlier.

"Typical," Julie said as she wiped dribbles of applesauce off Aaron's chin.

"Coop told me about him ticketing you for a rolling stop," Trey put in.

"Did Coop also happen to mention that Spoley used to hit on me all the time before he and I got together?" She gave her husband a teasing look.

"I might have left that part out," he admitted.

"The guy's obsessive," she went on, rescuing Annie's cup of milk from the edge of the table. "He doesn't like to take no for an answer. I used to dread going to Apple Jack's until Coop and I started dating."

"It took a while but Spoley finally found some other female to pester. Lately he's been after—shoot—" Cooper looked at Julie. "What's her name again? She was in your class."

"Baylee Westring. Nice girl. She's friends with his brother. But yeah, ever since her divorce, Spoley's been after her."

"Baylee?" Trey asked. He set his spoon down and glanced from Coop to Julie and back.

"You know her?" Coop asked.

"She works for me."

"No kidding. Doing what?"

"Started out I needed someone to clean and stuff, but she's doing a lot more for me now. Personal assistant I guess you'd say."

A look passed between Coop and Julie, some private communication.

"What?" Trey asked.

"Nothing," Julie said. "Just that Spoley already basically hates your guts. Now you're spending all kinds of time with the woman he's been interested in for probably more than a year. Why don't you just go TP his house and sink some donuts in his front yard and be done with it?

"You all done, sweetie?" she asked Aaron. She wiped his mouth, removed his bib and released him from his booster seat.

"Me, too," Annie said. Julie gave her the same treatment and Annie slid off her seat by herself.

"You two go play or watch a video for a little while."

Trey pushed his empty bowl away and zeroed in on Julie. "He's not going to make trouble for Baylee, is he? Because of me?"

Julie's gaze flickered to Cooper in another of those private moments.

"You guys aren't dating, are you?" she asked.

Trey didn't know why he hesitated before he answered. "No."

"Uh-huh," Julie said knowingly. She picked up her glass. "All I can tell you is Spoley's a bit of a loose cannon. You probably don't have anything to worry about nor does Baylee. On the other hand, I wouldn't put anything past him. So, you might want to watch your back. Hers too."

"Great," Trey muttered. They all pushed back from the table and began gathering dishes.

Aaron approached Trey dragging a bedraggled blanket with him, his thumb in his mouth and a book tucked under one arm. He tilted his head back to stare up at Trey offering him the book. "Read," he commanded, which sounded more like, "Weed." He removed his thumb from his mouth just long enough to get the request out. "Pwease."

Both Coop and Julie jumped in to thwart their son's demand, but Trey waved off their objections. "It's okay. I don't mind." He crossed to the sofa and opened the book. Aaron crawled up next to him. Annie watched warily from across the room. Trey patted the sofa cushion on the other side of him. "Do you want to help me, Annie? I might not know all the words."

Annie looked at her mother who nodded encouragement. She pretended reluctance but took the seat Trey indicated. He opened the book and began to read. Cooper and Julie disappeared into the kitchen.

The book was about brightly colored dinosaurs and dragons who spoke in silly rhymes in an effort to get each other to accept their differences. Trey thought it was ridiculous but both kids seem to find it great fun.

When he got to the last page, Aaron's thumb popped out of his mouth. "'Nother one." He scooted off the couch and ran from the room. Annie raced after him. They reappeared in seconds with another book. Inwardly Trey groaned. He could hear Cooper and Julie chatting in the kitchen. Entertaining their kids for a little while was probably the least he could do to repay them for dinner.

"Okay, one more," he agreed. "But then I have to go. It's past my bedtime."

He winked at Annie and she giggled. He opened the book.

That could have been me, he thought on the drive home. If he hadn't made it into the NFL, hadn't left North Carolina, he'd probably have a life very much like Cooper's or Brad's. A wife and kids and house with a mortgage and a job in the family business. He tried to imagine himself working side by side with his father at the hardware store. He'd never wanted to, but now it didn't seem like it'd be so bad. Not that his father would ask for his help.

Besides he'd had a wife. A beautiful wife who adored him and supported him, and he'd tossed her aside without a second thought during the worst of his addiction. Hayley had moved on, married someone else and adopted a little boy. She and her new husband would probably add to their family soon.

If he hadn't ruined things it could have been him and Hayley who adopted her nephew and gone on to have more children.

He turned into his driveway at the same time his thoughts turned to Baylee. Something about her unsettled him. She got under his skin without even trying. He wanted...what? To impress her? No, that wasn't it. Not exactly. He wanted her approval? Not that either. Acceptance. That's what he wanted from her. No judgment. No preconceived ideas about who he was based on local gossip and his public persona. He'd like, for once, to just be himself and have that be enough.

Baylee slunk down in her seat, propped her knees on the seat in front of her and tried to enjoy the movie, but it proved impossible.

"What's the matter?" Dusty whispered without taking his gaze away from the action on the screen.

"Nothing," she whispered back. "I'm fine."

Except her concentration kept breaking and her thoughts kept wandering in Trey's direction.

At least she had popcorn, she comforted herself, as she munched contentedly. She and Dusty were sharing an extra-large Coke with lots of ice.

She had noticed Trey and Ryan in the crowd at Apple Jack's earlier, but luckily there was enough of an after-work crush to make it unnecessary for them to acknowledge each other. She'd been aware, however, of Trey's gaze on her, his contemplation of her companion.

If he'd asked, she'd have told him the truth. She'd known Dusty since he'd been a band geek in high school and they'd gone to college together. Even though Dusty was in the science department and Baylee was studying business and finance, their paths continued to cross and they'd found themselves hanging out more and more often with mutual acquaintances and then just the two of them.

It had never occurred to Baylee that she could have a guy who wasn't gay as a platonic friend, but that's what Dusty was. They saw each other once or twice a month for a movie or a meal or just to hang out and do nothing. Dusty was a certified gemologist and he worked for one of the largest jewelry-making outfits in the state.

While Baylee adored Dusty, she'd never cared for his twin brother Justin, who'd always seemed a bit too full of himself for her taste. Ever since her divorce, he'd been asking her out. She'd made it clear she wasn't interested but Justin hadn't given up. She wished Dusty would tell his brother to lay off. Even though Dusty and Justin weren't close the way twins were expected to be, she'd learned early on that Dusty didn't take criticism of his brother particularly well.

While she'd talked and laughed with Dusty, sipped on her drink and listened to his stories, a part of her tracked Trey. She knew he'd leaned against a pillar and she sensed his gaze boring into her before he turned back to the game.

She sighed and took a sip of the drink and admonished herself to concentrate on the movie. Trey probably wouldn't give her another thought until she showed up for work the next time. If only she could do the same with him.

Matty stepped off the bus and began the walk up the street with a lightness he rarely felt. Today was the last day of school and he had all summer to basically do as he pleased, which meant he'd divide his time between the animal shelter and Mamacita's.

He groaned inwardly as he approached the house and saw the white compact parked in front of it and Jack Frost leaning against it.

The probation officer's gaze tracked his movements until he stopped a few feet away.

"Mateo."

"Hi."

"Need to talk to you."

"Yes, sir."

Jack Frost gestured at the porch steps. "Let's sit down."

Matty dropped his book bag as they took a seat side by side. Jack clasped his hands together and stared at the crumbling concrete of the sidewalk. "I hear you passed all your classes," he began. "In spite of missing quite a few of them."

Matty shrugged. School wasn't much of a challenge. It wasn't that hard to keep up even if he blew off a class here and there. He'd figured out how to stay under everyone's radar and maintain a B average.

"What are your plans for the summer?"

"Nothing." Matty knew better than to offer another shrug. Jack Frost might be an okay guy but there was a limit to his patience with non-verbal responses.

"Be a good idea if you could find a part-time job. The Dixie Cream hires at fifteen," Jack said, referring to the local ice cream shop. "So does Piggly Wiggly."

"Okay."

"You've got another fifty hours of community service at the animal shelter, too, because of your missed classes and curfew violations," Jack reminded him.

"Yeah," Matty agreed because Jack had already told him this when he'd done his last check-in.

Jack tapped Matty's shoulder and rose. "Try to stay out of trouble for the summer, all right? Finish your community service and you can be off probation by the time school starts up again."

Matty nodded. "Yes, sir."

Chapter Thirteen

♥

Trey limped along behind Mary Ann Simpson, whom he took to be the official animal shelter tour guide. She was a fifty-ish, no-nonsense type, dressed in baggy jeans, worn sneakers and a faded pink polo shirt with the shelter's logo on the pocket.

They'd just exited the building which housed the reception area, clinic and the temporary home for rescued and rejected felines. Trey'd never seen so many cats in one place.

As soon as she opened the door to a long, low barn-like structure and they stepped inside the barks of what sounded like a thousand dogs began. Trey resisted the urge to cover his ears since Mary Ann showed no reaction. She simply raised her voice over the din and kept up her constant patter about his duties.

"We keep the dogs as long as we can, but, of course, we're forced to euthanize a fair number of them." Trey winced as he glanced from side to side at the hopeful eyes and wagging tails of the miscellaneous mongrels. Most were barking, pawing at the cage doors, begging for a moment of attention. A couple stayed in the backs of their pens, defeated and resigned as if they'd given up all hope of being adopted or even let out of their pens.

"You'll need to hose down the pens when you come in," Mary Ann informed him. She'd come to a stop at a spigot and a hose. She unwound the hose and turned on the water. "No need to open the gate. Keep your hose low to the floor. The water will run off into the troughs on either side, see?" Trey nodded as she efficiently squirted water to wash off the excrement and urine. The occupant of the cage, a spotted hound mix, apparently knew the ropes and stepped aside as needed to avoid the spray.

"Then rinse the trough," Mary Ann continued while she demonstrated. "It'll wash out the other side. Then you'll have to go around and collect it."

Great, Trey thought. Fifty hours of cleaning dog urine and picking up puppy poop just because of his own need to pee. Talk about karma.

She turned the hose off and rewound it. "I'll show you."

On the other side of the pens, sure enough, there were grates for the water to drain out as it came through the trough. Any solid matter remained on top of the grate. Mary Ann donned a pair of rubber gloves, picked up a bucket and dumped the solid waste into it. "Course some days, one of the other volunteers might have already done this and you won't have to. But it's your job to check the pens and see that they're clean. You start with that. Any of them need to be hosed down, you do it."

"Got it," Trey replied.

"Then you make sure the water bowls are full of fresh water. Use the hose. The bowls are attached to the inside of the gates."

"Next thing is you check to see if any of the dogs are scheduled for pick-up." She showed him where that information would be. "See, now today, we've got two." She picked up a clipboard and scanned the paperwork. "Riley and Spanky. You'll need to bath them, walk them out in the yard afterward and then bring them to one of the holding cages in the main building. I'll show you where and how to bath them."

"I can do it, Mrs. Simpson," said a voice behind them.

Trey and Mary Ann turned at the same moment and Mary Ann gave a whoop of delight. "Speaking of volunteers," she said to Trey, "Matty here is one of our best." She enveloped the boy in a motherly hug which he awkwardly allowed. A smile hovered around his mouth until his gaze met Trey's and Trey could have sworn he blushed.

The boy looked to be about sixteen or seventeen, tall and slender with straight black hair that needed the attention of a barber. His golden-brown skin mixed surprisingly well with his hazel eyes.

Mary Ann released him and patted his shoulder. "I'm glad you're here today. This is Trey Christopher. You can show him the ropes."

Trey stretched out a hand and Matty shook it. His grip was firm but he seemed unsure about the gesture, as if he were feeling his way along through the maze of social niceties.

After Mary Ann let them alone, Matty gestured for Trey to follow him. He picked up a leash and opened one of the cages which held a medium-sized mixed breed with short, mottled fur and long droopy ears. The dog's tail twirled round and round as he squirmed in excitement at the attention Matty showed him.

"Hi, Riley. Hi, there boy." He let the dog lick his neck and face while he rubbed its neck and chest. "You found a family, huh, boy? Somebody to love you? Lucky you."

Trey watched in silence wondering if he imagined the trace of wistfulness in Matty's voice as he spoke to the dog.

"Okay, come on." He looped one end of the leash around Riley's neck and the dog leapt and bounded, doing his best to trip Matty in his excitement.

Matty gracefully led the dog back the way they'd come to the room with a large, low stainless steel tub and a spray arm attachment above it. He handed the dog off to Trey. "You want to hold onto him while I get the water ready?"

Since squatting to pet the dog was an impossibility, Trey sank onto a nearby chair. He stroked a hand over Riley's head. The dog gazed at him in adoration. "Sit," Trey told him. Surprising him, the dog sat. Trey grinned. "Hey, good boy." He held up a hand. "High five." Riley lifted a paw and swatted at Trey's hand. "Are you kidding me? Somebody trained this dog."

"Yeah," Matty agreed without turning around.

"What else can you do, boy, huh?" Trey pointed to the floor. "Down." Obediently, Riley laid down, his eyes bright and alert.

"I don't get it," Trey said. "This was somebody's dog. Somebody was interested enough to train it. How'd he end up here?"

Matty shrugged and spoke over the sound of running water. "Maybe they couldn't keep him or didn't want him anymore. People throw out things all the time. Pets. Kids. A dog doesn't have any say in what people do. One day he's got a roof over his head. The next day he's roaming the streets." Matty shrugged again.

"Well, yeah, but it just seems like if they took the time to teach him stuff they must have valued him, must have wanted to keep him. Otherwise, why bother?"

Matty apparently considered that a rhetorical question. He turned and took the leash from Trey. "Want to come and watch?" He led Riley back to the sink, picked him up and lowered him into the tub of water. Trey moved closer.

Matty pumped dog shampoo from an industrial-sized container and began to lather Riley's fur. "Start up by the neck and go all the way around. Just in case they've picked up any fleas. This stuff will kill them. Then work your way down all over." He demonstrated, although it wasn't like Trey'd never bathed a dog before. Before Bo, his parents had another golden retriever named Buster with whom Trey had been inseparable.

Riley looked like he was in heaven as Matty worked the lather from his neck to his tail and then rinsed him. Matty kept the dog in the sink until the last of the dirty water had drained. Then he picked up a threadbare towel and draped it over the dog. "You want to dry him off? Then we'll take him outside."

Obediently Trey rubbed at Riley's fur, although the towel was no match for the moisture it was trying to absorb. He looked around for another one but Matty shook his head. "Miz Simpson says only one. Budget cuts." He slipped the leash back on Riley and lifted him out of the sink. Riley promptly shook himself spraying Trey and Matty with droplets of water. "Okay," Matty informed him. "Let's go."

They went out a back door to a fenced-in grassy area. When Matty released him, Riley trotted over to the nearest fence post and lifted his leg. Once finished, he put his nose to the ground then ambled across the grass and squatted to do his business. He came back to Matty and Trey and gazed at them expectantly, tail wagging.

"Wish we had a ball," Trey said. "Maybe he'd chase it." He made a mental note to bring one with him next time.

Matty patted Riley's side. "His new family will play with him. Right, Riley?" Riley gazed at Matty adoringly. "I'll take him in and get Spanky. You want to start filling the tub?"

Matty allowed Trey to give Spanky a bath under his close supervision. The kid wasn't afraid to offer helpful hints or point out that Trey needed to bathe the dog *everywhere*, including his undercarriage. Spanky wasn't as thrilled to get a bath as Riley had been. He squirmed and fought the restraint and shook himself off every chance he got until Trey's mid-section was soaked and Matty was more than damp.

"A plastic apron or some rain gear would have been nice," Trey commented after Matty lifted Spanky from the tub and rubbed him dry.

"I think they used to have some, but—"

"Let me guess," Trey said dryly, as he rinsed the last of the dirty water down the drain. "Budget cuts."

Matty shrugged and they went outside. Spanky didn't seem to quite know what to with himself. He tentatively sniffed at the grass before moving away and finally deciding it was okay to let go.

"How'd you hurt yourself?" Matt asked Trey.

Refreshing, Trey thought. Someone who didn't know his history and wouldn't hold it against him. Matty was young enough to be his son, if Trey had been a teenage father. Matty had no idea who Trey was. "Old football injury," he answered. "Messed up my knee pretty badly."

"You gonna limp forever?"

"God, I hope not. I just started physical therapy again. Believe it or not, today's a good day for me."

Matty gave him an assessing look. "You play here? At Henderson High?"

"Yeah. When you were still wearing diapers."

"Team's going to suck this year," Matty informed him.

"So, what are you in for?" Trey asked to change the subject before Matty could ask more questions about his football career. "Mary Ann called you a volunteer, but you've got to be doing community service, same as me."

"Yeah. Me and some friends, we did some stupid stuff."

"What kind of stupid stuff gets you busted these days? Unless you'd rather not say." Trey was genuinely curious. Matty seemed like a decent kid. Mary Ann Simpson obviously thought highly of him. Maybe Matty'd gotten a bad rap. Or maybe a local cop had it in for him.

"Smokin' weed. Vandalizing school property. Stuff like that."

They were slouching against the outside wall of the building gazing at Spanky while he poked around in the grass. "Back in my day…" Trey hesitated. "God, I sound old, don't I?"

"You are old," Matty agreed, a smile flashing across his face giving Trey a glimpse of the little boy he'd been not long ago.

Pretending annoyance, Trey cleared his throat. "Back when I was your age, what are you, sixteen? Seventeen?"

"Seventeen."

"Weed wasn't all that popular but beer was. There was this old cop used to be on duty on the weekends. He'd bust us pretty regularly. Dragged my sorry ass home a couple of times. Always let me off with a warning. Probably because he knew my parents would give me a stiffer sentence than he could."

Matty glanced sideways at Trey. "Did they?"

"Oh, yeah. First, I'd get grounded. No car. No phone. No extra-curricular activities. My dad would invent all kinds of work for me to do, stuff he knew I hated. Helping him with inventory at the hardware store. Cleaning out the garage. Pulling weeds.

"Plus, he'd give me this sort of tight-lipped silent treatment to let me know how much I'd disappointed him."

"Too bad kids don't have something like that to let their parents know when they've disappointed *them*," Matty put in.

Trey turned to lean a shoulder against the wall so he could look at Matty directly. "Huh. I never thought about my parents disappointing me. They were great parents. Still are, actually."

"Lucky you," Matty said grimly. "What about your mom? Did she give you the silent treatment, too?"

Trey grinned. "My mom never stayed mad at me for long. She'd tell me what she thought about whatever I'd done and she'd go along with my dad's punishment. But she'd make up for it by cooking my favorite dinner and baking cookies. Hugging me when he wasn't around."

"That must have been nice." Matty's tone turned wistful. He gazed out across the fenced area.

"What about your—"

"Come on, Spanky." Matty clapped his hands, effectively cutting Trey off. The dog ambled over and Matty secured the leash.

Matty introduced Trey to a couple of the other staff members and showed him a few other things he could do to help out on the days he was there, one of which was cleaning the bathroom. Matty handed him a wad of paper towels and spritzed the glass front door with window cleaner indicating Trey could do the hard part.

"Missed a spot," Matty informed him when Trey thought he was done.

"Smart ass," Trey told him good-naturedly under his breath. Matty couldn't help the smile that escaped.

As they were leaving, Trey glanced at the clouds that had formed overhead. The air had cooled and a breeze had picked up. A few fat raindrops began to fall. He saw Matty removing his bicycle from the nearby bike rack. Trey unlocked the Cayenne with a click of the remote. "You want a ride?" he called to Matty.

Matty glanced at the sky and then at Trey's vehicle. More raindrops fell. Thunder rumbled and a flash of lightning streaked across the sky. "Come on." Trey lifted the hatch and lowered the back seat while Matty hustled over with his bike. He hoisted it in and jogged around to the passenger door.

He buckled his seatbelt and sat back, doing his best not to show his awe. A Porsche Cayenne? Silently Matty admired the buttery leather seats and luxurious interior. The racecar design of the instrument panel and gearshift. Matty decided the sound system probably had a manual all its own.

"Nice ride," he said as Trey pulled out of the shelter parking lot.

"You got a license?" Trey asked, glancing at him before returning his gaze to the road.

"Yeah." Matty didn't want to tell Trey he'd barely used his driver's license. He had no car and nowhere to go if he did.

"I'll make you a deal. You clean the toilets, I'll let you drive next time."

Matty shot a suspicious glance in Trey's direction. "Really?" Probably just another case of an adult promising something he wouldn't deliver.

"If you want."

Trey acted like it was no big deal, so Matty tried to do the same, but it didn't come easily. He'd learned to quell his excitement over promises made for the future, because he'd learned most of what was promised simply never happened. "Sure," he said as nonchalantly as he could.

"You hungry? I'm starving. I'll buy. Since you did all the hard work today."

Rain had begun to pelt the windshield. Matty refrained from pointing out the obvious. Stopping somewhere to eat meant they'd be soaked by the time they got inside.

"There's a Sonic out near the overpass, right?" Trey asked.

"Yeah," Matty acknowledged. "But I live on the other side of town."

"You in a hurry to get home? I don't want to get you in trouble."

"No. It's okay."

Trey parked underneath the drive-in area and killed the engine. He lowered the windows and asked Matty what he wanted. Matty'd only been to this place one time, over a year ago after it first opened. Because he wanted to act like it was no big deal he stuck to the basics. A hamburger, fries and a root beer.

"What are you doing all summer? You got a job?" Trey asked after he'd placed their order.

"No." Matty didn't want to admit to Trey that he slept as late as he could and then he hung out with twelve-year-old twins until their mother came home from work. The twins were as bored as he was. When Lisa came home, she turned into a drill sergeant, setting all three boys to work, cleaning the house and helping her with dinner preparation. Matty sensed Lisa didn't quite know what to do with him, so she treated him as if he were a twelve-year-old as well, assigning him tasks and serving him a meal. At some point during the day Dan would appear. He'd engage in half-hearted conversation with his son and grandsons while he rummaged in the refrigerator or pantry. He'd sit at the table and absently gaze at the newspaper while he ate a bowl of cereal or a piece of toast. His ghost-like presence had a dampening effect on the boys' normal shenanigans and cutting up.

Most evenings Matty biked over to Mamacita's to check up on her and keep her company.

"You can't spend every day at the shelter."

"No. Mostly I'm only there on Saturdays."

"You want a job?"

A flicker of suspicion flashed through Matty's head once again. Everything about this guy seemed too easy. "Doing what?"

"I'm living in my grandparents' old place. I need somebody to mow the grass and weed my grandmother's garden. There are a couple of outbuildings that are about to fall down. I thought between the two of us, we might be able to help them along. I haven't even looked in the barn, but I imagine there's a lifetime of stuff out there to go through and decide what to do with."

"What are you paying?" Matty already knew he'd do it. He could hardly believe a job had landed in his lap. Jobs for kids like him weren't very plentiful in Henderson.

"I guess minimum wage to start. What's that? Eight dollars an hour now?"

"Less than that," Matty told him. "A lot of places are paying way more."

Trey raised an eyebrow. "I'll start you at eight, anyway. See how it goes. If you're interested."

"I'm interested."

Their food arrived and they dug in, shelving conversation for a while. Trey selected tapped a couple of buttons on the console, and music poured from the speakers. Matty hadn't heard anything like it before, a mix of blues and rock, but he liked it.

By the time Trey drove back through Henderson following Matty's directions, the rain had let up.

"Right here's good," Matty said, indicating for Trey to pull over at the next corner.

"So where should I pick you up Monday morning?" he asked.

"Here's good," Matty assured him. "Thanks for the ride." Trey released the rear hatch lock mechanism and Matty removed his bike.

Trey lowered the passenger window. "Eight a.m. , right?" he called.

"I'll be here," Matty assured him.

Trey watched the kid mount his much-too-small bicycle and head down the side street. He couldn't help but wonder if there was something Matty didn't want him to know about where he lived.

"What's he doing here?" Baylee asked Trey on Monday morning. She was loading the dishwasher with everything Trey had allowed to accumulate in the sink over the weekend. From the window she had a clear view of the flower garden where Matty was toiling away pulling weeds.

Trey'd given him a pair of Grandpa Mike's gardening gloves and hauled a wheelbarrow out of the barn to cart away the unwanted vegetation. Trey hoped Matty knew the difference between a weed and a flower.

He followed Baylee's gaze out the window. "He's weeding the garden," he told her wondering why she expected him to state the obvious.

Baylee sent him a glance he couldn't quite decipher. "I can see he's weeding the garden. What I meant is why is *he* here. As in, 'where did you find this particular person to weed the garden?'"

"Is there a problem?"

"Not yet," Baylee muttered. She turned on the hot water, squirted soap suds into a pan and began to scrub.

Trey leaned against the counter cradling his nearly empty coffee mug. Wow. He barely knew her but he could tell by the set of her shoulders and her grim concentration on the pan she was scrubbing that something was bothering her.

His gaze flickered once more to the view from the window. "Do you know him?"

"Yes."

That probably shouldn't surprise Trey, but for some reason it did. Where would Baylee have run across a kid like Matty? "How?"

Baylee let a beat pass and then said, "He's my brother."

Trey took another good look at Matty who picked up a pile of weeds and dropped them into the wheelbarrow. He moved to a new section of the garden and started pulling. Trey brought his gaze back to Baylee. "Funny, he doesn't look anything like you."

"He's adopted."

"You're not pleased I gave your brother a job."

"You don't know anything about him."

"I didn't know much about you when I hired you." Trey felt compelled to point this out.

Baylee rinsed the pan and upended it on a towel she'd laid on the counter before she turned toward him.

"How'd you meet him?"

"At the animal shelter. I started my community service there on Saturday."

"Uh huh. Do you know why Matty was there?"

"He's doing community service, same as me." *What was her problem?*

"Did he tell you he's on probation?"

"No, but I sort of assumed he was."

"Do you know why?"

"Doing stupid teenage stuff and getting caught."

"That's right. He's kept doing it. Cutting school. Breaking his curfew."

"School's out now, so that's hardly an issue, is it?"

"My point is that Matty doesn't recognize authority. He's a loner and you need to watch out."

"I wasn't planning on giving him the pin numbers to my bank accounts."

"Ha."

"All I'm doing is giving the kid a summer job doing menial labor at minimum wage so he can earn a little bit of money. I like him," Trey added although it had nothing to do with anything.

Baylee glanced wistfully out the window once more. "I like him, too. Just—consider yourself warned. I'm going to start the laundry."

Trey lingered at the counter watching Matty as he worked. What was it, he wondered, that Baylee wasn't telling him. "I think I'll go see how he's doing."

After she put in a load of laundry, she went into the dining room to sift through, open, and prioritize Trey's mail. There were several bank statements and correspondence from a law firm in Jacksonville; a few ten-by-thirteen inch envelopes with the return addresses of investment firms; bills from credit card companies and local utilities and several envelopes that held checks from various entities.

Nothing of a personal nature from what she could see. She arranged them in individual stacks and then dusted the table's surface as best she could, maneuvering around the organized piles of papers and mail and magazines before moving on to the bookshelves.

Trey had unpacked more of his belongings since she'd been here last. She paused to check the titles of some of the books he'd arranged on the shelves. Several on Eastern religious practices, Zen and Tao, for the most part. A few biographies written by or about American business leaders or political figures. Some that appeared to deal with addiction and recovery as well as a few with self-help titles. "Huh," Baylee said to herself as she flicked her duster over them.

On a low shelf were a stack of black and white composition books. She lifted them up and set them on the corner of the table. She opened the cover of the top one and leafed randomly through it. The pages were filled with Trey's scrawling loopy handwriting.

She paused to read. *Haylee doesn't love me anymore. Not that I blame her. I lost the best thing that ever happened to me and yet I still can't figure out how I fucked it all up. She laughed at me when I told her I wanted another chance.*

She's changed. I thought she'd always be there for me. Jesus Christ I'm an idiot. I treated her like shit. Why would she sign on for more of the same? I don't think she hates me anymore.

The entries weren't dated and seemed to free flow from one into the next. Baylee set the notebook aside and picked up another one, opening it at random. *My fucking knee is killing me. Jesus Christ could they give me something? Anything? An aspirin for chrissakes. How do they expect me to live like this? I want to kill Brad. He sits there and repeats everything I say back to me like he expects me to figure it all out. Hell, if I could figure it out I wouldn't be here, would I? Isn't that what I'm paying him for? He lets me yell at him all I want and he just sits there. He doesn't yell back. When I calm down he says, "How do you feel right now?" And I tell him. I feel like a caged animal. I hate you but I hate myself more—*

Baylee slammed the notebook shut and put it back in the stack when she heard the back door open. She placed the entire stack back on the shelf where they'd been, wondering if Trey kept them in any kind of order, if he'd notice they'd been rearranged. She spared a glance at his table top filing system and decided he didn't.

She sped to the other side of the room, pretending to busy herself with dusting the windowsill.

When Trey's footsteps stopped, she turned to see him leaning against the doorway, arms across his chest, watching her.

The thought of how close she'd come to turning down this job returned. Trey's mere presence sent a sort of sick, fluttery feeling of anticipation through her. He'd done nothing untoward. He only mildly flirted with her in an offhand way. Hadn't hit on her. Yet she had the feeling that he was studying her while he kept his distance. Like she was a puzzle he couldn't quite figure out.

"How's it going?" he asked.

She ran her dust cloth along the window frames, then moved on to a small walnut cabinet nearby. "Fine."

Her back was to him but she knew Trey hadn't moved. Her senses prickled with awareness of him. She stopped dusting and turned. "Was there something...?" She lost her train of thought, derailed by his intent gaze which belied his relaxed stance.

"Something?" A corner of his mouth quirked up.

"Sorry. It's your house. Do whatever you want. I'm not used to being watched while I work."

"Then none of your clients are male."

Baylee frowned. "What's that supposed to mean?"

Trey blinked. Straightened. "Uh, nothing. Sorry. I just, um. Didn't mean to make you uncomfortable."

"No. You didn't. Never mind." Baylee reached for a different rag from her carryall and picked up a bottle of glass cleaner. She moved back to the China hutch, spritzed the glass and started to wipe.

Trey moved into the room behind her and took a seat at the table. In the mirrored glass at the back of the cabinet she could see him staring at the littered dining-table-cum-desk.

"I opened the mail," Baylee told him. "And organized it. I'll write checks for the bills after you check them over. Those investment reports can just be filed. There are some checks there that should be deposited. I can drop them off at the bank on my way home if you want. I wasn't sure what to do with the legal correspondence."

She'd finished with the glass and there wasn't anything left to clean except the floor which she'd do last along with all the others. She turned to find Trey's speculative gaze directed at her. He rubbed a thumbnail along his bottom lip which unintentionally drew her attention there.

There was a glint of something in his eyes, but she wasn't sure what it was. "What?" she asked, hoping he'd shed some light on whatever was going on his head.

He gave her his easy grin as if he were quite pleased about something. "I think you might be the best thing that's happened to me since I've been back." A jolt of pleasure washed through Baylee before he abruptly squashed it by gesturing at the neat stacks of paper she'd created. "Do you have any idea how much I appreciate this?"

Baylee pinned a smile on her face while swallowing her disappointment. His words had nothing to do with her personally. Just her capabilities as his personal assistant. "It's my job."

Chapter Fourteen

♥

Baylee stared at herself in the bathroom mirror. Was she seriously going to parade in front of Trey in this nightgown? She loved the chocolate satin trimmed in champagne lace. There was a matching robe. It wasn't like Trey was going to see anything more than he'd ever seen. Arms and legs—she wore shorts and tank tops to work almost everyday. If she put the robe on, which she certainly intended to, all he'd see would be her legs beneath the short hem.

You are being ridiculous she warned her mirrored reflection. Trey wouldn't care. He probably wouldn't even notice. She could hear the drone of ESPN alternating with the announcers from a baseball game on another channel as Trey flipped between the two. She'd have to pass in front of him to get to her bed, but so what? *Not like you're sexy, or anything* she reminded herself. *Not like guys ever think of you that way. Especially not guys like Trey.* She purposely pushed away the thought of Justin Spoley's unwanted attention.

Besides, she was the one who had screwed up the hotel arrangements, somehow making an online reservation for one room with two queen beds instead of two rooms with king beds. The hotel was booked solid, but the desk clerk had offered to obtain a room for her at the hotel's sister accommodation two blocks away. She and Trey had engaged in a brief, loudly whispered discussion where he'd stated his objection to her staying elsewhere. He obviously saw some need to protect her here in the big, bad city and Baylee called him on it.

"I'm a grown woman, Trey. I am perfectly capable of taking care of myself. I'm the one who screwed up the reservation. I'll be perfectly fine in the other hotel."

Trey wasn't convinced. "No."

Baylee threw up her hands. "It's either that or we can share your room."

Trey cocked his head. "Good idea. Let's do that."

Before she could voice an objection to her own solution, Trey turned back to the clerk and started signing forms. He handed her one of the key cards and turned toward the bank of elevators.

She'd had no choice but to follow him. *We're both adults*, she told herself now. There was absolutely no reason they couldn't platonically share a hotel room for a couple of days. Especially a hotel room that had two beds.

She put her glasses back on and slid her contact lens case into her toiletry bag. *Boys don't make passes at girls who wear glasses.* She grinned at her reflection. She had absolutely nothing to worry about. She opened the bathroom door, navigated the short hallway to the bedroom area and thought *Wrong!*

Trey's focus wasn't on the television, which he'd apparently muted when he heard the bathroom door open. His gaze lasered her as soon as she reached his line of vision. Her steps faltered slightly, before she strode as nonchalantly as she could to her bed which was about three feet from his. She bent to pull back the covers before realizing that was probably not such a good idea. She felt the heat of his gaze all along the backs of her thighs, even as the lace hem tickled her right below her buttocks.

What are you doing? She screamed in frustration but only inside her head. She hated this sense of being far outside her element. Unsure of what to expect. The sick sense of anticipation that Trey would make some kind of move on her had her on a roller coaster from which she was certain to fall. Her warnings to herself weren't doing her any good at all. Because the truth was, she wished he would. She wished he'd come after her, wished he found her desirable. Wanted her.

She slid between the sheets and grabbed the extra pillow to stuff behind her head, yanking the sheet up to her armpits. *Sex-y!* She stared at the now silent television set where an ad for one of the male sexual enhancement drugs played itself out to its natural conclusion and tag line of "Ready when you are."

A hot blush warmed her cheeks. *Please God, just kill me now.* From her peripheral vision she knew Trey was also staring straight ahead, but he made no move to change the volume setting. He'd also propped himself up with both pillows behind his head. He was still fully dressed except for his shoes and socks.

Baylee stared at his bare feet. No woman in the history of mankind got turned on by a guy's feet. Except for her. Maybe because it was safe. A guy's feet were hardly considered an erogenous zone. Why then was sucking his toes all she could think about at the moment? Maybe because his legs were attached to his feet. His calves and shins and knees. And if she kept moving up his legs, she'd reach the area where they joined the rest of his body. And that area certainly was considered an erogenous zone. If she had access, why she could use her mouth and her hands and her tongue—

Fingers snapped nearby, yanking her out of her fantasy. She turned to stare at Trey. He'd extended one arm toward her. Oh my God. Was this the invitation she'd hoped for? To join him in bed? Might her fantasies turn into reality?

"I'm going to go take a shower. Do you want the remote or not?"

"Oh, uh, sure." She took the remote she now saw was in his hand. When his fingers brushed hers another mini tingle slid through her. Her gaze locked with his until she forced herself to look away. She studied the unfamiliar remote control until she found the button to turn the mute setting off. Trey hadn't moved nor had he turned his head away. She could feel him studying her. Feigning nonchalance she hit the channel button until she found a *Sex and the City* rerun. How apropos. She could use some tips from the pros right about now.

Eventually Trey swung his legs over the side of the bed and pushed himself up. She watched him make his way to the bathroom, his limp barely noticeable. Only when she was certain he'd closed the door behind him did she let out a long shaky breath. Sharing quarters with Trey wasn't going to be quite as easy as she'd thought.

Trey stripped and stepped under the spray before it warmed up. Good, he thought. What he needed was a nice cold shower to get rid of the hard-on he'd evidently developed for Baylee. How? Why? When?

He had no idea except she'd somehow sneaked under his radar and wormed her way into his existence, tearing his defenses down as she went. What was it about her that got to him? He looked forward to her arrival at his house each day and he was sort of sad to see her leave. She wasn't his type for damn sure. She wasn't even classically pretty.

She had a slender, coltish body when he'd always gone in for the more voluptuous, curvy types. Her boobs weren't big, although they were certainly more than adequate. Don't need more than a handful, he reminded himself. Except he'd always liked an overflowing handful. But now here he was fantasizing about hers knowing there'd probably be some room left over. His hands were pretty big.

Where'd she get those sexy nightclothes, he wondered. Did she sleep in those all the time? He'd sort of figured her for the cotton tee shirt and boxers type. Not satin and lace. Showed how much he knew. About her. Himself. Anything at all.

She wasn't dumb. She had a way of concentrating all her energy on whatever she was doing. When she directed her focus at him, it was like being on stage under a spotlight he didn't want to step out of.

Those unflattering glasses just made her sexier. How was that possible? He'd seen her without them and he liked that look, too. She had sort of amber-colored eyes, from which her intelligence shown and humor glinted. Sometimes he wondered if she was laughing at him. He wondered if she knew how much of his energy it took to resist coming after her. Surely, she had no idea how awkward he felt without the blur of a couple of cocktails to help him ease into his comfort zone.

There was something there in her eyes, he thought he recognized. A sort of come hither look that invited while behind it lurked a wariness. Maybe it was her mixture of innocence and toughness that got to him. She wasn't shy. She could stand up for herself. She could certainly hold her own with him. But at the same time, he got the sense she wasn't as self-assured as her persona projected. She could be easily wounded.

Not going to go there, he decided as he turned the shower dial to the right for one more chilling blast of cold water. He'd caused too many people too much pain in the past. Unintentionally, yes, but his blind actions and self-centered behavior had hurt a lot of people. He'd hurt himself in the process. Along the way he'd lost relationships he should have cherished and protected.

He had to learn from those mistakes and stop barreling blindly ahead, taking whatever he wanted with no thought to the consequences. More than anything he wanted to stop hurting other people with his carelessness. Which meant hands off where Baylee was concerned.

Trey dried off and wrapped a towel around his waist realizing he'd forgotten to bring nightclothes or underwear into the bathroom with him. He was adequately covered by the towel. He started to brush his teeth before he opened the door with the toothbrush still in his mouth. Don't look at her, he warned himself. Don't get turned on, don't make a move, don't do anything. Get your stuff and get back in the bathroom.

He could hear the closing notes of the *Sex and the City* piano theme. He chanced a quick glance Baylee's way. She looked like she was asleep. "Baylee," he whispered. A big dollop of toothpaste foam dribbled out of his mouth to his chest. He ducked back into the bathroom to rinse his mouth.

When he came back out, she still hadn't moved. He approached her cautiously, like a panther sneaking up on its prey, not wanting to startle it or have it turn and attack him. "Baylee," he whispered again when he got closer.

Her head was turned to the side toward the light, but her eyes were closed, her breathing soft and even. The top of the sheet had slid down a little, giving him a tiny peak at her cleavage. He removed the remote control from under her limp fingers and set it on the nightstand between the beds.

Carefully he removed her glasses as well. She didn't move a muscle.

Her dark hair with its golden glints curled around the tops of her shoulders and teased the tender column of her throat. He moved a strand away from her cheek savoring the silkiness of it between his fingers. Her lashes made tiny shadows under her eyes. Her mouth, always ready with a smart comeback, looked soft and kissable now.

Trey groaned involuntarily. What would it be like, he wondered, if he had the right to slide into bed next to her. To press up against her and kiss that tender mouth, bury his fingers in the silk of her hair. Bury himself inside her.

Stop it he warned himself. It isn't going to happen. You have no right. Step back. Turn around. Walk away. By some strength of will he didn't know he possessed, he did. He grabbed stuff to sleep in out of his suitcase and went back into the bathroom where he leaned over the counter with his hands braced on either side.

Breathe.

Inhale.

Count of five.

Hold it.

Count of four.

Exhale.

Count of seven.

Again.

Trey had no idea how long he spent breathing, searching for the elusive Zen-like peace, but by the time he left the bathroom, he felt light-headed and drained. He kept his gaze averted, turned the light off and crawled between the cool sheets of his bed.

He woke up the next morning acutely aware he wasn't exactly alone. Even in the dim light seeping in through the heavy drapes, he could make out the outline of Baylee's shape in the bed next to his. She was turned away from him, but bits of her peeked out from the tangled bedclothes. The filmy robe had slipped off one shoulder. Her leg from the calf down had found its way out from under the covers.

Don't look. Don't look. Don't look, Trey warned himself. He took the clothes he'd hung in the closet earlier and closed the door to the bathroom behind him. He'd be shaved and dressed and in full command of his libido by the time he opened the door. Because anything else simply wasn't acceptable.

He'd suffered through training camps and numerous injuries. He played in all kinds of weather against all kinds of odds. He had nerves of steel on the field, focused on the goal, quick on his feet. He'd given up painkillers and booze. He'd survived his various surgeries and physical therapy.

He'd trained himself to block out the discomfort, the pain, the cravings. Baylee Westring wasn't going to get to him. She wasn't going to undermine his hard won-peace of mind.

Dressed, he padded barefoot back to the bedroom. She was still asleep and there was more light now, even though the drapes were still closed. The sounds of traffic twenty stories below was like a soft but constant buzz. Trey went to the window and parted the drapes to look out. It promised to be a sunny day, which, in New York City meant stifling. The buildings blocked breezes and trapped the automobile and truck fumes close to the ground.

He dropped the drape and turned back to the room just in time to see Baylee yawn and stretch, unaware of his presence. At least he hoped she was unaware because he couldn't take his gaze off her in spite of all his admonitions to himself. She arched her back and flung her arms overhead. A soft little sound emitted from her throat, as if she were satisfied with the results of the stretch.

She snuggled down in the bed, pulled the covers over her and hugged one of the pillows to her.

Trey turned away, disgusted with his voyeuristic behavior. He yanked the heavy drapes open with more force than necessary. When he turned back, Baylee was sitting up in bed, the sheet pulled up against her. She stared at him, her eyes wide and blinking. "I didn't know you were there."

"Where else would I be?" he responded irritably. He strode back to his suitcase and rummaged around for a pair of socks. When he turned back he found her in the same position, still staring at him. Her hair was messy and she looked sleep-rumpled. *Probably has morning breath, too.* But that didn't lessen her appeal one bit.

He yanked his socks on and slid into his shoes. He picked up his wallet, watch, and cell phone from the top of the television armoire. "You want to get breakfast?" he asked over his shoulder, doing his best to keep his voice neutral.

"Sure."

He didn't want to look at her again. "I'm going to the business center. I'll meet you in the lobby." He glanced at his watch. "A half hour enough time for you?"

"Sure."

As soon as the door closed behind him, Baylee swung her legs over the side of the bed and rolled her neck around a couple of times in one direction and then the other.

By the time the elevator deposited her in the lobby, she'd decided to ignore Trey's earlier mood, whatever had caused it. The lobby was abuzz with guests checking out or meeting each other. She wanted to sit and people watch. She wanted to eat. She wanted to be a tourist and wander the city and soak up the atmosphere. Two days wasn't going to be long enough to do much of anything, but she decided to enjoy every second of it. She wouldn't let Trey Christopher's attitude rain on her parade.

He either sensed or saw her coming toward him because he lowered his phone and watched her approach. Something about the way he did it made her think of a cat twitching its tail in anticipation of a particularly tasty canary that had somehow wandered into its path. Silly, she told herself. What he's probably starving for is eggs and bacon.

He stood and she stopped a couple of feet away, glad she'd dug out some of her old wardrobe. Her slacks and tops and shoes still fit her even if they were a couple years out of season. She'd gone for classics because she had a tight wardrobe budget even when she'd been in banking. Classics could be mixed and matched and they were timeless.

She wore a silky short-sleeved blouse in a rich rose shade. The sleeves hugged her biceps and a row of pearl buttons ran down the front. The cut left a vee at her neck and her silver necklace with the tiny heart dangled there. Lightweight black slacks and black flats should be ideal for her self-guided sight-seeing tour.

Trey seemed about to say something, but whatever it was, he thought better of it. "The restaurant's this way." He gestured and she turned to walk ahead of him.

What a fun trip this would be if they were a couple, she mused. They could have awoken in bed together. Made love this morning, maybe. There wouldn't be this weird, awkward tension between them. They wouldn't be walking on eggshells around each other. They'd spent the night in a hotel room. In separate beds. Big deal. Nothing had happened. Nothing was going to happen. Why couldn't they go back to the easy camaraderie they'd had before?

No reason as far as she could tell. She decided to do her best to get back there whether Trey wanted to cooperate with her or not.

"I'm starving," she informed him as they approached the hostess stand.

His stomach growled in response. It made her grin.

He flashed her a smile.

Everything was going to be okay between them. She was certain of it.

The following evening, the dinner meeting broke up and everyone headed to the bar which they had to pass through to get to the exit. Baylee excused herself for the restroom. Upon her return, she slid onto a corner barstool to wait when she saw Trey deep in conversation with one of the ESPN guys.

The bartender approached with a smile and a cocktail napkin at the ready, but she waved him off. "I'm just waiting for a friend."

He retreated but a man slid up next to her. "Is that all he is? A friend?"

She turned to see Collin Cassiday grinning at her. He'd been looking her way off and on during the dinner and he wasn't shy about broadcasting his interest. Baylee had learned at dinner that Collin co-anchored ESPN's hour-long daily sports round-up weeknights at eleven.

"A friend. And employer," she informed him. Seriously, could a guy like him be interested in *her*? Doubtful. Probably he was just making casual conversation until the group was ready to leave.

"That's what I hoped you'd say."

"Why? What possible difference could my relationship with Trey make to you?"

"Ooh. Spunky. I like that." He grinned at her again. "Well, if you're not with him, is there someone else?"

"Someone else?"

"A boyfriend back home?" He made a point of looking at her left hand. "No ring. You're not involved with Trey. I hope that means you're single. And available."

"Available for what?"

Is this flirting, Baylee wondered. Was she *flirting* with this guy? Was he flirting with her?

"A drink somewhere. Listen to some music?"

"Now?"

Collin looked around the room. Baylee did the same. The goodbyes were beginning, the small knots of people breaking up, shaking hands, clapping backs, some of them already meandering toward the door. Trey was still talking to the same two ESPN guys, but his gaze flickered her way. He seemed to also take in the fact that Collin had positioned himself quite close to her. Surely, she imagined the flicker of displeasure she thought crossed his handsome features. Why would he care?

Tonight was her last night in New York. She'd managed to visit a couple of museums and Central Park. She'd caught a matinee of an off-Broadway play and window-shopped along Fifth Avenue. But she hadn't been out for a drink and listened to music with someone who was obviously at home in the city. "I think I'd like that."

"Great. Let's go."

She slid off the stool and smoothed her skirt. He began to guide her toward the exit with a hand on the small of her back. "Oh, wait. I should probably let Trey know I'm leaving."

"Oh, I think he knows," Collin assured her. He came to a halt and Trey seemed to materialize in front of her.

"Excuse me, Baylee. A word?" He shot Collin an unfriendly look and without giving her a choice, clasped his fingers around her elbow and maneuvered her to a deserted corner.

"You're not leaving here with him."

Trey's tone fell somewhere between a statement and a question and Baylee found she didn't particularly care which it was.

"He asked me out for a drink."

"And you accepted?" Now his tone bordered on incredulous.

"Yes." She pressed her lips together to keep from saying anything else. Her chin came up.

Over Trey's shoulder she could see Collin slouched against the doorjamb, hands in his pockets as if he didn't have a care in the world. He winked when she caught his eye.

"Baylee, I don't think you should go out with him."

She brought her attention back to Trey. "Why?"

"Sheesh, Baylee. Because he's a player. He's got a reputation for taking advantage of women. He uses them and dumps them so fast they don't know what hit them."

"I appreciate your concern, Trey, but I'm a big girl. I can take care of myself. Now if you don't mind." She pointedly loosened his fingers which were still encircling her elbow.

Collin straightened as she strode toward him. He looked pleased. "See you around, Trey," he called. Baylee looked back to see Trey's silent glower.

"Let me guess. He told you not to go out with me," he said once they were seated in the cab.

"Yes. He said you were a player."

He barked a laugh at that. "Takes one to know one I guess."

"What do you mean?"

"Baylee, come on. Trey Christopher? Do you have any idea how many women he went through while he was a star quarterback?"

"No. Do you?"

Collin snorted and glanced out the window. "I didn't keep count personally, no. But from what I heard it was no small number."

"Wasn't he still married while he was playing?"

Collin swung his gaze back to her. "Surely, you're aware that marriage does little to keep a man faithful. Especially a guy like him."

"What kind of guy is that?" Baylee folded her arms across her chest. She found Collin's accusations against Trey annoying, but she didn't know why. She knew nothing about Trey's past history with women. Only that he'd passed out on top of *her* in high school and that he'd been married and divorced. Why did she now have this urge to leap to his defense?

"Can we talk about something else?" She asked, taking a moment to glance out the window herself. She'd been flattered to be asked out, but now she wished she hadn't been so quick to take Collin up on his offer. She almost wished she'd gone back to the hotel with Trey. Even if it meant another uncomfortable night watching television from their separate beds.

"Gladly. We're here, anyway."

The cab pulled to a stop on a narrow street. Baylee could hear bluesy instrumental music drifting from a narrow door nearby. Several patrons were gathered in small conversational groups outside, most of them smoking cigarettes.

Collin opened the door for her and ushered her inside. It wasn't a large place. A bar took up the entire length of one wall. A slightly elevated stage held a group of musicians in the far corner. There were small tables and chairs, most of them occupied, scattered throughout the open floor.

A saxophone wailed and a drummer kept up a steady beat, along with a piano and a bass.

Collin nodded to a couple of people as he took her hand and led the way to an empty table. Baylee wanted to stop and stare and look around. This is what she'd come to New York for. She was in a genuine jazz club, surrounded by what she assumed were native New Yorkers. Fighting her instinctive desire to gawk like a tourist, she took the seat Collin held for her and turned her attention to the musicians.

A petite waitress wove her way through the nest of tables with a tray held overhead, pausing to take orders, clear empty glasses and collect money. She arrived at their table and Collin asked Baylee what she'd like.

When Baylee hesitated, Collin suggested something called a Fuzzy Peach. "Being a Georgia girl, you're probably partial to peaches, right?"

"I'm from North Carolina," Baylee reminded him.

"Oh, right. Maybe you'd prefer an appletini instead? They grow apples in North Carolina, right?"

It was all Baylee could do to keep from rolling her eyes. The waitress was getting antsy. "I'll try the Fuzzy Peach."

She rarely drank, something she attributed to Trey's influence on her at that high school party. If he hadn't passed out when he did, and sometimes she still thought that was surely God's way of protecting them both, she might have actually had sex with him. God knew her inhibitions were lowered enough, her judgment practically nil after the few plastic cups of beer she'd consumed that night. Plus, she hadn't been able to believe her luck. Trey had singled her out, put his arm around her, taken her up to the hayloft. She'd been stupidly flattered, too young and dumb to know it wouldn't have mattered to him who she was. He wanted a willing female. She'd stepped into his line of vision, been the right gender, and she'd blindly followed his lead.

Jenny had been livid with her. Even now, Baylee could hear her best friend's words in her head. "My God, Baylee, do you know what could have happened? You could have got pregnant. Or worse."

Jenny's displeasure with her did not help Baylee's roiling stomach or pounding head. They were in Jenny's bedroom, squished together in a bed slightly larger than a twin, but smaller than a full, barely big enough for the two of them.

"What could be worse?" Baylee had asked before she thought better of it. Surely an unplanned pregnancy at age fifteen fell into the "worst" category.

"STD's," Jenny hissed. "Herpes. HIV. Did you learn anything in health class last year?"

"Trey doesn't have herpes," she'd argued.

"How do you know? He's slept with at least four girls this year. And I don't know how many before them. He could have herpes and not even know it. He could have given it to you."

Baylee couldn't think of anything to say. Probably because Jenny was right."So lucky for me nothing happened."

"You're damn right," Jenny growled as she turned on her side presenting Baylee with her back. "You better wise up before something bad does."

In minutes Jenny fell asleep, but Baylee stayed awake much longer playing the entire evening over in her head before concluding she was sorry Trey had passed out. Sorry she was still a virgin in spite of the risks. Dumb or not, she wanted to know what it'd be like, what the big secret was. The truth she only admitted to herself, never to Jenny, was how much she'd wanted to be the girl Trey didn't dump. The one he fell head over heels in love with for good.

Their drinks arrived and Baylee took a small sip of hers. It wasn't bad.

Intently, he watched her lick her lips afterward. Do you like it?" he whispered close to her ear.

She smiled at him and nodded. "It's pretty sweet."

He reached for her hand and squeezed. "Just like you."

Baylee sipped her drink and listened to the music while taking in her surroundings. She wasn't sure she'd ever learn to appreciate jazz, but most of the other patrons appeared rapt with attention to the skill displayed on the small stage.

When the musicians took a break, she excused herself for the restroom. Not because she had to go, because she wanted to see if it resembled the one she'd seen on *Sex and the City* last night. Maybe she'd overhear some interesting tidbits of conversation like Carrie and her friends sometimes did.

Sadly, such was not the case. The tiny, dingy ladies' room had only two stalls and one sink. A woman finished drying her hands and left as soon as Baylee entered. She stared at herself in the faded mirror over the sink. *What am I doing here?* She silently asked her reflection. She didn't want to be here. She wasn't interested in Collin, and she was pretty sure he wasn't all that interested in her. Except maybe he thought she was dumb enough to fall for his fake flattery and his practiced seduction techniques.

In the middle of the set, he'd trailed his finger from her shoulder to her wrist. She'd had to repress a shudder of annoyance. Then he'd slid his fingers beneath hers and rubbed his thumb in a circle on the top of her hand.

Maybe she didn't have a lot of experience with men, but she knew enough to know this one wasn't turning her on at all. As soon as she could, she withdrew her hand from his on the pretext of picking up her drink. She gave him a smile as fake as he was. He signaled to the waitress for another round.

She should have listened to Trey. She shouldn't have come out when he'd warned her not to.

Unfortunately, his objection to her going only reinforced her resolve to do it. It wasn't like he owned her. He signed her paycheck every week, but she didn't belong to him.

A wave of loneliness and longing swept through her. She sort of wished she did belong to Trey. To anyone. She wished there was a man who wanted her, who had a right to warn other men away from her.

But she didn't belong to anyone but herself, and she didn't fit in anywhere. Soon she'd be a thirty-year-old single woman, divorced and childless and still a virgin. If she'd tried to imagine a fate for herself on that long ago night when Trey had disappointed her with his lack of performance, she doubted she could have imagined a scenario like this.

"Stop it," she whispered to herself as she applied some lip gloss. She had to stop thinking like this. Two women came in together, barely acknowledging her presence as they practically climbed over her to get to the stalls.

She'd go back to the table, finish her drink and inform Collin she'd like to leave.

Chapter Fifteen

♥

Trey drummed his fingertips on the taxi door, his gaze fixed on the entrance to All That Jazz.

"How much longer you gonna wait?" The cabbie caught his eye in the rear view mirror.

"As long as it takes." They'd already been sitting here for thirty minutes. The meter clicked over again adding to the fare. Trey ignored it. He and Hiram were on a first-name basis now, and he'd assured the cabbie there'd be another generous tip on top of the one he'd already given him.

Hiram slouched down behind the wheel and closed his eyes. "You wake me up when you ready to go."

"Will do."

If what Trey had heard about Collin Cassidy's M.O. was true, he wouldn't have to wait long. He hated the feeling in his gut right now. He'd had this sick churning sense of loss ever since Baylee had left the restaurant and it worsened after he told the cabbie to stop outside the club and wait.

He couldn't stand the thought of Cassidy's slimy hands on her. The guy was a sleaze. How could Baylee not see it? He was smooth, for sure. Trey supposed women would find him good looking with his tall build, dark hair, and white smile.

If she'd been more sophisticated, she'd have seen that behind the smooth exterior lurked a womanizing asshole. She'd have blown him off in two seconds, seen through his false charm.

She hadn't liked his warning to stay away from the guy one bit. The truth was he had no right to tell her what to do. No claim on her at all. None. He had only to pay her the agreed upon amount for the time she spent working for him each week. His obligation to her ended there. She was, as she'd told him, a big girl. She probably even believed she was capable of looking out for herself. Maybe that was true when she was in Henderson, North Carolina. New York City was an entirely different ballgame. The Big Apple ate naïve women like her for lunch and spit them out by dinner time.

Trey hoped he was wrong about Cassidy. He sincerely hoped everything he'd heard about the guy was a lie. But the world of professional sports was relatively small. There was a surprising amount of truth behind even the smallest bit of scuttlebutt.

The door to the club opened and several people spilled out. Trey concentrated on the group, not wanting to miss Baylee if she was a part of it. But she wasn't. He sat back against the cracked leather seat and drummed his fingers some more. The cab's on-duty light was on, but the engine was off. He'd rolled the window down to let in the warm night air. A hint of moisture tinged the fading heat of the day.

The club door opened again and this time he sat up and watched as Cassidy exited first and Baylee followed. She almost fell against Cassidy and he put an arm around her when she wobbled. They began walking, although even from this distance, Trey could see Baylee was none-too-steady on her feet. He couldn't have got her drunk already, surely. They hadn't been inside for even an hour.

Trey reminded himself he had no idea how Baylee reacted to alcohol. Maybe she was a lightweight, the type who got tipsy after one glass of wine.

Would Cassidy hail a cab and take Baylee back to the hotel? If so, Baylee would never know he'd followed her. He planned to simply arrive back at the room shortly after she did with no explanation.

If Cassidy had other ideas, however, Trey's plan would change. The fact that Baylee appeared not to be in charge of all of her faculties only reinforced his resolve to step in if necessary.

When they reached the cross-street Cassidy hailed a cab. Trey nudged his driver. "Hey, Hiram. Let's go." Hiram came to attention, started the engine, and put the car in gear. "See the couple up there getting into the taxi?" Hiram nodded. "As they say in the movies, follow that cab."

Hiram did as instructed. Trey wasn't terribly surprised when it pulled to a stop several blocks later. Hiram got stopped at a red light a half block behind. When he thought he saw Cassidy half drag, half carry Baylee toward an apartment entrance, he panicked. "Pull up outside that building." He opened his door. "And wait for me," he told Hiram.

Trey sprinted to the corner, anxiously waiting for the traffic to clear so he could cross against the light. He strained to see what had happened to Cassidy and Baylee. If they'd already disappeared inside the building, Trey might have a helluva a time gaining access and tracking them down.

As soon as he could he dodged across the street and ran to the building entrance. The double glass doors were locked, of course. They rattled when Trey tried yanking on them. Giving up, he rapped hard on the glass, peering inside to see if there was a doorman.

There was. An older man, dressed in a uniform, ambled toward the doors, his expression hovering between annoyance and curiosity. He hit an intercom button nearby. "Can I help you?"

"A guy just came in. With a woman. Collin Cassidy."

The doorman was no dummy. He neither acknowledged nor denied Trey's statement. Trey thought of everything he knew about doormen in a building like this. They were paid to assist and protect the tenants by limiting access to the building.

How could he convince the man to give him access? The guy was older. Probably had a family. Children. Grandchildren, maybe. "That woman? That's my—" *What*, Trey thought wildly? *Little sister? Cousin? Girlfriend?* "Sister. Did you see her?"

This was taking too long, but Trey had to be patient. He had to say the right thing or the doorman might just walk away and leave him standing here.

"I saw a woman come in with one of the tenants."

"Tall, slender, dark hair? Kind of pretty?"

The guy nodded.

"Look, I'm afraid—" what? What would work here. The truth? Another lie? He decided to go with a lie. "I'm afraid he might have given her something. You know? Put something in her drink, maybe, so he could—"

The door buzzed briefly, and the doorman pushed it open. Trey could hardly believe his luck. "Look, buddy, it wouldn't be the first time, but—"

Trey was ready for this. He pressed several bills into the breast pocket of the man's jacket. "What apartment?"

"Twelve B."

Trey started past him, but the guy blocked him. "You get your sister and you get out. That's it. You rearrange

Mr. Cassidy's face or anything like that, you and me got a problem. Capisce?"

Trey nodded. The doorman stepped aside.

The elevator bumped to a stop on the twelfth floor and in seconds Trey pounded on 12B's door. "Cassidy? Goddammit, if you've touched one hair on her head, I swear to God, I'll—"

The door burst open. "What the hell do you think you're doing?" Collin glared at him and then switched his attention over Trey's shoulder when a door across the hall opened.

"It's okay, Mrs. Barry. Just a friend who's had too much to drink. Sorry to have disturbed you."

Trey heard the door behind him click. He was barely aware of his fists flexing in anticipation of beating the hell out of Collin Cassidy. But he quelled that desire.

He took in Cassidy's appearance. His shoes were off, his shirt untucked. Trey clenched his fists again. "Where's Baylee?"

Cassidy stepped back and with a sweeping gesture, motioned Trey to enter.

The apartment wasn't large but it was dimly lit. He saw Baylee slumped in the corner of a black leather sectional sofa in the living room. Most of the row of tiny buttons down the front of her dress were undone. He saw flashes of flesh, the black lace of her bra. The hem of the dress rode above her knees but not high enough to be indecent.

She didn't acknowledge Trey's presence even when he put his face close to hers and said her name. Her eyes were glassy, the pupils dilated but unfocused.

"What's wrong with her? How much did she have to drink?" He didn't spare a glance in Cassidy's direction. He started buttoning Baylee's dress.

"That the only way you can get a woman to come back to your place? By getting her drunk?"

"No. It's just more expedient," Cassidy stated without a hint of remorse.

Trey slid a glance his way to find him leaning against the wainscoting in his stocking feet, arms crossed over his chest. Never in his life could Trey recall wanting to rearrange another man's face as much as he wanted to at this moment. Not in all the games he'd played, not after all the bad calls, the sacks, the unsportsmanlike conduct he'd seen on the field. Not even when Spoley had pulled him over for speeding and handed him a sheaf of citations.

That had all been personal, behavior directed at him. This was about someone else and he was angrier on Baylee's behalf than he'd ever been on his own. He'd figure out why later. Right now, all he wanted was to get her out of here, away from the scumbag standing less than ten feet away, into Hiram's cab and back to the hotel.

He finished with the buttons and tugged the hem of her skirt down. One of her shoes had slid off her foot and he put it back on. "Come on, baby."

He helped her up from the couch and as soon as he did her knees sagged. He kept her upright by using both arms to hold her against him.

He thought of all the things he wanted to say to Collin Cassidy, of what he'd like to do to the guy, but he wouldn't. He didn't look at him or say anything. He got Baylee out into the hallway and let the door slam behind him. Guys like Cassidy would get their due without any help from him. Karma would take care of it. Although smashing his fist into Cassidy's face would have been much more satisfying.

Hiram turned to look at them when Trey got into the backseat with Baylee. "She all right?" he asked.

"Yeah. I think she'll be okay. Take us back to the hotel."

Hiram nodded. Trey placed a grateful number of bills into Hiram's hand when he dropped them off. He still had to half drag, half carry Baylee through the lobby to the elevator. He hoped the surreptitious looks he received from the staff and the few guests lingering about meant they understood Baylee'd had too much to drink, but he couldn't concern himself with the thoughts of strangers.

In the room, he got Baylee to her bed. He pulled back the covers and laid her down. She was like a rag doll. It was a little scary and not at all a turn-on for him. He wondered how a guy like Cassidy could perform with a woman in such a state. Personally, Trey liked his sexual partners to be enthusiastic participants, not nearly co-matose victims. The entire evening had left a bad taste in his mouth.

He slipped Baylee's shoes off her feet. She could sleep in her clothes. He sure as hell wasn't going to undress her.

He covered her with the sheet and supposed she'd sleep now. He had a feeling she was going to feel like hell during their trip home tomorrow.

The bedside alarm clock glowed three-thirty-four in red when Trey came awake. He sat up trying to figure out what had awakened him. He could see the glow of light surrounding the closed bathroom door, and Baylee's empty bed. He pulled a tee shirt on over his pajama bottoms and listened for a moment outside the door. He heard water running and thought he heard her utter an unlady-like oath.

"Baylee?" He tapped on the door. "You okay?"

She opened the door and stared at him. She had on those same sexy nightclothes from the previous evening, but frankly, she looked like hell. Her hair was a mess and there were dark circles under her eyes. Her eyes themselves were red and puffy. God, he hoped she wasn't crying. He hated when women cried. He never knew what to do and whatever he did or said always seemed to be the wrong thing.

"Are you okay?" he asked again.

She shook her head. "I don't know what's wrong with me." Her voice quavered. "I feel really weird. I'm super thirsty and I've got the mother of all headaches."

"Come on." He led her back to her bed and tucked her in. "Did you take anything for the headache?"

"No. I don't have anything to take."

"I've got over the counter stuff. It might help." He went back to the bathroom and got his bottle of ibuprofen and retrieved a bottle of water from the mini fridge. The rage he'd felt earlier came back to boil below the surface. The image of Collin Cassidy's face beaten and bloody, complete with a broken nose, a black eye and minus a few of those white teeth, swam before his eyes. The thought of it sent an exultant river of potential satisfaction through him. But he wasn't going to get a chance to see it happen. His concern now was the same as it had been before. Baylee's welfare. He shook tablets into his hand and she took them along with half the bottle of water.

"I keep drinking water, but it doesn't seem to help. My mouth's like a ball of cotton."

He went back to the fridge and found a sports drink and another bottle of water.

"I don't know what you had to drink, but it's got some nasty side effects."

He opened the sports drink and handed it to her.

She took a gulp and massaged her temple with her fingers. "Everything's kind of a blur."

Trey sat on his bed across from her. "What do you remember?"

She thought for a moment. "Being at some club with Collin. He ordered me a drink. Something sweet that tasted like peaches. I went to the restroom."

"Was the drink there when you came back?"

"He'd ordered another one for me."

"Did you finish it?"

She frowned. "I don't remember. But even if I did I only had two drinks." Her voice rose in her own defense.

He leaned forward, his gaze locked with hers. "Baylee, you didn't do anything wrong."

"But I don't understand. I shouldn't be this messed up from two drinks. What aren't you telling me? What did he do to me? What don't I remember?"

Trey moved to the edge of her bed. He patted her calf through the sheet and kept his hand there, hoping to offer some kind of comfort. "He didn't do anything. I—sort of busted up your date."

"You did? You were there?"

"Yeah."

"But if you hadn't been—then he could have—oh, Jesus. You told me not to go."

Trey shrugged. As far as he was concerned, she never had to know how close Cassidy had come to getting away with whatever he had in mind.

"Nothing happened. We came back here. I stuck you in bed."

"Thank you," she told him, her voice a soft caress.

"My pleasure." The truth warmed him. For the first time in a long time, he got to be the hero instead of the failure. He patted her leg. "Drink up. Try to get some sleep.

"Okay." She chugged some more of the drink and then set it next to the water on the nightstand. She slid down beneath the covers.

Trey turned off the bathroom light and got into his own bed.

"Night, Trey."

"Night."

The sense of disorientation dogged Baylee the following day. She awoke to a fully dressed Trey pushing her shoulder back and forth with such force her entire body moved from side to side. Even so, getting her eyes open and her brain to kick into gear was like swimming up through a sea of mud.

Her head felt thick. Her ability to concentrate had deserted her. Somehow, she'd managed, with Trey's help to get herself and her things together. Her eyes were sticky since she hadn't had it together enough the night before to remove her contacts. She knew from looking in the mirror after her shower she looked like hell.

Oh, what did it matter, anyway? Trey wasn't interested in her and neither was any other man other than Justin Spoley, who she found to be a major turn-off, and Collin Cassidy, who apparently only wanted one thing from her and used some truly questionable methods to try to get it. She shuddered every time she thought of what might have happened.

How lucky for her that not only had Trey prevented it, but he also got how awful she felt. He didn't try to carry on a conversation with her. He was more solicitous than usual, doing his best to make her comfortable.

Once they were on the plane, she closed her eyes. Bits and pieces of the previous evening flashed through her head, but they were out of order and didn't make any sense.

A taxi ride.

An elevator.

A dimly lit room.

Trey buttoning her dress. Or unbuttoning it. She wasn't sure.

Trey holding her against him. She thought it was him, anyway. Not Collin.

She recalled Jenny's long-ago warning about the worst thing that could happen to her.

Wouldn't it be worse if the first time she had sex was with a man who took her and left her with this vague sense of unease? This sick, disoriented feeling. Worse if he took something he had no right to take, and she had virtually no memory of the encounter. What had been in those drinks Collin had ordered for her? She might never be able to enjoy anything peach-related again.

She sniffed and rubbed her fingertips against her eyes beneath her glasses.

"You okay?" Trey bent his head close to hers and spoke softly near her ear.

She nodded without opening her eyes.

"Come here." He guided her head to his shoulder.

Her thoughts had been chasing themselves around in her head ever since she'd woke up this morning, but one thing had crystallized overnight. Trey was no longer that seventeen-year-old boy who'd passed out on her. She'd allowed that one incident to cloud her judgment about men and to make her doubt her own appeal. She thought she saw both herself and Trey more clearly than she ever had before. Last night he'd proven himself in a way she'd never expected. Her insides hummed whenever she was close to him. Being around Trey made her *happy*. What, she asked herself, could be wrong with that?

She lifted her head and planted a kiss on Trey's cheek.

He looked at her in surprise.

"You're my hero," she said softly.

He flashed her a quick grin while several emotions warred for dominance in his expression. The tips of his ears turned pink.

He bent toward her and crooked a finger beneath her chin. His gaze dropped from her eyes to her lips. He gave her a quick, light kiss on the mouth, so fleeting she wasn't sure she hadn't imagined it. But there was a flare of something in his eyes when he looked at her again.

Maybe, just maybe, he was interested in her *that way*. Whether he was or not she planned to take every opportunity for contact with him, every moment she could touch him, no matter how innocently.

She slid her arm beneath his and made herself comfortable against him in case this was all of him she'd ever get.

By mid-afternoon the plane had landed in Asheville and they were on their way back to his house where she'd left her car. She'd dozed off on the plane, but she hadn't really slept. She dreaded going home where she'd be surrounded by but mostly ignored by her family.

On the outskirts of Ednaville, she broke the silence between them. "Could I ask you a favor?"

Trey took his gaze from the curving road for only a second to glance her way. "Sure. Anything."

"Could I stay at your place for a little while? Maybe take a nap before I head home?"

"Damn, I didn't even think of that. I can take you home and pick you up tomorrow."

"No, no. It's okay. We're almost to your house. I understand if you'd rather I didn't stay. You probably have stuff to do."

"Hey, no. You're welcome to stay. Stay as long as you want. Whatever you need."

Baylee didn't have to fake a yawn. "Thanks. I think I just need a nap." *Liar. What I need is you.*

Once she'd made herself comfortable in Trey's bed, she couldn't fall asleep even though she desperately wanted to. Her thoughts kept returning to *what if?* in a way they never had before. What if Trey hadn't rescued her?

She'd always considered her virginity something she controlled, something she'd share with a man of her choosing. Scott hadn't wanted it, even though she had chosen him. She could only think of one other man she'd choose. The same one she'd sort of chosen at fifteen. Except now she wasn't even slightly inebriated. She wasn't fifteen any more, either. She was an adult woman, dammit, and she had needs. Needs she put on hold for too long. She made a decision. She didn't know exactly how or when. But she was going to rid herself of her troublesome virginity with her eyes wide open, fully conscious, with a man of her choosing. And she was going to do it soon.

Chapter Sixteen

♥

"Baylee?" Trey spoke softly from the doorway. She hadn't answered when he'd lightly tapped on the door seconds earlier. He couldn't believe she was still asleep.

The hall light spilled into the room behind him as he stepped closer to the bed.

She was curled on her side, the same way he'd seen her sleeping before, the sheet pulled up under her arm, her hands clasped beneath her chin.

She hadn't wanted anything on the plane except the small bottles of water the flight attendant brought her. Trey lost track of how many she'd had. She'd bought another bottle before they left the airport and drank it and there was a half a bottle sitting on the nightstand.

Trey wondered if anything besides alcohol had been in those drinks Cassidy had ordered for her last night. Whatever was in them had dehydrated her and knocked her out. Surely, she needed to eat something.

He sat down on the edge of the bed and gently shook her arm. "Baylee? Baylee?"

Her eyelids fluttered. She moaned softly. Then she blinked her eyes open and gazed up at him and smiled. "Hi," she breathed.

Every thought in Trey's disappeared, chased away by the vision of her waking up, all soft and warm. In his bed. Her eyes dreamy from sleep. With a smile just for him.

"Come here," she whispered. She half sat up and tugged on his shirt. She kissed him!

Stunned, Trey couldn't think what to do. Although he'd been unable to stop thinking about that brief kiss he'd given her on the plane, he hadn't expected her to respond like this. Had he?

Her soft lips pressed against his, teasing him, sending him a signal. In seconds his body roared to life. Everything he'd been holding inside for such a long time welled to the surface, begging for release.

He kissed her back, deepening the kiss instantly. He heard a soft little moan from her direction and a sigh of surrender before she met him full force. She didn't play games or go to war with his tongue. She took it and held on, sucking it as if she couldn't get enough.

Sexually, he'd always been the aggressor, but he felt weirdly out of control. His mind couldn't seem to catch up with his body or its reaction to the feel of hers. But like riding a bike after an extended absence, his body operated without him telling it what to do. He found buttons and zippers and clasps, and he knew how to dispense with such things as clothes.

He should probably stop kissing her and use his mouth to explore her elsewhere, but he didn't want to stop and if he wasn't mistaken, she didn't want him to. So, he used his hands instead, roaming them all over her back and her bottom and her breasts.

She was doing the same thing to him, exploring everywhere she could reach, everywhere she could touch while their mouths were locked together. Everywhere, that is, except his cock. She brushed by it, around it, but her shy hand slid away each time. Waves of excitement washed through him.

Had he ever had sex before? Everything seemed new and different. Even though he knew what to do, employed the same practiced moves he'd perfected over the years, it was almost like he'd never used them before.

"Baylee," he whispered. He slid his fingers between her legs to discover the slick, hot wetness of her. Her gasp of pleasure thrilled him.

He lowered his head to suckle a nipple and she arched against him, her legs parted, giving his fingers easier access.

"Touch me," he whispered. He fumbled for her hand and brought it against him. "Please."

Her breathing quickened as she circled the length of him. It wasn't a knowing, practiced touch, but more an exploration of uncharted territory. Yet she was hitting all the right spots and if she kept it up, the show was going to be over before it started.

"Okay, babe. Okay." He eased away from her to open the nightstand drawer. From long habit, he kept condoms there, whether he thought he'd have a need for them or not. He sure as hell hadn't thought he was going to need them tonight.

There was enough light from the half open door to see what he was doing. His hands shook. He stared at them for a second in amazement. Imagine that. But he got the condom on in record time anyway and got back to business.

He ran the flat of his hand down her tummy from beneath her breasts to her pubic hair. He kissed her just above the navel. "You're hot," he whispered. Her skin felt like a fire burned just beneath the surface, protecting him from a burn, but hot just the same.

"I want you."

Trey froze, his hand stilled where it was, splayed against her, her pubic hairs tickling him. He could see the depths of her amber eyes. She'd said the words clearly, directly. A statement of fact.

Maybe her tone should have killed the mood, but blatant honesty turned out to be another turn-on for him.

He could have told her she didn't need to state the obvious. He could have told her he wanted her, too. But he supposed she'd already figured that out.

He kissed her again. Slow and hot. It was a wonder the bed didn't burst into flame, he thought wildly. He pressed as much of her as he could as close to him as it could get until he couldn't stand it anymore.

"You'll have to be on top, darlin'."

"Mmm?"

"Come here."

He rolled to his back taking her with him, their positions making it all too clear how this would play out. Still, it took her a second before she acted on his direction.

He watched, fascinated, as she braced herself above him and ever so slowly sank down against him, taking him inside her bit by agonizing bit. He didn't realize he was holding his breath until he let it out when he was completely, deeply inside her. She'd sunk her top teeth into her bottom lip while she'd lowered herself onto him. But once it was done, he could feel her relax a bit, although she was sheathed around him so tightly, he wondered how long he could last.

Then she gave him the most beatific smile he'd ever seen, like she'd accomplished something magnificent, and took immense pride in herself for doing it.

"Wow." She knocked his socks off and it wasn't like she was even trying. Was she? Somehow whatever was happening, he got the idea it was more about her. What she needed. Or, as she'd said a minute ago, what she wanted.

"What do you want, darlin'?" he asked, his gaze never leaving hers. He stroked her thighs, her tummy, her breasts.

"You. I just want you."

"You've got me, babe. Now what are you going to do with me?"

That brought a sort of choking giggle out of her. "To tell you the truth, I have absolutely no idea."

He grinned at her. "I've got a couple. Want to hear them?"

She nodded.

He eased his fingers in where she sat atop him. "Ease up there, a bit, darlin'."

She did. He pressed his thumb against her and watched her reaction. Her eyes widened. Her internal muscles flexed around him. "Feel good?"

"God yes."

"Okay. We're cookin' now."

Trey let her chase her orgasm while she rode him, madly frantically, until she caught it, bucking and rocking against him while he drove into her again and again and again.

Then she collapsed against him a shaking, shuddering mess.

His mind idled while he caught his breath. He liked the weight of her on top of him. She fit there, her torso a perfect match for his. Her hair tickled his chin and his neck. Her warm breath fanned against his shoulder and upper arm.

He brushed her hair back with his fingertips, enjoying the silky feel of her skin. Again, that intoxicating fragrance wafted beneath his nostrils, a tiny, fleeting scent, not enough for him to grab it and hang on and figure out what it was. All it did was make him want more.

Just like her. The thought was there in his brain, and he found he couldn't reject it. That elusive scent was exactly like Baylee, sneaking into his senses, teasing him, eluding him.

Baylee chose that moment to slide away from him, though she stayed close. He glanced down. Her eyes were closed, a peaceful expression on her face.

Trey did not want to move a muscle. He didn't want to get out of this bed for a good long time. Not while

Baylee was in it with him. But he needed to attend to business. Dispose of the condom and the uncomfortable stickiness. Maybe they could jump in the shower together.

"Baylee?" he whispered.

She sighed but didn't answer. Had she fallen asleep? In just these couple of minutes?

They could always shower later. Maybe after round two.

He slid out of bed as quietly as possible and tread softly to the bathroom, trying to avoid the floorboards he knew were the creakiest. After closing the door, he turned on the light. He paused in the act of dropping the condom into the wastebasket. What was that? Reddish streaks. Blood?

He stared down at himself to see what looked like more of the same. This had only ever happened to him one time that he could recall. The first time he and Hayley made love. She'd told him in advance, warned him really, she was a virgin. That had pleased him immensely, knowing he was her first. How she'd made it to college without giving it up to some other guy, he never quite figured out. But he'd fallen hard for her and knowing she hadn't been with anyone else made her that much more special to him.

Okay, but Baylee was an entirely different story. She'd been married. She had to be close to his age. No way was she a virgin. Probably, she was getting her period and didn't realize it. Should he tell her? Ugh. Maybe he could hint that she might want to visit the bathroom instead. Yeah. That was better.

He finished cleaning up and left the bathroom light on. He hoped she hadn't fallen asleep for real. He opened the door to discover her still in bed and wide awake.

She tracked his movements as he made his way back to the bed.

"You want the bathroom it's free," informed her as he lay back down.

"Nope. I'm good," she replied.

He slanted a look down at her. "You sure?"

"I'm sure." She shifted closer. He curled an arm around her trying to figure out what to say. Already he could feel himself stirring. He wanted her again.

He stroked her back with the tips of his fingers. "I think you started your period or something." *Or something?*

"Nope." She slid the palm of her hand back and forth across his chest. She shifted in order to kiss his shoulder, the crook of his neck. He came to full attention when she pressed the length of her body against his. Her knee slid intimately between his thighs, causing him to groan.

"Then there's something else wrong," he informed her. She kissed him full on the mouth. He didn't want her to stop, but his brain told him he needed to know what was going on with her before they went any further.

"What could be wrong?" she whispered.

Trey held her a little away from him. "I don't know. But there was blood. You're bleeding."

She stared at him. He could see her debating with herself about what to say to that. "It's not a problem," she assured him, dipping her head to kiss him again. Her arms slid around his shoulders. Those soft breasts with their erect nipples pressed against his chest. Her knee brushed against him, and her hand slid down his side.

Let it go, his body insisted.

Find out what's going on, his brain argued.

She said it's not a problem, his body fired back.

I thought you were going to stop thinking with your cock.

"Okay, wait." Trey somehow managed to get a few inches of distance between them. "There was blood on the condom and on me. It's not your period. Then what is it that's 'not a problem'?"

He watched her debate. Saw the uncertainty in her eyes. "I've heard sometimes there's a bit of bleeding the first time."

"The first time? The first time what?"

He thought he saw a flash of disappointment in her eyes. He realized he didn't want yet another woman to give him that particular look. He scrambled to save himself. "The first time...you have sex?"

Her gaze stayed steady on his, like she might break in half if it didn't. She nodded.

There was no danger of him looking anywhere else. Shock wouldn't let him. "But—but you were married. You're—you're—"

"I'm what?"

"Old!" he exploded. Immediately he knew it was the absolute wrong thing to say.

Surprising him, Baylee started to laugh. Completely tickled by his remark, her laughter seemed to bounce around the room, off the walls, reverberate through the house.

Trey tried to recall a time when he'd been so completely out of his element and couldn't. He had no idea what he should do, no idea what she found so funny or why. Had she just shared her virginity with him, and hadn't he just told her she was old? Shouldn't she be insulted instead of gleeful?

Finally, her laughter dissipated. She lay on her side facing him with her hands tucked up under her chin, tiny bits of moisture visible in the corners of her eyes.

"Thank you. You can't imagine what a relief it is to not be a virgin anymore."

"A relief?" he echoed.

She nodded vigorously. "And don't worry. You don't ever have to sleep with me again if you don't want to."

His erection reminded him it was still there. "Oh, I want to. I just don't—"

"You do?" She slid in close to him again, her eyes shining. She smiled at him with such delight it took his breath away. When she kissed him, he forgot the questions he wanted to ask. He forgot to think about anything at all. Except how much he wanted her.

This time there was no trip to the bathroom afterward. No way was he leaving this bed. Tissues from the box on the nightstand did the trick. He spooned up behind Baylee and wrapped an arm around her. She nestled back against him like she belonged there. A perfect fit.

He played with her hair, discovering it was weirdly curly and wavy when unleashed from its ponytail. Mesmerized, he let the thick, silky strands drift through his fingers, much the way his mind drifted off point. He didn't want to start a conversation. Didn't want to ask questions but he needed answers.

Except maybe not right now. Not while Baylee was all warm and soft, his thighs tucked up under hers, her bottom nuzzling against his groin. He wondered if she'd be up for a third time. Because he'd abstained from sex for such a long time it was almost new again for him. Although not quite as new as it apparently was for her.

He stroked her with his hand, along the flat of her tummy and down along her side to her hip. He tugged the sheet way from where it was tucked around her and yanked it off to the bottom of the bed.

"Hey," she objected, although she made no move to retrieve it.

He turned on the bedside light and regarded her from behind before he started stroking her again. Down her side to the indentation of her waist, along her hip to her thigh. And further, down her leg to her knee and along her shin.

"What are you doing?" she asked sleepily.

"You've got a great body."

"Hmm." She managed to make that non-committal utterance sound disbelieving all the same.

He nudged her over to lie on her stomach and traced the flat of his palm up her leg, pausing to tickle the back of her knee. She flinched and he noticed her buttocks flex at that touch.

"What are you doing?" she whispered, more alert now, her voice muffled by the pillow."

"Nothing." He smiled. She had a great ass. He slid his hand up the back of her thigh, letting his fingers trail between her legs.

He heard her quick intake of breath and he smiled again. He massaged the backs of her thighs, his fingers sliding closer and higher against her. He kneaded the soft round mounds of her buttocks, all the while letting his fingertips brush lightly against her. He felt her muscles clench in reaction to his touch.

"Open your legs a little."

She made another sound in her throat, but she complied. His fingers brushed against her moist flesh while his thumb teased against the cleft of her bottom. Another one of those sounds from her, her legs separated more, welcoming his touch.

It was the sexiest damn thing he'd ever witnessed.

"Turn over," he whispered.

She rolled without losing contact with his fingers. Her eyes glittered up at him, her whole body seemed consumed with a rosy glow. He wanted to watch her. He wanted to see what his touch did to her.

"Spread your legs," he encouraged.

She complied. He hiked one of her knees up and let it fall against him and without him telling her she did the same with the other one, completely open. He gazed down at everything that made her a woman, stroked against the slick engorged bud between her legs. With the fingers of his other hand he took some of the slickness and stroked her nipples.

She arched her back and a long "Ahhh," slid from her lips. She writhed against him, urging him on as he kept touching her. He waited, waited, like he had all the time in the world, gauging her reactions to everything he did, fascinated by her innocent passion.

When she was close, really close, he lowered his mouth to her, touched her with his tongue, just there, just that little bud, coaxing the ultimate response from her. In seconds she gave it to him, her exultant cries of ecstasy better than any cheers from fans at a packed stadium.

By the time he'd kissed his way back up her body, she'd quieted some, but she wrapped herself around him, leaving no doubt as to what she wanted. His cock rooted against the wetness between her legs. He wondered if his knee could survive him being on top. Maybe he could shift most of his weight to his other leg.

While he briefly debated the wisdom of attempting this, he discovered Baylee had maneuvered her body against his so that he slid inside her. Even as her tight heat closed around him he knew he couldn't do it. "Baylee, no," he told her softly, bracing himself away from her.

She looked up at him, a rapturous expression on her face. Her knees hitched higher and she clasped him closer still. "Oh, but it feels so good, doesn't it?"

Good? Good didn't begin to describe how it felt to be this deeply, completely inside her with nothing between them. He doubted he could hold this position for long, even though at the moment most of his weight was on top of her. Tentatively he bent his knee. She responded by hiking even higher against him. He groaned. If she kept that up, he wouldn't have to worry about what position they were in because he'd come in about two seconds.

Carefully, he started to ease out of her, forcing her to let him go. Her lower lip puffed out and she frowned like a little kid who didn't get her way. Trey laughed at her and kissed her nose and then teased her lower lip with his tongue, before rolling onto his back and reaching into the nightstand drawer for a condom. She propped herself on one elbow and watched him roll it on.

"My way was more fun," she informed him. "I'm not crazy about these condoms."

He laughed again. "Me either. It's the curse of the responsible adult. Come here."

She straddled him like she'd been riding him forever. He watched her lower herself, her eyes widening as he filled her. He cupped her breasts, noting how perfectly they filled his hands, nothing to spill over, while he teased her nipples with his thumbs.

Her breathing changed. He loved watching her every reaction and couldn't imagine he'd ever tire of it. He sat up halfway and suckled first one and then the other nipple. Her fingers threaded through his hair as they rocked together. When he lay back down, he brought her with him, kissing her, ravaging her mouth as he surged inside her. He guided her movements against him, maximizing, he hoped, her pleasure as well as his.

It worked, he thought, for she collapsed against him when it was over, both of them panting from exertion. He liked her against him, liked her weight on him, the feel of her skin, the unique scent of their mingled sex in the air.

He wrapped his arms around her and hugged her tightly, feeling weirdly, oddly connected to her. He'd never have guessed, not in a million years, that Baylee could get to him this way. She made him feel something he hadn't felt in a long time. He'd never imagined he'd want her the way he did.

Eventually, he eased her to the side and dealt with the condom. He was already heartily sick of those. His thoughts drifted back to when he was married to Hayley. She'd put herself in charge of birth control early on, because, as she told him, she'd be the one bearing the physical consequences if it failed. They hadn't used condoms since those first couple of months in college and he sure as hell hadn't missed them.

He'd behaved in ridiculously stupid ways with other women since and he'd known enough to use them. He didn't want any surprises, and he was quite sure, neither did they.

He'd sworn off hurting and using women. All of a sudden he wondered if he hadn't just done exactly what he'd been trying not to do.

"Are you okay?" he asked. "Have I hurt you?"

Baylee's eyes blinked open. She saw the care and concern in Trey's eyes, and for a second she couldn't speak. Whoa. What brought this on?

"Of course, you haven't hurt me. Those were moans of ecstasy not pain. I thought you'd be experienced enough to tell the difference." She grinned at him, but it didn't lighten his mood.

"That's not what I meant."

He continued to regard her intently, searching for something. But what?

They were facing each other, pillows beneath their heads. Already she wanted to reach out and touch him again. He'd given her what she knew she'd been missing, what she'd craved for such a long, long time. She was afraid she might be able to understand addiction, like what someone hooked on crack goes through. She wanted more and more and more of Trey. Of being with him like this. Of being physically connected to him. After being deprived for so long, how would she ever get enough?

"I don't want to hurt you."

Wow. This was turning serious. She didn't know what else to do except reassure him. "You haven't."

"I've got a lousy track record."

What could she say? She knew firsthand about his track record. "I know."

When he didn't say anything else, she decided she should. "I don't—I'm not expecting—uh, that is, I don't expect anything from you—"

"Why not?"

He sounded mildly insulted and curious at the same time.

Baylee tried to backtrack, to get her addled thoughts together. "I mean like a *relationship* or something. Just because we, because you—"

"What?"

Wow. How had she lost the thread of this conversation? What were they talking about anyway? Why oh why hadn't she simply kept her mouth shut? Why did she always feel like she had to smooth everything over, make it all better, keep everyone happy?

It wasn't her job in life to keep other people happy. When did *she* get to be happy? When did she get to take what she wanted and screw what everyone else expected from her?

"Nothing."

"Nothing? You're saying this was nothing?"

"No, that's not what I—"

"Because I've got news for you, Baylee. This was something."

"I know it was." For some reason, she felt perilously close to tears. She shifted closer to Trey. Her head ended up below his chin. He moved a little and wrapped an arm around her so she could be right where she wanted to be.

His fingers played idly up and down against her skin. Somehow, he managed to snag a corner of the sheet and tugged it over them. "Feel like talking?"

Baylee angled a look up at him. "Shouldn't you have rolled over and fallen asleep by now? I thought that's what guys are known for after they have sex."

"Huh. But you don't know this from personal experience, do you?"

Her answer came out on a sigh of resignation and regret. "No."

"How is that?" Trey moved around so he could see her. "How could any guy be married to you and not want you twenty-four/seven?"

"Would you?" A lump of emotion began to form in her throat. There were those insistent tears again.

"Hell, yes."

"Really? You'd want me? In bed?"

Trey frowned. "I thought I just proved that. Must be losing my touch."

"No. No." She shook her head in vehement denial. "I just thought—that was maybe because you hadn't had sex in a while. I've heard when a guy doesn't get any—"

"Hey." He grabbed her hand. "I haven't had sex for a while because I made a conscious decision not to, not because I couldn't if I'd wanted to. Believe me when I say, with you, I wanted to."

"Okay." The tears spilled over. She knew they were coming and didn't try to stop them. Even though he didn't know it Trey had given her a gift she'd never expected to get. No one could ever take it away from her.

"Baylee. Awww." He gathered her close again and let her cry all over him, shoving tissues at her until there was a small pile of them littering the bed. Eventually, she quieted.

He turned the bedside light off, leaving the light from the bathroom to break up the darkness. She thought he'd start asking her questions, but he didn't, though she could sense his desire for an explanation. She certainly owed him one.

"I didn't know Scott was gay when I married him, although I certainly should have, I suppose. He was in denial, I think, of his sexuality. He thought marriage would somehow fix him. It didn't.

"His family would never accept his homosexuality, and that would have crushed him then.

"I thought the reason he didn't press me for sex before we got married was because he respected me. That sounds stupid, doesn't it? But we were both involved in our church youth group, we'd both committed to abstinence before marriage. I know a lot of kids sign up for that but don't take it seriously, but I honestly thought Scott and I were on the same page.

"Which we were, but for different reasons. Fast forward to the honeymoon. I was ready. More than ready. I loved him. Thought I'd be with him for the rest of my life, that he'd be the only man who'd ever touch me that way.

"But, he didn't want me."

Trey squeezed her against him in sympathy.

"The sad thing is I wasn't smart enough to figure it out. We'd kiss and stuff, you know? He'd get excited. But when it came time to, you know. Penetrate?"

"Yes. I know."

"He'd lose it. All the desire fizzled."

"You figured it was you."

Baylee nodded vigorously. "Oh, you betcha. What else could it be? There wasn't anything wrong with him, obviously. He just didn't want *me*."

"Oh, Baylee." He gave her another squeeze. "He never told you?"

"Not for a long time. Years. I tried everything. Sexy lingerie. Stuff like that. Nothing." She shuddered remembering how humiliated she'd felt trying to turn Scott on with her various bag of tricks. How the harder she tried the more distant and, it seemed to her, disgusted he became.

"Until I couldn't take it anymore. I insisted on marriage counseling. Either that or a divorce."

"Why the hell did he put you through that? Why not choose the divorce?"

"It would have devastated his family. His father's a minister, a very staunch conservative, traditional kind of man who ruled his family with his beliefs. Scott loved him and admired him, but he also feared him. Feared the possible repercussions. I understand it now, but at the time it was like living in hell."

"What happened in marriage counseling?"

"The inevitable. Scott finally admitted he was gay. I was able to vent my anger and frustration and disappointment. Telling his family we were getting a divorce was the lesser of two evils as far as Scott was concerned."

"You mean his family still doesn't know he's gay?"

"He's never told them as far as I know."

"Am I allowed to say something?"

"Of course."

Trey shifted so he could see her. He cupped her face with one hand, his fingers sliding back into her hair. "That was an extremely shitty and cowardly thing he did to you."

She wrapped her fingers around his wrist. "I know. But I let him do it. It's hard to explain to someone else, but I loved him. I think maybe I was scared, and he was safe."

"What were you scared of?"

Of having a man who only wants to use me. Of passion. Of my feelings for you.

But hadn't Scott used her, too? For his own purposes? And in a way, hadn't she used him, as well? To play it safe rather than risk going after the kind of man she really wanted? Oh, it was such ancient history. She didn't want to talk about it anymore, so she took the easy way out. "I let a lot of things scare me. Doesn't everybody?"

Chapter Seventeen

♥

"Hey. You awake?" Trey whispered.

She was though she didn't want to be. She'd been happily drowsing, enjoying the feel of Trey's warm skin next to hers. Her stomach growled. She hadn't eaten all day. Plus she was thirsty and she had to pee.

"Time is it?"

"I don't know. I'm going to make coffee. Maybe get something to eat."

"Okay." She scooted out of bed. Her clothes were scattered around the room. She'd look for them later. In the bathroom she stared at her reflection. She didn't really look any different, she didn't think. Her hair was its usual tumbled mess. Maybe her lips were a little swollen. Wait there *was* something different. The knowing look in her eyes.

She smiled at herself. Finally, good God, at last, she knew what "it" was all about. She was a fan.

When she finished in the bathroom, she found her panties in a twisted tangle buried near the bottom of the mattress. The rest of her clothes were in various crumpled heaps. She opened Trey's second dresser drawer and helped herself to one of his vee-necked tee shirts. The hem hit the tops of her thighs. She found the baggy soft cotton comforting.

Barefoot she padded down the hallway to the kitchen. The aroma of brewing coffee tinted the air. Trey's head was in the refrigerator. He backed out with his arms full of sandwich makings. He stared at her.

"I borrowed one of your tee shirts. Hope you don't mind." She came toward him.

"Uh, no. Help yourself." He set everything on the table. Then he stared at her some more.

"What?" she finally asked.

"I had you figured for a tee shirt kind of girl. You know. To sleep in."

"So?"

"But you walked out of the bathroom in New York in a silky, sexy nightie."

"Well, I wasn't planning on sharing a room with you when I packed."

"I know. It threw me."

"It did?" Her lips curled into a smile.

"Oh, God. Do you have any idea how sexy you are?"

"Not really. No."

"Sharing a room with you about drove me crazy."

"It did?" The smile returned.

"Why do you think I was cranky the first morning?"

"Because of me?"

"Honey, let me tell you something. You want to turn a guy on, you put on that sexy outfit and give him one of your 'you can't touch me' looks. You'll drive him crazy in about five seconds."

"I have a 'you can't touch me' look?"

Trey grinned. "You did." He pulled her to him. "Not so much anymore."

He dropped a kiss on her lips. "Let's eat."

They put plates together and went outside. Trey set his coffee on a small table next to the swing, but Baylee opted to keep her bottle of water next to her.

Crickets chirped. The night air was cool but not un-comfortable. Trey set the swing in motion, and they ate in companionable silence. He set the empty plates on the table and picked up his mug.

Replete with sex and food, Baylee knew she needed to crash and really sleep for six or eight hours. Her eyelids drooped. She yawned. "I have to get some sleep," she informed him.

"Come here." She climbed into his lap. He wrapped his arms around her as if he were rocking a small child. The soft cotton of his pajama bottoms and tee shirt were like a security blanket. She could fall asleep here wrapped in such warmth.

"If I fall asleep, you're going to have to carry me to bed," she warned him after a few minutes. "Your knee won't like it."

He chuckled. "Okay. Let's go in then."

Trey came awake the next morning with a raging need, his too-long-denied libido ready for action. In the past, when he found himself in this position, with a woman in bed next to him, he'd make his desire known and let nature take its course.

Baylee was curled on her side with her back to him. He could tell she was still asleep. He debated waking her. He wanted to. *Desperately.* But in his new *mature* outlook, the one he'd been trying to develop for more than a year, he reminded himself everything wasn't about him. His needs. His wants. His desires.

Less than twenty-four hours ago, Baylee was still a virgin. For all of her enthusiasm last night, he doubted she'd appreciate him coming at her first thing this morning, nudging her awake with morning wood and expecting her to accommodate him.

He laid a hand on her hip, just for a second, before he got out of bed and took himself into the bathroom. He could get used to cold showers, he supposed. Not that they did anything to relieve his discomfort long-term.

In fact, he spent the entire time in the bathroom, all through showering and shaving, reliving scenes from last night in his head.

Baylee!

He'd never suspected she was interested in him. Never suspected she was a virgin, either, or that she'd choose him to relieve her of what she apparently viewed as a burden.

But what a welcome surprise. Still, he should tread carefully, shouldn't he? She might think all they were doing was having sex, but he knew sex involved emotions. More for women than men, but whether women wanted to believe it or not, men had emotions, too. They could be hurt, as he knew only too well from first-hand experience.

He'd promised himself he'd appreciate the next serious relationship he had with a woman. Being a selfish s.o.b. had become second nature to him, but it wasn't beneficial for long-term interaction with a woman.

Whoa. Long-term? Relationship? Commitment? He was getting ahead of himself here, wasn't he? He didn't know where this thing with Baylee was going. He suspected she didn't either. Best to take it slow.

He yanked on underwear and jeans and opened the bathroom door to find her awake, still in bed, tracking his every move. Every thought of taking it slow went right out of his head. The cold shower he'd just endured had been a waste of time. Desire tore through him just seeing her there in his bed with that sleepy gleam in her eye.

"Come here," she said.

He stepped to the edge of the bed.

"What's this?" She reached up and tugged on the waistband of his jeans.

"What's what?"

"You're dressed?"

"Yeah."

"Why?"

She sat up. The sheet fell away to pool around her waist leaving the top half of her naked.

He stared down at her. "Uh."

"I thought you'd wake me up first. Don't guys get what they call 'morning wood'?"

"Uh. Yeah."

"Is that what this is?"

Her hand slid over his crotch, cupping the bulge now pressing for release.

"Jesus, Baylee."

"What?"

Her expression held knowing innocence mixed with genuine curiosity. What a massive turn-on.

"I thought maybe after last night you'd had enough," Trey choked out.

She grinned up at him. "I've got lots of lost time to make up for, remember? I'll probably never get enough. Can we undo this?" she unsnapped his jeans and slid the zipper down.

"Take these off."

Trey complied. The jeans dropped to the floor.

"And these," she whispered, tugging at the leg of his boxers.

They dropped and his erection sprang free.

"Oh, wow."

Baylee touched his stomach and he flinched, his startled abs reacting, his entire body rigid with need and anticipation.

Her hands explored him, caressed his groin, the tops of his thighs. Trey held his breath. She gripped him tightly in one hand and looked up at him, uncertainty in her eyes. "I want to try something. But I've never done it before, so you might have to give me some pointers."

He couldn't speak, spellbound by what she did to him, her touch, her apparent fascination with his reactions.

When her mouth closed around him, he sighed in ecstasy. She scooted closer. He buried his fingers in her hair. Had anything ever felt this good? He couldn't remember. Couldn't think. Everything he had was concentrated right there in her mouth.

She stopped only once to ask, "How am I doing? Any suggestions?"

She didn't need much direction and what little he gave her, she took so well, in seconds he had to ease her away from him. She let go with a sad little sound of disappointment. "I wasn't done yet," she informed him.

"You were close enough," he told her dryly. "Lay down there,"

She grumbled some more but complied. Trey got a condom in place and yanked the sheet off and gave her the same treatment she'd just given him. He breathed in the musky scent of their earlier mating.

His knee be damned, he was going to be on top this time, the one in control. He had another knee after all, and enough upper body strength, he was pretty sure he could make it work.

Her eagerness inflamed him, though. The way she had of wrapping herself around him, moving against him, beneath him, had his control slipping away before he knew it. Her fingers dug into his buttocks. Her lower body arched against him meeting each of his thrusts until he was spent.

Could you really pass out from euphoria, he wondered a few minutes later? He doubted it, but he seemed to have blanked out. When he came to, he found her crushed beneath him, her fingertips playing idly up and down his back like she didn't have a care in the world.

He propped himself up on his forearms to look at her. She matched his direct gaze. No coyness or shyness there. He'd been about to say something, hadn't he? He couldn't remember, couldn't think of anything appropriate or meaningful or necessary.

Instead, he kissed her lips tenderly. Her arms came around his neck and she kissed him back.

Finally, he rolled off her, keeping one arm crooked around her. "You're going to kill me, you know that?"

"Death by sex?"

He chuckled. "Something like that."

"How's the knee?"

"What knee?"

She giggled.

"I'll let you know when the feeling returns."

She propped herself up to look at him. He returned her gaze, sifting his fingers through her hair. She didn't say anything, just continued to study him until he said, "What?"

She shook her head. "Nothing. I'm going to go take a shower, okay? And then, since you've been such a good boy, I'll make you breakfast."

"Okay."

He watched her walk naked into the bathroom and close the door. What had he gotten himself into here? Whatever it was, he had absolutely no desire to get out of it.

Baylee stood under the warm water letting it soak her hair and skin while she sorted through her jumbled thoughts.

Had she planned this, whatever this was with Trey? From the moment she'd set foot on his porch perhaps she had sub-consciously decided to seduce him. The very idea made her giggle. She had no idea how to seduce a man. She'd never had to and her attempts at seducing Scott had left her with little faith in her own appeal.

No, she assured herself, all she had done was take matters into her own hands and decide for herself what her first sexual experience was going to be and who it would be with. She'd come too close to having something so intimate occur with a sleazeball like Collin Cassiday.

She'd chosen Trey for her first time again, and for better or worse, the experience was permanently implanted in her memory bank.

She made him breakfast, cleaned up the dishes and picked up her purse.

"You could stay the rest of the day, couldn't you?"

"Nope. I have a couple of commitments I made before I agreed to work for you full-time. I've got to check on the Shriver's cat and then I'm taking Mrs. Willoughby to her doctor's appointment and to run some errands."

Trey slid his arms around her. She'd already pulled her hair up in a ponytail. He'd decided he didn't like her ponytail. He liked her hair down so he could run his fingers through it whenever he wanted. He kissed her. He liked kissing her. A lot. "You could come back tonight."

"Can't. I have plans."

"How about tomorrow?"

"I'll be here tomorrow. It's my regular day to be here."

"How about tomorrow night? Are you busy? You could stay. We could go to dinner."

She eased away from him. "I don't know."

"Don't know?"

"That's what I said."

"Don't know what? Whether you can stay tomorrow? Whether you want to eat dinner with me? What?"

"All of the above."

That directness of hers which he found appealing in bed disconcerted him out of it. What was she saying? She didn't want to be around him? *Unless* they were in bed? Was she *using* him? For sex? The outrageousness of the thought almost knocked him over. If that was what she was doing, he was having none of it.

"Okay. I'll see you around then."

He walked away from her before she could walk out the door. How was that for having the last word?

By supper time Trey had to acknowledge the truth. He missed Baylee. He wanted to call her. Just to hear her voice. How pathetic was that? He wanted to ask her again if she wanted to come over, which, they both knew, translated into, did she want to spend the night?

He held his cell phone in his hand and accessed her number. He stared at the display until the screen went black. One touch of a button and it would reappear. Touch one more button and the phone would automatically dial. And?

She'd turn him down again. He'd be in the position of begging. Trey Christopher did not beg.

She'd rejected him this morning. He hadn't particularly cared for the experience and had no wish to repeat it less than twelve hours later. He set the phone down and did what he often did when he was frustrated and lonely and not ready to sleep. He worked out. He did the exercises the P.T. recommended for his knee. He meditated. He wrote in his journal until his hand cramped. He watched some television, idly flipping from sports to movies to news and back. He took some ibuprofen, brushed his teeth, and got into bed.

The sheets were rumpled. He imagined he could still smell her scent on the pillow next to his. In his head he replayed all of last night, which did not, in any way, help him to relax. He tossed and turned and shoved the pillow she'd used onto the floor. If only he could just as easily shove thoughts of Baylee out of his head. Apparently, once she'd taken up residence, she wasn't easy to dislodge.

In her sunny yellow kitchen with its bank of windows looking out over the backyard Jenny poured iced tea into two glasses. She handed one to Baylee. "I'm glad you came over. Ryan has that monthly bar association meeting. Seth's finally in bed. I'm ready for some girl talk."

Baylee followed Jenny outside to the back deck. She and Ryan had bought their house shortly after they married, and they'd worked hard to make it their own. In fact, there was always some new project ready to be tackled, from major renovations to minor stuff like painting the woodwork. They'd installed the wood deck last spring. Baylee had to admit it complemented the house perfectly, giving them extra space to entertain and overlooking the big back yard where soon, according to Jenny, there would be a swing set for little Seth.

"So, what's up with you?" Jenny asked, giving Baylee an assessing look as she took a sip of tea.

Baylee rocked in the white wicker rocker. Of course, she'd tell Jenny everything. They'd been telling each other secrets since the fifth grade. But she wasn't sure how Jenny would take the news that she'd finally, blissfully, slept with a man.

"There's something going on. You're different."

Baylee couldn't help the knowing little smile. "Am I?"

"Yeah. Spill."

"I slept with him."

Jenny spewed her sip of iced tea all over herself, the chair cushions and the deck below."

"What? Him who? Oh, no. Don't tell me." She stared at Baylee in disbelief. "Trey? Are you serious?"

Baylee nodded, unable to wipe the grin off her face.

"Oh, Baylee," Jenny moaned. "What were you thinking?"

"I was thinking I've had the hots for him since I was fifteen, he's unattached and willing. Can't you just be happy for me? Can you for once not lecture me?" Baylee set her glass of tea down on a nearby table and picked up the pace of her rocker.

Chastened, Jenny backed off. "I'm sorry. I worry about you. You've been through a lot. With Scott and every-thing—"

"Exactly. And you know what happened in New York? I went out for a drink with a guy. I don't know what was in them but after two drinks I was so out of it I couldn't have stopped whatever he had in mind. I wouldn't even have remembered it probably. But Trey stopped him."

"That doesn't mean you owe him—"

"God, Jenny, it isn't about me owing him. It's about me, making my own decisions, making my own choices. I *chose* to sleep with Trey. And you want to know some-thing? It was *fantastic.*"

"Okay. Well, that's good, but—"

Baylee let out an exaggerated sigh. "Why does there always have to be a 'but?' Why can't anything good ever happen to me without you looking at the worst case scenario?"

Jenny seemed to consider the question. "I don't know. Because I worry about you, I guess. I don't want you to be hurt. You almost slept with Trey Christopher years ago, and then—"

"I know my own history, Jen. You don't have to remind me. After I *didn't* sleep with Trey during our teenage drunken encounter, I scared myself into never sleeping with a guy outside of marriage. Except I went one better and married a guy who wouldn't sleep with me in a million years.

"It's my life and my choices. My mistakes, too. If I get hurt, I get hurt. I'm not a child, Jen."

"I know."

"Then stop treating me like one, okay?"

"Okay. But if you think Trey Christopher's going to take you seriously after you jumped into bed with him, think again."

Baylee laughed and retrieved her glass of tea. "I don't expect him to take me seriously. I don't want him to. I was tied to a man for too long because I took everything too seriously, because I thought that's what I had to do. I'm free now, and this is what I want. It's all I want right now. My freedom. To do what I please, when I please, with whomever I please. I'm tired of being the serious girl, the good girl. I'm going to try being me for a while and see how it works."

"You're happy," Jenny stated.

"I am," Baylee agreed.

"You don't care if this, uh, situation with Trey turns into anything more than what it is?"

"I haven't given it a lot of thought, to be honest with you. I'm tired of trying to plan a future that doesn't work out the way I thought it would. Right now, what I want to do is—I don't know—live for the moment, I guess. Take whatever bit of joy and happiness that comes my way and just go with it, you know? I just want to be free."

"Along with freedom comes responsibility," Jenny quipped in an ominous tone, both quoting and imitating her mother.

"Jen."

Jenny stood. "Okay, Miss Freedom I Can Do Anything I Want To Do When I Want To Do It. What do you think about ordering a pizza, getting whatever toppings we want on it and enjoying many moments of pigging out?"

Baylee followed her into the house. They decided on the pizza and phoned it in. Jenny opened a bottle of the inexpensive red wine they both liked and poured them each a glass. For all of Jenny's mothering behavior, Baylee loved her like a sister. Luckily, when Jenny overdid her tsking and lecturing, Baylee could tell her to back off and she did.

They took their glasses of wine out to the front porch to wait on the pizza.

"So?" Jenny asked after a few minutes of companionable silence. "You said sleeping with Trey was fantastic, I believe?"

Baylee nodded, knowing Jen was fishing for more details. Up until that moment, Baylee thought she'd be unable to keep any of her encounter with Trey to herself. She'd planned to tell Jenny every detail. But now she realized she didn't want to share that kind of intimacy with even her best friend. Not even her more knowledgeable and experienced best friend. She wanted to keep it all for herself, to take out every nuance, every touch, every kiss, every memory and examine it or relive it whenever she wanted to. She didn't want any of it watered down or judged by someone else.

But she knew she had to give Jenny something. "It was so easy, Jen. So—I don't know. Natural, maybe? He was there, I was there. I wanted him, and—" she stuttered to a halt.

"He wanted you?" Jenny finished for her gently.

A lump of emotion clogged her throat and brought tears to her eyes as she remembered her conversation with Trey about a man wanting her.

She could only nod, afraid if she said anything the tears would spill over.

Jenny reached over and covered Baylee's hand with hers. "If he makes you happy, I'm happy for you."

Is this what happiness feels like? Baylee asked herself on the drive home. This buoyant sense of well-being? Of near giddiness? Is this all it took? Sleeping with Trey? Having sex. *Finally.*

No. There had to be more to it than that. Sex did not equal happiness. Surely there were plenty of happy people out there in the world who weren't having sex for one reason or another.

Maybe it was the sense of connectedness that went beyond just physical? Baylee considered this as she parked in front of her house.

Maybe it's finally getting something you want.

That thought slapped her upside the head as she unlocked the door. She closed and locked it behind her and leaned against it for a minute. Could it be that simple? Hadn't she ever gone after what she wanted before?

Hadn't she ever felt this bone-deep sense of satisfaction? Ever?

If the answer to that question was no it was almost too depressing to think about. She went into her makeshift bedroom to get ready for bed.

She tried to remember when she'd felt this way. The only moment that came to mind was that party at Jimmy Macklehorn's place. When they'd gathered around the bonfire and Trey dropped his arm over her shoulders. She'd loved the delicious feeling of being close to him, of him singling her out, zeroing in on her. Showing interest in *her*. Wanting *her*.

If he hadn't had so much to drink what would have happened? She brushed her teeth staring at herself in the mirror. Would he have remembered her the next day? Would she have been his final high school conquest before he moved on to college girls? Another notch on his bedpost?

Why, she wondered, had she been ready to give herself to him then? Was it the influence of the alcohol? Or something more?

Was it truly mere coincidence that all these years later, she'd chosen him for her long-awaited first time?

Or had she simply been waiting for *him*?

"You're overthinking this, Baylee," she told her reflection in the bathroom mirror as she patted her face dry. She smoothed on moisturizer and turned out the light.

She crawled into bed and pulled her pillows around her. They were a poor substitute for a hard male body, but tonight they'd have to do. They didn't stop her from thinking about Trey as she fell into a deep, satisfied slumber.

When Matty woke it was almost one a.m. Most nights he left around nine-thirty and was home by ten. But tonight, Mama had been uncomfortable and restless, moaning and thrashing in her sleep until she'd finally settled down around eleven-thirty.

He peeked into her room to make sure she was okay before letting himself out and locking up.

It had been warmer earlier in the day, but the night was cool and pleasant. There were hardly any cars on the road. He coasted down Marshall Avenue where the pretty Victorian homes stood behind their tidily manicured lawns. Along Palmer Street, the porch lights glowed and the wide verandas of the B and B's beckoned visitors to relax.

Matty'd never been on vacation, never been anywhere really, except the occasional trip to Asheville and once a trip to Atlanta to see the Braves play the Yankees.

Back when he'd first come to live with the Westrings they'd signed him up for Little League. They'd come to every game. He and Dan played catch almost every night. Matty had no natural athletic ability, but he'd tried his hardest sensing his success on the ball field was important to Dan. Perhaps Dan had appreciated the effort even if he'd been disappointed in the results couching the trip to the Braves game as a reward of some sort.

Matty took a right at the red light on Benson Street, pedaling easily past the hodgepodge of small businesses and residences before he became aware that lights were flashing behind him. He looked over his shoulder to see a sheriff's department patrol car. He hadn't done anything wrong as far as he knew. Except violate his probation. Again. He told himself the cops in Henderson couldn't possibly care one way or the other about a kid like him breaking curfew. But Henderson wasn't a large city. Maybe Jack Frost had told them to be on the lookout for him.

Maybe the cop wasn't even after him, he told himself as he slowed and braked and came to a stop in front of a car parked on the street near the corner. No. He couldn't be that lucky. The cop car pulled to a stop even with the parked car and the door opened.

Matty crossed his arms over his chest and waited. He took a couple of deep breaths to calm himself but he had that sick feeling inside that something bad was about to happen.

"Out kind of late, aren't you?" the officer asked.

Matty turned toward him. He knew enough to show respect whether it was genuine or not. Cops despised teenagers and he'd never found mouthing off to one beneficial to his cause. "Just heading home, Officer."

"Got some I.D. on you?"

Matty took a better look at the guy while he reached in his back pocket for his painfully thin wallet. He was tall, the cop was. Looked like he was in fairly decent shape, but there was something about him Matty didn't like. A meanness in the set of his mouth, that look of dissatisfaction or disgust with his lot in life. It wasn't the first time Matty had seen that look.

"Did I do something wrong, Officer?" Matty inquired, forcing politeness into his tone as he handed over his driver's license. He hardly ever got to use it, but his dad had taught him how to drive and took him to get his license the day he'd turned sixteen. Matty thought he'd have a future as his dad's designated driver, but Dan preferred to walk to the bar which was only a few blocks from home. He usually found a ride home with a drinking buddy or with the owner of the bar on the nights he closed the place down.

Matty hardly ever had any cash. He couldn't afford gas. He wasn't allowed to hang out with the few friends he'd gotten into trouble with, so he had no reason to borrow his dad's truck and he hadn't exactly proved himself trustworthy to use anyone else's vehicle.

"We'll see," the officer said as he shone a flashlight on the license.

J. Spoley his nameplate read. Matty filed that away in his memory.

"Stay here," the officer told him. He returned to his car.

Matty thought he knew what would happen next. He supposed his record and probation would show up on the cop's dashboard computer. He'd nail him for violating his curfew. Maybe take him down to the jail and call his dad to come get him. Jack Frost would be informed. Maybe he'd have to go before the judge again and explain himself. At the rate he was going he'd be on probation until he was twenty.

Straddling his bike, Matty realized how tired he was. He leaned over and rested his arms on the handlebars. If he hadn't been stopped, he'd be home by now. He'd have brushed his teeth, stripped down and fallen into bed. No one would have known or cared what time he got home. They only knew or cared when they were inconvenienced by him *not* coming home when he was supposed to.

Although it was probably only a few minutes it felt like half an hour before the cop exited his vehicle and came back with Matty's license. He held it by two fingers and extended it to Matty. "You're not by any chance related to Baylee Westring, are you, son?"

It wasn't what he'd expected the cop to say. "She's my sister," he answered cautiously.

"Thought she might be. I s'pose you're aware you're violating your probation being out this time of night?"

"Yes, sir. I was heading home. I know I'm late." Matty made himself stop talking before he said any more. If he got in trouble, he might not be able to watch over Mamacita for Des.

"I can take you in. I can notify your probation officer. Your family."

The sick feeling returned in full force. He tried not to look as panicked as he felt.

"But I'm going to let you off with a warning this time. You go on home now, all right?"

"Yes, sir. Thank you, sir." Matty slid the license back into his wallet and took off, desperate to put as much distance as he could between himself and Officer J. Spoley. It wasn't until he got home that he began to wonder why he'd been let off the hook. He was pretty sure it wasn't because Officer Spoley was a nice guy. Why had he asked about Baylee?

The sick sense of dread returned.

Chapter Eighteen

♥

Trey woke up viciously early the next morning with an unfamiliar hum running through his system. An excited, anticipatory kind of feeling that energized and unsettled him at the same time. He couldn't wait to see Baylee again.

One look at the clock told him he had a couple of hours before she'd arrive. She'd be there to work. She'd expect to work. Sort through the mail, balance the checkbooks, help him stay organized. She'd vacuum and do laundry and make the bed. He hated the idea of her cleaning up after him.

Well, isn't that what you're paying her for, his brain inquired.

Yes, but.

But what? What do you want to do? Pay her to have sex with you instead?

Yikes! He shied away from the thought. Maybe he could pay her *not* to clean. But to spend time with him instead.

Great.

A paid escort?

That wouldn't work. She'd be insulted if he suggested such a thing and he'd feel like a pimp sampling from his own stable. He'd hired Baylee to do a job. They had an agreement. He'd have to stick by it.

He did his P.T. exercises followed by a light workout. His knee did seem to be responding to the P.T. The swelling was down. The pain was manageable. Maybe he'd walk without a limp one day soon.

In the kitchen he brewed coffee and retrieved his current journal from the table/desk in the dining room. He'd take his coffee out to the back porch, journal and then meditate. Maybe today he'd find that elusive center, that calm he was always searching for.

He'd read the books and followed the practices. Maybe the breathing helped. The journaling. The meditation. But he never felt really at peace. He was always chasing after...something. Something more. Something less. Something different. He didn't even know what it was. But he had a feeling he'd know when he found it.

Settling himself in the chair, propping his leg up on the one next to it, he took a deep satisfying sip of coffee and opened his journal. He never read back through his entries. The one time he'd tried, it had been too depressing. Had he really felt that way? Had he been that miserable? He knew, of course, that he had been. He'd lived it. But he'd come a long way since and he didn't plan on going back. Ever. Move forward. One day at a time. One step at a time. That was his mantra now.

He stared at the first word he'd written without even thinking about it. *Baylee.* What was there to say about Baylee? Hell, he could probably fill page after page about her. The scent of her skin, her direct manner, what it felt like being inside of her. Well, why not? The journals were to put down whatever was on his mind. Whatever was bothering him. And Baylee bothered him. A lot. Trey wrote. About all of it, starting with Collin Cassiday in New York, about following Baylee, rescuing her from the apartment. How it felt to have her head on his shoulder on the plane, seeing her in his bed. He spilled his guts onto the page, knowing no one would ever see these pages, but him.

When he put the pen down and flexed his fingers to uncramp them, he thought maybe he'd discovered part of Baylee's appeal. She renewed him.

He went into the kitchen and tossed his cold coffee down the drain and poured a fresh cup. Leaning against the counter he sipped it, reanalyzing the thoughts that had come to him during his journaling session.

He'd known of course, that he was starting over, starting a second life in a way. After leaving the NFL, surviving rehab, losing any chance he ever had of reconciling with Hayley, and then moving back here, he'd been like a blind man feeling his way along in unfamiliar territory.

Living without the buffer zone created by booze and pills, dealing with physical pain, and some emotional as well, he had to face himself in the mirror every morning. There were too many days where he saw himself for what he was—a washed up former pro athlete, alone and lonely with no one to blame but himself.

Except when Baylee was around. Something about her presence made him think starting over wasn't so bad. Being with her in bed—*wow*. He wondered if it wasn't the first time he'd been fully present with a woman. The first time in a long time, that was for sure.

Baylee had been hurt, certainly, but she wasn't jaded. Regretful, perhaps, of what she'd been through with her ex-husband, but she wasn't bitter.

He still couldn't get over the fact that she'd been a virgin, that she'd *thanked* him for relieving her of what she viewed as a burden. Had she specifically chosen him for that task?

He shook his head. Doubtful.

He heard her car pull up outside. Damn. He hadn't showered. Hadn't even looked in the mirror. His hair was probably stuck up in six different directions. Plus, he had morning breath *and* coffee breath. He thought about hightailing it into the bathroom, but he realized what his accelerated heartbeat meant. He couldn't wait to see her.

He'd left his journal on the table outside. Had he closed it? He couldn't remember. What if she saw everything he'd written? About her? About his feelings? *Yikes!*

He took a step toward the door just as she opened it. She stopped short when she saw him. They stared at each other across the expanse of linoleum floor for a few seconds. Her hair was in the ponytail. He wanted to release it from the elastic and let it tumble around her shoulders. He tightened his fingers around the handle of his mug instead.

"Good morning," he managed.

"Hi," she breathed. She gave him a small, uncertain smile and set down her bucket of supplies and bag of rags.

Neanderthal thoughts ran through his head while arousal pushed against the fly of his pajama bottoms. Could he seriously pick her up and drag her back to his bed and have his way with her?

That's what he wanted to do. He wondered if that's what she wanted him to do.

No way to tell. She was dressed for work, in shorts and sneakers and a tee shirt, her hair pulled up. He ought to get out of her way and let her get to work. Except it was his house, his kitchen, and he didn't want to leave. He wondered if she'd mind if he watched while she cleaned? If she'd talk to him while she worked? Or maybe she'd let him help.

He smiled at the thought. He'd never done housework and had absolutely no inclination to start now.

"Are you okay?" she asked.

"Sure. Why?"

"You're staring."

The disarming directness again. Trey grinned. Maybe he could learn a thing or two from Baylee. "That's because I like looking at you."

"Oh." Baylee glanced down at herself then back at him, a glimpse of uncertainty in her eyes. "Really?"

Her tone somehow combined both bravado and innocence. He lifted the carafe of the coffee pot. "Want some coffee?"

"O-okay. Sure."

He poured her a cup and walked it over to her. He set it on the counter. "Here you go."

"Thanks."

They continued to regard each other. Trey caught a whiff of the scent she wore that made him think of ripe fruit and fresh cut flowers. Raw need tore through him, and he didn't think about what he was going to do before he did it.

"Can you take this thing out of your hair?" His voice sounded husky even to his own ears, as he indicated the elastic band of her ponytail.

She kept her gaze steady on his as she reached up and with one motion, pulled the band away allowing her hair to tumble free.

Trey buried his hands in it and lowered his mouth to hers. She met him full force with her body and her mouth. He'd never known such lust, such need, such *wanting*.

He wanted to be inside her. *Now.* He unsnapped her shorts, lowered the zipper. They fell away to her ankles, and he went to work on her panties pushing and shoving them away, allowing access for his exploring hands over her buttocks, then between her legs. All the while their mouths glued themselves to each other. The way she sucked his tongue made him think of the way he'd been in her mouth. Was it just yesterday? Twenty-four hours ago?

She shoved the elastic waistband of his pajama bottoms away, her hands exploring his raging erection.

He swore softly, while a tiny part of his brain wondered where, how, here in the kitchen? Up against the counter? But the majority of him knew only need.

Logistics fell way, somehow her legs wrapped around him, they were braced against the wall or maybe the countertop, he only knew he was where he wanted to be: inside her. He couldn't stop touching, caressing, kissing, fucking her. Pleasure so intense he was certain he'd never felt anything like it before washed over him as he pounded against her, thrusting again and again and again, and oh, God, again.

That was the thing about sexual encounters. They started out so hot and delicious. But they always ended. Often leaving the participants feeling vaguely foolish, certainly disheveled, and forced to face each other.

Trey didn't want to let go, even as he felt himself wither and Baylee's legs slide down his own until she was back on her own two still-sneakered feet.

He buried his face in her neck, not quite willing to face the truth of what he'd just done. For one thing, he'd taken her almost fully dressed standing up in the kitchen. For another, he hadn't used a condom.

Idiot!

Now he'd have to face her. Apologize for his uncontrollable lust. Deal with the consequences.

"I think I'm in love with you," he whispered over her shoulder. *What? Where had that come from?*

He coughed and straightened, attempted a smile though he wasn't feeling very cocky at the moment. "Sorry. I mean I think I've definitely got the hots for you."

Baylee stared at him as if she were trying to figure something out. She wasn't exactly frowning but there was a slight pucker between her brows.

"Are you mad at me?"

She shook her head.

"I didn't use a condom."

"I know."

"Think it will be a problem?"

"I don't know."

Trey bent and pulled his pajama bottoms up. Except for her sneakers, Baylee remained naked from the waist down and made no move to cover herself. She continued to regard him

"What are you thinking?"

His question seemed to pull her out of some sort of reverie. She grinned. "I like that you have the hots for me. I like having sex with you."

Trey moved in and slid his arms around her again. He kissed the tip of her nose. "Good. Want to do it again? *With* a condom?"

He slid his hands under her shirt and cupped her breasts. He heard her sharp intake of breath. He doubted that coupling just now had done much to satisfy her although it had slaked his lust. Temporarily. He whispered in her ear about what he'd do if she'd let him take her back to the bedroom.

Her nipples beaded against his fingers. He smiled and maneuvered her down the hallway.

This was what it was like to be at the mercy of your sex drive, Baylee decided over an hour later. Her work ethic had flown out the window along with every ounce of practicality she'd ever possessed. She'd be perfectly content to stay in bed with Trey all day and do nothing but have sex with him.

Once they'd reached the bedroom earlier, he'd relieved her of her sneakers first, cradling her feet and ankles in his hands, before sliding his hands all the way up to caress the moist skin between her legs with his thumbs, one on either side, then dropped a kiss there before taking off her tee shirt and bra.

Then he'd yanked off his tee shirt and pajama bottoms, so they were both naked and it was like what had happened in the kitchen had never occurred. That lustful mindless coupling had nothing on what happened now.

Like he'd downshifted from sixth gear into first, Trey took his time, lingering over her breasts, kissing and suckling them, before stroking between her legs, first with his fingers and then with his tongue. He liked spreading her legs, liked looking at her, watching her reaction to him. That in itself was a turn-on. This was what it felt like to have a man interested in *her*.

She couldn't have chosen anyone better to help her explore her own sexuality than Trey. The fact that he not only wanted her, but that he seemed to like her, allowed her to shed any inhibitions she might have had. With him, she found, she had very few. With Scott, she'd had a ton, because she'd been sure his lack of interest was her fault. She'd kept trying to change herself, to make herself sexier, to find a way to appeal to him. Until she'd discovered his lack of interest had nothing to do with her.

But Trey's interest seemed to have everything to do with her. As he'd said, he could have had sex any time he wanted to. But he hadn't. Until her.

So, there was something there, between them. But Baylee didn't want to define what. Trey's earlier whispered words had threatened to throw her even further off balance. She didn't want him to be in love with her. She didn't want to be obligated to him or to worry about hurting his feelings. She just wanted to be with him. Like this. With mutual affection and lust and enjoyment. She didn't want to be weighed down by yet another relationship or expected to give more than she had to offer.

So when Trey's tongue found her, when he nudged her over the edge, she indulged herself, let the deliciousness of her orgasm wash through her, let herself go mindless with the pleasure of this right now moment. Of Trey in bed with her.

When her body settled down again, she turned her head. Trey lay on his back next to her, his eyes closed. She turned on her side and propped her head up on one elbow. She caressed his chest. She loved his body, the broad shoulders and chest that tapered down to tight abs. The muscles, the strength, even with his various injuries. His skin was covered with blondish-brown hair everywhere. She ran her hand through the extra crisp portion on his chest.

He turned his head and opened his eyes. Those clear laser blue eyes pinned her and for a moment she lost her breath. The thought flittered through her brain before she could stop it, but she didn't say it aloud. Thank God. *I love you.* She could almost understand why Trey had whispered almost the same thing to her earlier. There was something about being close this way, about sex or making love, or whatever name you wanted to call it that could make you think those thoughts.

But sex and love were two very different and separate things. She knew that very well. Trey probably did, too. He'd been married. He'd surely loved his ex-wife. She'd loved Scott. But it hadn't been enough to save either relationship. With or without the sexual component.

What was love anyway? She loved the way Trey made her feel. She loved looking at him. Touching him. Having sex with him. But love *him?* She couldn't answer that. Couldn't define what that meant.

"You're thinking deep thoughts," Trey told her.

He picked up the hand she'd laid on his chest and kissed it. Then he slid forward for an embrace. "What are you thinking about?" he whispered.

"How much I like you," she whispered back. "How much I like being with you like this."

He eased back so he could see her face. "Really?"

"Really."

He hugged her to him again. "Even though I'm a Neanderthal who takes you up against the kitchen counter as soon as you walk in the door."

"I love Neanderthals." She nearly choked on her whispered reply as emotion swept through her. She didn't think she'd ever be able to make Trey understand how much him *wanting* her that way meant to her.

She hugged him back hard, hoping to convey her acceptance of *him*.

His erection pressed between them, and another delicious thrill went through her. She pressed her lips to his neck. Then her tongue, then her teeth. She eased the embrace to slide a hand between them and wrap it around him.

Trey groaned and she smiled.

She nipped his earlobe. "I think we need a condom."

An hour later they sat across the table from each other good-naturedly arguing. They'd eaten breakfast and now lingered over the last of the coffee when Trey said, "I want you to know that if I distract you from your work, you still get paid for your time."

"But I allow you to distract me. I could have said no."

"Not if you don't have a chance."

"I wouldn't have anyway."

"I know." Trey grinned at her, and Baylee chuckled.

"You can't pay me to have sex with you."

"I know." Trey drummed his fingers on the table. "Could I give you a bonus?"

"Like a retainer? Like I'm your mistress?" Baylee bristled.

"No, no, no." Trey frowned. "You get the salary we agreed on every week no matter how many hours you're actually working."

"But the sex is free?"

"Right."

"Okay." Baylee slid her chair back and dropped a kiss on Trey's lips as she walked by. "Besides, you couldn't afford me."

He smacked her bottom before she got out of range. "That's probably true."

He let her get to work then, but from his seat at the dining room table, surrounded by correspondence she'd sorted and checks she'd made out for his signature, he was always aware of her presence. He made some calls, sent some e-mails, paid some bills, all the while listening to the clink of dishes, the hum of the vacuum and the washing machine and dryer cycles.

Occasionally he heard her voice as she sang a few lines from whatever song played in her ears. Each time it made him smile, as he imagined her doing her impromptu dance steps to go with the music.

He got corralled into a long conference call with his agent and a couple of the ESPN executives. It was winding down when Baylee tapped on the woodwork and stuck her head in. "I'm leaving," she mouthed.

He held up a finger to keep her there until he got off the phone a few minutes later.

He came around the table. "How about dinner?"

"Don't you mean lunch?"

"No, I mean, how about going to dinner with me. Tonight?"

Her gaze fell away from his. "Oh. Um."

"What, Baylee? If you don't want to go to dinner with me, just say so." He didn't know why her hesitation annoyed him, but it did. She'd done the same thing the other day when he'd suggested she stay or come back that night and she'd told him she had plans.

"It's not that exactly."

At least she looked him in the eye when she said it. How, he wondered, could a woman be so direct in the bedroom and so non-committal out of it? Maybe he should only ask her questions when they were naked between the sheets.

"Then what is it exactly?"

"Henderson's a pretty small town."

"I'm aware," he drawled.

"I don't want it to look like we're, um, dating."

"We're not."

"But if we go to dinner together—"

"Why do you care what other people think?"

Baylee pressed her lips into a thin line. "Fine. Have it your way. No. I don't want to go to dinner with you." She turned on her heel, her sneaker making a squeaking noise on the clean floor.

"Baylee." Trey hit just the right note, part command, part plea, to stop her in her tracks. She turned back to him. He came toward her. "Just tell me, okay?"

"I like this." She waved a hand at their immediate vicinity. "I like you, and—the sex." She took a shaky breath. "But I don't want *expectations.*"

Trey's eyebrow rose. "Expectations? From whom?"

"You. Me. Anyone."

"Expectations of what exactly?"

"Anything. That this—us—is anything more than what it is."

"And what it is is sex between two unattached consenting adults?"

"Maybe more than that," she conceded.

"But not much more."

"See this is what I don't want! I don't want to be obligated or pressured or made to feel like I *should* do something when I don't want to!"

"You're saying you don't want to have dinner with me?"

"No! I do."

Trey lowered his voice. He stepped closer and ran the palms of his hands up and down her arms. She shivered. "Baylee, tell me what you want."

"Can we go to dinner somewhere else? Asheville, maybe?"

"Of course. Anywhere you want."

"Okay."

"I'll pick you up."

Baylee shook her head. "I'll meet you back here. It'll be easier."

She slid away, picked up her things and left.

Easier for who? Trey wondered.

Chapter Nineteen

♥

Matty opened the gate which led through Mamacita's front yard to the door. Des had told him it'd be best if he parked his bike on the front porch and if he had a bike lock to use it. Even though Mamacita was well-known throughout the neighborhood and beloved by her long-time neighbors, crime ran rampant, especially among the disadvantaged and unemployed youth of Henderson.

He closed the gate behind him and startled when a voice he didn't recognize said, "Hi."

Warily he looked in the direction from which the voice had come. "Over here."

Matty squinted against the brightness of the sun toward the house next to Mamacita's. A figure rose from a rocking chair on the front porch and a young woman came into view. She held an infant against her shoulder and gently patted its back. When she smiled at Matty he realized he knew her. Correction. He knew *of* her. Jasmine Kendall was in his class at Henderson High, but so far above him in social status, he'd never even said hello to her. She was an honor student, a varsity cheerleader and class secretary. Although he had no yearbook of his own, he'd seen she'd been voted Best Smile as well as Most Likely to Succeed in the class of juniors.

He took a couple of steps up the crumbling walkway and paused. "Hi."

"I heard you're helping Mamacita." She'd walked to the end of the porch and sent him one of those winning smiles.

"Yeah," Matty said. He ambled closer to Mamacita's porch. There was no reason he could think of that Jasmine Kendall would start a conversation with him.

"My cousin Cecily had twins. She's staying here with my Aunt Micheline until her husband gets out of the military. My mother decided I should help Cecily with the babies because it will discourage me from having any of my own any time soon." Jasmine grinned at him. He didn't know why. But he found himself smiling back.

"I could come over later maybe. Visit with Mamacita."

"Okay."

"You're Matty, right?"

"Yeah."

"I'm Jasmine. See you later, then." She awarded him another smile and went into the house.

Matty stayed where he was a moment longer trying to recover from the surprising fact that Jasmine Kendall knew his name. Maybe Mamacita had mentioned it to her aunt when Matty wasn't around. He proceeded up the steps and leaned his bike against the porch railing and secured it with the rusty bike lock marveling over the fact that Jasmine had acknowledged his existence. Jasmine *saw* him. He had an odd tingly sensation inside at the thought that he might be in Jasmine's company once again before the day was through.

Jasmine presented herself at seven-thirty that evening with a plastic bowl filled with chunks of fresh melon and sliced strawberries. She'd greeted Mamacita with warmth and allowed herself to be held against the older woman's bounteous bosom. Over Mamacita's shoulder she grinned and winked at Matty. He couldn't help but smile back. He had the thought that he'd smiled more in the past couple of hours since Jasmine had said hello to him than he had in the past month. There was something about Jasmine that made others want to smile, he thought. Like she was sharing a joke everyone wanted to be in on.

In Mamacita's kitchen she dished up the fruit like she'd been doing it forever. She knew which cupboard held bowls and where the spoons were. She treated Mamacita like an old friend, answering her questions about school and her family and going into detail about helping with her cousin's babies.

Matty relaxed when he realized nothing would be expected of him conversation-wise. He only had to blush and duck his head when Mamacita told Jasmine how much his help meant to her and Desmond. "Your mama would be proud," Mama told him.

Around nine-thirty, Mamacita went to bed admonishing Matty and Jasmine to behave themselves. What did she think was going to happen, Matty wondered. Jasmine probably couldn't wait to get back to her aunt's house.

"We could sit on the porch," Jasmine said after Mamacita's bedroom door closed.

"Okay."

Outside the heat had dissipated, bringing a welcome coolness to the air. Crickets chirped and a light breeze stirred the scent of warm flowers. They took seats side by side in the old metal chairs.

"Mamacita's the best, isn't she?" Jasmine asked. "She used to babysit me when I was little."

"I think she babysat everyone at one time or another."

"Is that how you know her?"

"Yeah."

"You know, I've seen you around at school. We were in World History together last year."

Matty offered a non-committal grunt. He'd taken notice of her in history class. He'd never imagined she'd noticed him.

"You weren't very friendly," Jasmine informed him.

Matty turned to look at her. He couldn't think of anything to say.

"You aren't shy, are you?"

"Am I?" He'd never thought about it. He wasn't afraid to talk to anyone. But he found it prudent first to gauge the recipient's level of interest. Otherwise, conversation was a waste of time and words.

"I don't think so." Jasmine tilted her head to one side studying him. "I haven't quite got you figured out yet."

"Why would you want to? A girl like you?"

"A girl like me?" Her teeth gleamed in the dim light. "What kind of girl is that?"

"You know."

"No, I don't. I'm a girl. You're a boy. Why does it have to be complicated?"

Matty shifted in his chair and gazed out at the street. Only a few cars passed by. Down the street two young boys took turns dribbling a basketball and good-natured-ly taunting each other. Somewhere nearby a screen door slammed.

"I think you're cute."

Matty thanked the darkness that surely covered his blush.

She tiptoed her fingers along his arm electrifying his skin. "Do you think I'm cute?"

He could tell she was smiling, teasing him, waiting for his answer. "No."

She withdrew her fingers. "No?"

"Cute's like a puppy or a, I don't know, what girls say about clothes. You're more than that."

"Okay, then, what am I?

Matty turned to look at her. In the dim light he could see the curve of her cheek. He'd already memorized every facial feature she possessed, her coffee-colored eyes, the slope of her eyebrows, her smile. "You're beautiful."

Chapter Twenty

♥

"Every year my parents throw a Fourth of July party. Want to go?" They were watching *The Hangover* which was one of Trey's favorite movies. The irony had not escaped either of them. Baylee had to admit the movie was mindless, ridiculous fun. She finished chewing the popcorn she'd just put in her mouth and set the bowl on the coffee table. The Christopher's Fourth of July parties were local legend. Baylee had never been invited but it seemed half the county had. Friends and relatives contributed food, drink, live music, and fireworks. She'd heard about the barbeque pit and the fireworks display.

She still wasn't comfortable being seen with Trey in public unless it was work-related. Luckily most of his "work" took place via conference calls and e-mails or meetings in New York or Atlanta. She didn't mind running errands on his behalf as part of her job or driving him to his doctor or physical therapy appointments if his knee was bothering him. But the few times he'd insisted on taking her to dinner, at her insistence they'd driven to various restaurants in Asheville or Shelby.

She knew Trey was humoring her and she couldn't explain to him why she didn't want anything about their personal relationship made public. Maybe he had shaken off the small-town minds and eyes, but she hadn't. He'd escaped the confines of Henderson, North Carolina for a time, but she had quite publicly lost her job, her husband, her career, and every dime she had. At least Trey had made it big before he fell from grace. She'd been scrambling to obtain some kind of status and security in her hometown, and she'd ended up flat on her face. There was no way to hide her father's drinking nor Matty's juvenile record.

She wished she didn't care, but she was pretty sure there were rumors about why her marriage had failed. Even if Scott spent most of his time in Asheville, even if he didn't "come out," there were whispers about his lifestyle even Baylee couldn't ignore. Bottom line, she was embarrassed to have every mistake she'd made scrutinized and examined and tutted over by the community she'd grown up in. Realistically she knew they probably didn't give two cents about her predicament, but she couldn't shake the sense that if she gave them more to talk about, they would. They'd positively salivate over the possibility of her liaison with the womanizing former town hero.

"It's okay if you don't want to. I know you're ashamed to be seen with me."

Baylee turned to stare at Trey. His gaze was fixed on the television screen. Sometimes she had a hard time telling if he was teasing her or if he was serious.

"I'm not ashamed to be seen with you," she said. *I'm just waiting for the other shoe to drop.* A further truth, if she were willing to admit it, wasn't that she feared what others were saying or thinking about her. It was Trey she didn't trust. He was too good to be true and if she'd learned one thing the past few years it was when something appeared to be too good to be true it probably was.

While she would like to believe the fantasy she sometimes fed herself, that Trey was her Prince Charming and they'd live happily ever after, cold hard reality had taught her otherwise. What they had now, this no-com-mitments-necessary relationship and mind-blowing sex could not continue forever. Trey had admitted up front his track record with women was not good. At the time she thought it didn't matter. But it did. When it fell apart, she'd prefer to pick up the pieces in private. That was all.

He turned his attention away from the television and pinned her with his gaze. "Yes. You are."

She'd hurt him, she could see. Telling him the truth would hurt him more, but she didn't see a way around it. "I'm scared."

He muted the television. "Of what?"

"I'm not sure. Remember when you told me you don't have a good track record?"

Trey nodded.

"What if it continues?"

Trey's jaw clenched. His gaze cooled. "I screwed up and everybody in the whole damn world knows it. I crawled back inch by inch. It wasn't easy, but I cleaned up my act. I hurt a lot of people, but I've tried to make amends. None of that matters. No one wants to give me a sec-ond chance. All they remember is that I let them down. Everybody's so sure I'll do it again, they're waiting for it to happen. I thought with you—ah, hell, forget it." Trey stood and stormed out of the room.

Baylee scrambled after him. "Don't you walk away. You thought with me what?"

He made it to the kitchen where he whirled on her so fast, she skidded to a halt and had to take a step back. "I don't have a history with you. I get to start fresh. Get it right the first time."

"You have a history with me."

"What?"

"Come here." She took his hand and led him to the swing on the back porch. He sat willingly enough and she sat sideways facing him tucking her knees up near her chest and wrapping her arms around them. "I used to come here as a child with my grandparents. Millie and Rufus Gruber. Do you remember them?"

"Grandma J and Grandpa Mike had a lot of friends."

"It doesn't matter whether you remember them or not. What matters is I came with them a few times when they visited, and you were here, usually with a bunch of your rowdy boy cousins or friends. I don't know who they were, but none of them wanted anything to do with me. Including you."

"We were kids," Trey said defensively.

She nudged him with her toe. "Stop interrupting. But there was one time when I came with my grandparents, and you were here by yourself. You asked me if I wanted to go down to the creek with you." Baylee could still remember the blond, blue-eyed Trey, stubbing the toe of his sneaker in the dirt, pinning her with his gaze when he offered the invitation.

Maybe that's when her crush started. She'd been wary, but without his gang around, Trey'd seemed as vulnerable and unsure of himself as she was. She fell into step with him, and they'd cut through the orchard to the trickle of water that ran through the Pritchard's land. He and the other boys had built a crude treehouse in the branches of an old oak tree. She hadn't thought about what he'd show her if she followed him up the unstable pieces of wood they'd hammered into the trunk for steps. In any case, after Trey clambered up swiftly and sure of himself, she'd taken hold of the highest plank she could reach and pulled herself up first one rung and then to the next. Trey peered over the edge of the crude platform and motioned her up. "Come on. I've got something to show you."

Baylee looked up at him, at the shock of hair falling over his forehead, at his laser-blue eyes, reached for the next hand hold, hoisted herself up and screamed when the crude piece of wood came away from the trunk. She fell awkwardly, with an "Oomph" of surprise, her right ankle twisting when it hit the hard dirt, the wind knocked out of her.

Trey sent her one horrified look, then swung himself off the platform and climbed down the planks like a monkey, jumping to the ground from the second one.

"You okay?"

Baylee nodded even though she was having trouble getting air into her lungs. From behind, Trey pushed her into sitting position. He gazed up. "We're going to need some more nails. And another piece of wood." The broken one lay in two pieces on the ground nearby.

"We can catch tadpoles," he informed her, quickly offering an alternative form of entertainment.

"Okay." Baylee would have agreed to just about anything to remain in his company.

He offered her his hand to help her to her feet, but when she stood she yelped and fell against him. She lifted her foot and stared at her ankle which was swollen to twice its normal size.

Trey stared, too. "Wow, cool. Look how big it is. I bet you sprained it. High five." Baylee stared at his offered palm. He wasn't kidding. Her injured ankle evidently garnered some sort of boy respect. She slapped his palm with hers.

She was still leaning on him, holding her injured ankle off the ground. She could smell his unique boy scent, a mix of perspiration and heat from the sun, and something else, something underlying it all that was just him. "I bet I can carry you."

"Back to the house?" Baylee asked incredulously. He was two years older and almost a head taller, but she doubted he'd be able to carry her very far. A quick vision of him dropping her and injuring her further flashed through her head. "I don't think so."

"Let's see." He wrapped his arms around her thighs, hoisted her up and staggered a few feet. "You're right. You're too heavy." He lowered her until she was back on one foot. "Here, then." He brought her arm over his shoulder. "Walk on that foot. I'll carry half of you."

In this manner, they made their way back to the house. The double sets of grandparents fussed over Baylee while Trey told the story of her fall. Trey's grandmother made up an icepack for her ankle, settled them on the swing and handed them each a Popsicle.

"If you tell me you remember that, I'll know you're lying," she concluded with a grin.

He lifted a hand in resignation and let it fall. "I don't. Not specifically. It was what? Twenty years ago?"

"I know I didn't make much of an impression on you, but that's one of my favorite childhood memories."

"That's not much of a history, Baylee."

"There's more."

"Crap."

"High school."

Trey stared at her. "Wait a minute. The first time I saw you, when you showed up to work, I told you I thought you looked familiar. I was sure I remembered you from somewhere."

"It might have been your grandmother's funeral."

"You were at Grandma J's funeral?'

"Yes. Look, my grandmother was her friend. I had memories of her from childhood. My mother had known her as well. I wanted to pay my respects."

"That was kind of you."

"What I'm trying to say is I knew you in high school. You were two years ahead of me and didn't know I was alive."

"How can you expect me to—"

She poked him with her toe again. "Don't interrupt. Do you remember your senior year? Jimmy Macklehorn had a big party at his place?"

"Maybe. Not really."

"You were drunk."

"Which explains why I don't remember."

"I remember."

"Baylee—"

Ignoring him as if he hadn't spoken, she went on. "I was there with Jenny and her cousin. I never drank, but I had a few beers. A bunch of us gathered around the bonfire. You came up and put your arm around my shoulder."

Trey made a sound in the back of his throat, but he didn't interrupt. Baylee's voice softened as she lost herself in the memory. "It was the most delicious feeling in the world. Your arm around my shoulder. I'd had a crush on you since I don't know when, and you'd picked me out of the crowd, put your arm around me. I was in heaven."

Trey set the swing in motion and the chain squeaked and moaned.

"We went up to the hayloft. You were drunk. I was too, but I was beyond excited. You kissed me, got me half out of my clothes—"

Trey brought the swing to a halt. "You're sure as hell not going to tell me I stole your virginity that night."

"I'm sure you would have if you could have, but we both know you didn't. You passed out."

"Lucky for you." Trey gazed out into the darkness.

"You'd think so, wouldn't you?"

He turned back to her, his eyes glinting in the dim light from the kitchen. She scooted closer to him. "I know you don't remember our history, but I remember it. I was disappointed that night in the hayloft. I think, in some weird way, I've been trying to find my way back to you all this time. Now that I have, I'm afraid—"

"I'll disappoint you again? I'll let you down."

Baylee nodded. "I'm afraid to let this, us, be more than it is."

"Maybe we should end it right now."

Baylee couldn't help the sound of distress she made, but she caught herself. "If it's what you want."

"It isn't. But I don't want my past mistakes thrown in my face every time I turn around. I don't want you waiting for me to screw things up, either."

"Maybe it won't be you. Maybe I'll screw it up."

"Maybe. I can't predict the future, Baylee. I can't change the past. Neither can you. We can take life a day at a time, which is all anyone can do. If you don't want to do that, we're done."

"I don't want to be done." She looped her arms around his neck and kissed him. She smiled. "I'm not done with you."

"The Fourth of July?"

"I'll be there. With bells on."

Chapter Twenty-one

♥

"I guess you've got plans for the Fourth, huh?" Matty had somehow managed to bring up the subject, stealing himself for Jasmine's confirmation that she did indeed have Fourth of July plans with her friends or her family. He'd met her aunt CeeCee and her cousin Cecily and the twin babies, of course. Jasmine wasn't helping her cousin every day, but she was there quite a bit. He knew when she wasn't that she hung out with her girlfriends. Maybe she even had a boyfriend for all Matty knew. He hoped not. She never talked about one.

"I don't know for sure. Maybe we'll go to the lake and watch the fireworks. Seems kind of lame, though, you know?"

"Yeah." Matty agreed, although he hadn't been to the fireworks at the lake since Diane's death. Holidays were hardly noted in the Westring house anymore. Jonah and Josh often spent a good part of the summer with their paternal grandparents in Charlotte.

"What are you doing?"

This was it. Now or never. No guts no glory. "The guy I do work for sometimes? Trey? He invited me to this big party at his parents' house. He said I could bring a friend. If you want to go."

There. The invitation was out there. Matty held his breath, his heart pounding in his throat.

"That sounds like more fun than going to the lake. I'll ask my mom if it's okay and let you know."

"Okay. We, um, might need a ride, though. I don't have a car and it's out in the country near Ednaville."

"Maybe I can drive. I'll ask."

The Fourth of July was a hot, hazy summer day. The sun in the cloudless sky bore down on the residents of Henderson County, so that by late afternoon all anyone wanted was relief from the heat. Trey had left early to help his parents set up for the party. Baylee offered to help, but he assured her his mother would have plenty of help with the food. Baylee suspected Trey's father would have plenty of assistance from other sources as well, but Trey was trying his hardest to get back in Andy Christopher's good graces.

By the time she arrived, a good-sized crowd was already assembled. The driveway was packed with vehicles, so Baylee parked behind several other cars along the side of the country road. Party guests spilled out of the house onto the porch. Several picnic tables had been set end to end. Beneath a party canopy were more tables set up buffet style and laden with food. Round metal bins held ice and cold drinks.

Some distance away smoke rose from a long cylindrical barbeque grill of the sort Baylee had seen at the county fair. Clusters of men were gathered nearby. Sections of the sprawling lawn had been set aside for horseshoes, croquet, and volleyball. There were people everywhere and Baylee wondered how she'd find Trey in the crowd. She wove her way across the grass looking for him. She greeted several acquaintances before she spotted him in conversation with another couple who were accompanied by a little boy.

He saw her approach and turned to include her. "Baylee, this is Hayley and Ray Braddock and their son, Fletcher. Baylee Westring." She smiled and shook hands with them wondering how Trey could so casually introduce his ex-wife and her husband.

Hayley Braddock was, there was no other way to say it, gorgeous. She had the sort of effortless beauty Baylee had always envied. Although her sun-streaked hair was surely the result of an expensive salon visit, it looked completely natural. She had curves in all the right places, and she was in the best physical shape a woman could be in. Plus, she exuded warmth and genuineness.

Her husband and little boy were both dark-haired handsome fellows who obviously adored Hayley and were happy to be in orbit around her.

Hayley wore a blue-and-white striped sundress and strappy sandals. Baylee envied her perfectly manicured nails as well as her pedicure. A significant diamond ring sparkled on the third finger of her left hand accompanied by a wedding band encrusted with smaller diamonds.

Even when Trey linked the fingers of his hand through hers, making it obvious they were a couple, Baylee stared down at her own outfit wishing she'd worn something entirely different. The denim skirt and red, white and blue polka dot tee shirt had seemed fun and perfect for the occasion when she'd put them on along with a pair of flipflops. But next to the stunning Hayley, she felt ridiculous and gauche. Although she'd painted her toenails, that's all she'd done. There was never a reason for a professional manicure, either. Not in her current line of work. As for her hair, she was lucky to get it cut every few months.

She'd left it down today, because she knew Trey preferred it that way. A narrow band kept it out of her face, but the uneven curly waves were no match for Hayley's highlighted blond perfection.

"Hey, Uncle Kurt's here." Trey turned to greet a handsome, fortyish man. He and Trey gave each other a man hug clapping each other on the back. Kurt greeted Hayley enthusiastically. She then introduced him to her husband and son. Trey introduced him to Baylee before Kurt said, "I'd like you to meet a friend of mine. Scott Givens."

Baylee had seen Scott walking half a step behind Kurt before they'd joined the group. She offered him a weak smile now, her enthusiasm for the day dwindling by the second.

While the others chatted, Baylee merely smiled and nodded or murmured agreement when it was necessary. She was embarrassed to the tips of her toes to be standing here with her ex-husband and the man he was obviously involved with. The man he'd left her for.

Kurt was the Asheville art gallery owner Scott had mentioned. Baylee hadn't wanted details. She hadn't spoken to Scott in months in any case. But to be faced with him now, so shortly after meeting Trey's beautiful ex-wife? It seemed grossly unfair. Trey had wanted her here with him. She'd promised to accompany him. But all she wanted to do was flee.

She untangled her fingers from Trey's. "I'm going to go get something to drink." She forced a smile and made brief eye contact with everyone but Scott. "Excuse me."

She fled.

She stopped near the buffet area and swiped an icy cold soda from one of the metal containers. She had no idea where to go. Where to hide. Behind the Christopher's house was a modern-looking metal structure meant to house tools and equipment. It was where Andy Christopher stored his fishing boat, lawnmower, a small tractor, and other items.

Since it seemed to be deserted, Baylee headed toward it. The building was open on one side and she ducked into the shade provided by the roof. Half of the structure offered a loft area. *Perfect.*

She climbed the metal rungs quickly to discover a wide open space at the top. On the opposite end of the loft was a rectangular opening big enough to load bales of hay through. Andy Christopher didn't raise cattle or horses as far as Baylee knew, so he probably had no need of the access. There were a few bales of hay stacked haphazardly near the opening, though.

Baylee took a seat on one and popped the top on her soda. She took a sip of the cold liquid, glad to be away from the crowd. She gazed out the opening at the apple orchard beyond and the mountains in the distance. From here she could hear the musicians, but that was all. The party seemed very far away.

What had ever possessed her to think that whatever this was she and Trey had going could turn into something real? After seeing his ex-wife, she understood Trey was most likely just passing time with her until someone better came along. Someone more his type.

Isn't that what she'd wanted anyway? She'd never wanted Trey to take her seriously. She just wanted to have fun with him. Have sex with him. She hadn't wanted a relationship. She didn't even want to stay here in Henderson. She was dying to leave, right? She was saving her money with that intent. Unless she got a job offer soon, she planned to move to Orlando and start fresh in a place where no one knew her, no one would talk about her, no one would pity her. Even if the voices she imagined she heard were her own, the internal monitor that judged her, changing environments might quiet it. She'd have something new and different to focus on.

Maybe a change of scenery was the answer and maybe it wasn't. She tried to imagine what she might miss if she left Henderson. Certainly not her self-involved family. Not her lumpy daybed mattress or the drudgery of the jobs she'd been doing the past year. She'd miss Jenny, of course. But mostly, if she were honest with herself, the person she'd miss most was Trey.

Stupid, she warned herself. If she left, he'd move on so fast her head would spin if she were here to see it. He'd find a willing, available woman. There were lots of them in Henderson or further afield in Asheville. She'd miss his house, organizing his office. His bed.

She took another sip of soda. She straightened her spine and squared her shoulders. She needed to get back to the party even if it was the last thing she wanted to do. There was no reason she couldn't paste a smile on her face. She'd promised Trey.

"Baylee?"

Trey!

"Are you in here?"

"Yes, I'm up here," she called back. She stood up and brushed the back of skirt. "I'm coming down." *Smile*, she warned herself. *You came here to—to what?*

While she was trying to formulate an answer to that question, Trey's head appeared at the top of the ladder. "Hi there." He climbed the rest of the way up. "You okay?"

She bit her lip and shook her head as he approached.

"Seeing the ex sucks, doesn't it?" He hugged her and dropped a kiss on the top of her head. "Believe me, I know how you feel."

"You do?" Her question was stifled by his chest.

He gave a humorless laugh and let her go. He moved to look out the window, propping himself up with one hand on the wall.

"I thought..."

He glanced over his shoulder. "Thought what?"

"You were over her," she said in a tiny voice.

"Me too," he agreed softly.

"Oh." She sank back to the bale of hay she'd been sitting on earlier.

"You know what's weird?" He turned to her and smiled. "It isn't about her, exactly. Hayley. It's that seeing her reminded me of everything I lost. She's the most obvious symbol of how badly I screwed up. I think that's what got to me."

"When you were talking to her, you didn't act like it bothered you at all."

He grinned. "I was faking it." He sat next to her.

"When you called to me just now? I was trying to think of what to tell you about why I was hiding out here."

"I'm sure it wasn't pleasant to discover your ex has hooked up with my uncle."

"How'd you know he was my ex?"

Trey gave her a look. "You clammed up the second he appeared for one thing. Hightailed it out of there as soon as you could. His name is Scott." He tapped his temple. "I figured it out."

She nudged her shoulder against his. "Hayley's beautiful." She glanced up at him from beneath her lashes to gauge his reaction.

"Yeah."

When he didn't say anything else she plunged ahead. "I don't understand how you can—" she stuttered to a halt the moment she realized she didn't want to know the answer.

"How I can what?"

Yes, she did want to know. "Go from being married to someone like her to sleeping with someone like me?"

He cocked his head. "What do you mean?"

She didn't want to, but she'd have to spell it out for him. "She's gorgeous and I'm—I'm—"

"Stunning."

She stared at him. Was he joking? Teasing her? "No. I'm not."

"Are you kidding? You've got these gorgeous, amber-colored eyes, which by the way, have this mischievous glint in them and every time I look at you I always wonder what you're up to."

She smiled at his description.

"This hair." He pushed her headband back until it slid off. "Wild. All I want to do is run my fingers through it."

"This mouth. This very sexy mouth." He leaned in and brushed his lips against hers. "This mouth drives me crazy. So do these." He cupped her breasts and kissed her again. "And this." He squeezed her bottom and pulled her into his lap.

The next thing she knew, she was on her back in a pile of straw and Trey loomed over her. He twined strands of her hair around his fingers and let them go while gazing into her eyes. "If I had a condom on me, you know what I'd do?"

She held his gaze with hers. "You don't need one. I'm on the pill."

"Since when?"

"Since a few weeks ago."

"Man, this party keeps getting better and better." He kissed her again. "Want to give me another chance in a hayloft?"

"I'd like that."

Later, their clothes in rumpled disarray, they lay together, Baylee's head on Trey's shoulder, his hand sifting through her hair. Twilight had dimmed the bright sun of the day. A cool breeze blew across them from the opening nearby.

"We should go back to the party. They'll be setting up the fireworks soon."

"Okay."

They straightened each other's clothes and brushed each other off.

They left the barn hand in hand. The first person Trey saw was his father who was replacing the trash liner in one of the garbage cans. He frowned as he watched them approach.

"Hey, Dad. Need some help?"

"Wouldn't mind it," Andy replied. He handed Trey a roll of trash bags and fixed his gaze on Baylee.

"Baylee, this is my dad. Dad, Baylee Westring." Andy shook Baylee's hand. "Dan Westring's girl?"

"Yes, sir."

"You got a piece of straw in your hair." Andy tugged a long piece of straw loose and let it drop to the ground."

"Oh! We were just, um, nothing." Baylee could feel her face turning red.

"I'll help, too." She nudged Trey. "Nice to meet you, Mr. Christopher."

He nodded. His frown stayed firmly in place.

Chapter Twenty-two

♥

*D*amn it! Matty had been extra careful lately, or as careful as he could be on the dark streets of Henderson in the wee hours of the morning. As soon as Mamacita fell asleep, Matty and Jasmine found time to be truly alone with each other. Mostly they sat on the front steps of her aunt's house talking quietly while the chemistry between them grew. Or at least Matty thought it was chemistry. One thing he knew for sure, he never felt more alive than he did when in Jasmine's presence.

A couple of times they'd lain on an old sheet in her aunt's back yard and stared at the stars. Jasmine knew all of the constellations and pointed them out to Matty, describing their history and their outlines. Matty found himself mesmerized by the sound of her voice, the scent of her, the fact that she thought him worthy of her time.

He hadn't minded the scratchy grass poking through the thin cotton into his back or the smell of dust from the dry ground beneath them.

She'd taken to touching him, casually. Bumping her shoulder against his or caressing his forearm. He didn't know what to make of these gestures because the very idea that a girl like Jasmine could be attracted to him was so foreign, he hardly dared to dream of it. He figured she was just bored, and he was convenient and they had a few things in common. Like attending the same school. Being of mixed race. Loving Mamacita.

At the Fourth of July party, she'd discovered a handful of friends she knew from school, so instead of the one-on-one situation Matty had envisioned, they'd been part of the group of teenagers in attendance. At least Jasmine hadn't abandoned him. She'd gracefully made sure he met the other kids. Most of them he was acquainted with in one way or another. In a town like Henderson, it was hard to escape crossing paths with other kids around his age.

Every night while he pedaled home, he allowed his thoughts to run wild. Like what if Jasmine was seriously interested in him? What if she was his girlfriend? Then he mentally slapped himself for such ridiculous thoughts.

But tonight she'd given him reason to hope. She'd actually kissed him. On the lips! He'd been so startled he'd barely had time to react. The touch of her soft lips against his burned through his psyche and he decided it was a good thing he hadn't reacted because he'd probably have ruined the moment by saying or doing something stupid.

She'd smiled at him after and drifted back into her aunt's house like it was no big deal. Like she dropped kisses on guys all the time. To him, though, it was a very big deal.

Now his perfect night was about to be ruined because as careful and watchful as he'd been to avoid that cop Spoley, he hadn't been careful enough. The guy was sitting in his squad car with the lights off and Matty cruised past him before he'd registered the cop was there. Next thing he knew, the high beams came on, trapping him in their bright light from behind. The red and blue lights twirled and Matty knew he'd have to stop.

Spoley had cornered him twice more since that first time, each time acting like he was his smarmy best friend.

I'm not going to bust you this time even though we both know I could. One call to your probation officer and you'll be heading for juvenile detention. Matty did not want to go there. He bit his tongue, pretended respect, all the while his skin crawled and that same sick sense of dread built inside him. There was something not right about Spoley's behavior. He *should* call Jack Frost. One warning maybe, but tonight was the fourth time he'd caught Matty out after curfew. He didn't know why, but Spoley had targeted him specifically.

Matty braked his bike and waited for Spoley to pull alongside and kill his headlights and his red and blues. He even turned off the ignition. Which meant he planned to have more than a brief chat. Straddling his bike, Matty crossed his arms over his chest and waited.

"Hey there, Matty." That fake friendliness. Matty wanted to throw up.

He gave the cop a quick nod. "Sir."

"How's it going?"

How's what going? "Okay, I guess." Proceed with caution Matty warned himself.

"Out pretty late, again, aren't you?"

"I'm just heading home."

"You hear about the break-in at The Worley Inn over on Palmer Street?"

"No, sir."

"You wouldn't know anything about that, would you?"

"No, sir."

"Even though Palmer's on your way home?"

Matty had no answer for that. He pretended he wasn't sweating. Pretended his heart wasn't racing.

"I'd hate to think me going easy on you, not turning you in for all these curfew violations led you to believe I'd tolerate other sorts of violations."

"I—" *didn't do anything.* But before he could continue, Matty somehow knew it would be wiser to keep his mouth shut. Spoley was leading up to something.

Spoley smiled at him. In the thin light of the streetlamp on the corner, Matty caught a flash of his teeth which made him think of the ferret his third-grade teacher kept as a class pet. The thing had pretended to be warm and friendly the one time Matty got close to it. Right before it bared its teeth and bit his hand. He tried not to shudder. Whatever Spoley was after it wouldn't be good. "You what?" he asked softly. "Didn't do anything?"

Matty couldn't help the glare he sent the cop.

"Well, see that's the problem," Spoley went on. "You can say you didn't do anything, you didn't break into the inn, didn't steal anything, but a cop like me finds a kid who's already on probation breaking his curfew, being in the same neighborhood where a crime's been committed, you can see why that might arouse suspicion."

Matty stared determinedly ahead afraid if he looked at Spoley he'd be tempted to show the loathing he felt for the guy and that would only make things worse.

"Kid like you," Spoley began again, "with no proper supervision, who's already been in trouble with the law, gosh, might even be tried as an adult. You're almost eighteen, aren't you? You know what that means, Matty? Grown-up prison. With adult men. Bet they'd love to get their hands on a fresh young piece like you."

Matty was so revulsed by the thought of that, he lashed out. "What do you want?" His gaze locked with Spoley's and he could see the cop's satisfaction in his gaze.

"I want you to do me a favor," Spoley said softly. "One little favor. That's all. Then you and I are done."

Bile surged in the back of Matty's throat. He forced it down even though his stomach lurched at the idea of what "the favor" might be.

"What?" he ground out when he felt in control enough to speak again.

"Not so fast. Either I haul your ass in right now. Call your probation officer. Make it clear you were in the vicinity of The Worley Inn. Or you do one thing for me. Do we have a deal?"

As if his whole life were flashing before him, Matty thought of what would happen if he didn't agree to do whatever it was Spoley had in mind. No more community service at the animal shelter. He loved those damn dogs with their hopeful eyes and pathetic wagging tails. He wouldn't be able to help Mamacita. What if she fell again? She'd call and no one would come. His fledgling relationship or whatever it was with Jasmine would be snatched away before it ever got started. His budding friendship with Trey, the chance to earn some money, so maybe, if he ever got up the nerve, he could ask Jasmine out on a real date—maybe Trey would even let him borrow his Cayenne—all of that would be lost to him forever. His dad would probably give up on him for good.

No one would come to visit him in prison. He'd lose the possibility of everything. All because months ago he'd done one stupid thing wrong and been dumb enough to get caught. Now an asshole like Spoley had power over him.

Never again, he vowed to himself. He'd do this one thing, whatever it was, no matter how revolting it might be, and then he'd wise up. He'd figure out a way to stop breaking his curfew. Maybe just tell his Dad and Baylee and Lisa and Jack Frost the truth. Maybe he could spend whole nights at Mamacita's house with their permission. Ride his bike home in the morning. Finish up his community service and get off probation for good. Stop cutting class when school started again in the fall. Never do anything dumb for the rest of his life. Never get in trouble again. Never have to kowtow to a jerk like Spoley. "Deal."

Baylee startled awake when her cell phone rang. She glanced around the deserted emergency department waiting room. According to the clock over the automatic sliding exit doors, it was three forty-eight a.m. She stared at her phone for a moment before depressing the send key. "Hello." Her voice was barely audible even to her own ears.

"Baylee?"

Trey! Why would he call at this hour? "Yes." She answered using her still uncooperative vocal chords.

"What's wrong?"

"I'm in the hospital."

"What happened? Are you hurt?"

"No."

"Baylee, I can hardly hear you. What's going on?"

Baylee cleared her throat. "Hold on. I'm going outside." She thought her voice was slightly stronger. She stepped out into the damp air of the pre-dawn darkness. A sidewalk led around to the main hospital entrance. She followed it for a few feet until she was away from the glare of the lights in the emergency parking area.

"Okay. That's better." She heaved a sigh of relief, glad to be out of the oppressive waiting room.

"Are you at the hospital in Henderson?" Trey asked.

"Yes. It's my dad."

"What happened?"

"I don't know exactly. The cops think he got mugged or beat up or something. They think he was trying to walk home and he was hit by a car."

"Is he badly hurt?"

"I don't think so, but I only saw him for a minute. They took him for X-rays and I don't know what else. You know how long everything takes in an ER."

"I'm on my way," Trey informed her.

"No, please. You don't have to. I'm fine."

"Of course, you are," Trey agreed. "I'll be there in a few minutes."

He disconnected. Baylee stared at her phone for a long time, a tiny smile tugging at the corners of her mouth. A nugget of warmth took up residence in her heart. She hadn't realized how alone she felt, how alone she always felt until Trey had come into her life. Since her mother's death, she hadn't had much in the way of a support system. Scott had hardly been a supportive spouse, although if she'd needed him, he'd have put in an appearance. She'd never been close to her father and he now preferred the company of the bottle over anyone else's. Lisa worked like a dog and was preoccupied with the twins. She had little left over to give anyone else. Even though they were best friends, Jenny's priorities were Ryan and Seth.

Trey didn't ask if she wanted him here. He'd simply informed her he would be there. For her. Because of her. *Where have you been all my life?* she wanted to ask him.

She hovered outside the emergency room entrance to wait for Trey, so she'd be visible if any of the hospital personnel came looking for her. Tendrils of warmth spread from the soft spot in her heart as she anticipated his arrival. His presence alone would be a comfort. He didn't have to do anything or say anything. She could lean on him. But for how long?

She always came back to that question. How long before he grew tired of her? Or bored? Surely it wouldn't be long before he went after someone more his type. He'd let her down. He wouldn't want to be there for her indefinitely. Would he?

Fairy tales, she warned herself. She wanted a fairy tale. But surely even Prince Charming couldn't live up to his princess's expectations forever. Who knew what their life was like after "the end."

Her thoughts didn't keep her heart from lifting when she saw the headlights of Trey's Cayenne sweep across the parking area. He parked and came toward her dressed in jeans and a tee shirt. She wanted to run to him like the woman in that crazy hair color commercial. Leap into his arms and he'd swing her around after he caught her. Stupid fantasies. They had to stop.

She made herself stand still. She couldn't think of anything to say. Her heart did a weird flip-floppy thing right before Trey gathered her in his arms. His lips grazed the top of her head and every ounce of tension seeped out of her. She clung to him and let him hold her. She had no idea how long they stood together. At some point he brushed his fingers through her hair and whispered, "It's okay." A little while later she let go of him.

Back in the waiting room he took the seat next to hers. "How long have you been here?"

"A couple of hours." Baylee smothered a yawn behind her hand. "I might be late for work."

"Good thing you have an in with the boss."

"By the way, why were you calling me at four a.m.?"

Trey ducked his head which put Baylee in mind of a little boy caught doing something he knew he shouldn't. "I woke up and couldn't get back to sleep. I started thinking about you and all the times you've cooked me breakfast and I thought maybe you'd like to meet me this morning here in town and I'd buy you breakfast for a change. I didn't think you'd have your phone on. I didn't want to wake you up. I was going to leave you a message."

"Oh." Baylee got stuck on *I was thinking about you* and barely heard the rest of his explanation.

Trey stood. "I'm going to see if I can find out what's going on." He approached the nurse's station. Baylee watched him use what she'd come to think of as the Trey Christopher charm on the thirty-something nurse seated at the desk behind the glass window.

How lovely to let someone take over. She couldn't hear exactly what Trey said to the nurse, but she could tell by the woman's body language he'd found a soft spot. The nurse would cooperate. Baylee watched her pick up a phone. Trey leaned forward, propping his arms on the counter. Baylee would bet a hundred bucks he was offering one of those endearing grins to the nurse.

She spoke into the phone for a minute briefly before hanging up and returning her attention to Trey. Whatever she told him appeared to satisfy him. After a few more minutes of conversation, Trey sauntered back to his seat.

"Your dad's got a broken arm and a concussion. It sounds like he's pretty banged up otherwise as well. They want to keep him overnight. The doctor will be out to talk to you in a half hour or so."

"Thanks."

"Has this happened before?"

"Not this bad. He's had disagreements with some of the guys who frequent the tavern. No one's beat him up, though. Usually, he finds his way home or sometimes Buzz drops him off."

"Buzz?"

"Buzz owns the tavern. He and Dad were in school together."

"Ah."

"How long's he been drinking?"

"Always. As long as I can remember. It got worse after my mom died. When Matty started getting into trouble, it's like Dad gave up. He doesn't care about anything or anyone anymore."

"He's an alcoholic. An addict. He needs help."

Baylee made a sound Trey couldn't decipher. "He won't get it."

"He will if you don't give him a choice."

"How would that work, exactly? I'm in no position to issue ultimatums. I live in his house rent-free. Besides, he's never been interested in me or in my opinion about anything. If I tell him he has to get help for his drinking he'll laugh in my face or ignore me more likely."

"I'll talk to him."

Baylee stared at Trey. "You don't even know him. What makes you think he'd listen to you?"

"I've been there," he said simply.

"Oh." Baylee shut her mouth. Trey rarely alluded to his past issues with drugs and alcohol or his stint in a rehab clinic. Much of what she knew about his recovery was what she gleaned from watching his behavior and what she'd read in his journals. Still, she doubted he could reach Dan Westring and get him to agree to seek help for his problem.

At the same time, she wondered what her father might be like when he wasn't under the influence. His relationships had all been distorted by his view through a bottle.

A youngish-looking man in green scrubs arrived in the waiting room a few minutes later. He introduced himself as Dr. Barber. He reiterated what the nurse had told Trey before he fixed his gaze on Baylee. "Miss Westring, your father has a severe alcohol addiction. He's a prime candidate for treatment."

Before Baylee could respond, Trey covered her hand with his and said, "We're aware."

"He can be transferred directly to a treatment facility when he's released tomorrow, but it has to be voluntary."

Again, Trey replied. "We'll talk to him."

Dr. Barber's glance moved from Trey to Baylee and back before he rose. "Very well. Mr. Westring is, ah, resting. He'll be released late tomorrow morning, so you'll need to speak with him first thing."

"We'll take care of it." Trey and Baylee stood. They shook hands with the doctor and thanked him. When he left, they were alone together.

"Let's get out of here." Trey steered her toward the exit and in the direction of his Cayenne.

"Wait. I have my car here."

"It will still be here when we come back to see your dad in a few hours. Until then, you can come home with me and get a couple hours of sleep."

Baylee didn't resist. She was, she realized, tired of being alone. If she were in Trey's bed, she doubted she'd get any sleep. Even though she was drooping with exhaustion, she wasn't sure sleep was what she needed or wanted.

By the time they reached the house, Baylee had changed her mind. She kicked off her shoes and the jeans she'd donned when the hospital had called and crawled into Trey's bed. She didn't wait for him to join her. In seconds she was asleep.

Trey congratulated himself as he got into bed twenty minutes later. Baylee was asleep, just as he'd hoped she'd be. His plan had worked. Although it was unlikely he'd get any more sleep before they had to be back at the hospital, he was willing to give it a try.

Two hours later the alarm on his phone beeped softly. Trey turned it off quickly. Baylee didn't move a muscle. She was still curled on her side as she'd been before. He stretched a little then slid out of the bed and headed for the kitchen.

When he returned to the bedroom, he sat on her side of the bed and gently pushed a few tendrils of hair behind her ear. He bent and whispered, "I brought you coffee." He nuzzled her, breathing in the scent of her, reluctant to move away.

She made a murmur of reluctance and pushed at him half-heartedly.

He kissed her neck. "It's seven-thirty," he informed her before nibbling his way back to her ear. "If you get up now, I'll make you toast, too."

An intense wave of desire shot through him. Was it desire or lust? Maybe they were the same thing. All he knew was he wanted Baylee. Constantly. Even when he was trying to be practical and in control and not give in to every base instinct she aroused in him, he wanted to fuck her, own her, possess her. This morning, knowing she'd had about two hours of sleep all night, that she was upset about her father, and nervous about confronting him this morning, Trey wanted to undress her the rest of the way and bury himself inside her.

He commanded himself to remove his lips from her skin and sit up. Breathe, he warned himself. Get a grip. Think about her instead of yourself for a change.

She gave him a soft, sleepy look. She was rumpled and gorgeous. "That's a nice way to wake up," she said. "If I skip the toast, do we have time for sex?"

No wonder he was in love with her. The thought flitted through his mind when she reached for him at the same moment he came down on top of her. As unlikely as it may have seemed at one time, Baylee Westring was exactly what he needed. Wanted. Was fast realizing he couldn't live without.

He dispensed with her tee shirt and bra in seconds, mesmerized as he always was by the silky feel of her skin, her scent, her sensitive nipples. He wanted to take his time, explore, arouse, but she drove him crazy. Only when he encountered the dampness of her panties did he slow. He drew them down and off and gently parted her legs. This particular part of her fascinated him more than anything. He didn't know why. He'd seen others. Explored others. But something about the way she'd responded to him from the very first, that he'd been her first, she'd waited for him, maybe that was it.

He loved touching her there, first with his fingers, sliding back and forth against her slick wetness, watching her facial reactions, her eyes closed to slits as she watched him touching her and taking her over the top with his tongue.

He buried himself thickly, deeply inside her. She groaned in delight as he rolled to his back.

She liked to move at a slow, sensual pace which drove him even more insane with need. He did his best to be patient, because he liked watching her move while he caressed her thighs, her breasts, her belly. When he could stand it no more, he rolled with her so she was beneath him once more, her knees high and tight against him while he slammed into her. Faster, harder, higher he drove into her until he couldn't hold out any longer. His exclamation of triumph sounded foreign even to his own ears. He collapsed on top of Baylee who was panting beneath him. She held onto him tightly with her arms and legs wrapped around him. She kissed his shoulder, his neck, wherever she could reach, between breaths.

Trey didn't know what was happening to him. He couldn't recall ever having this overwhelming sense of need for another person. The self-control he'd worked so hard to achieve and maintain deserted him when he was with her. He wasn't sure what to do about it.

"Why don't you let me talk to him?" Trey asked two hours later as they rode to the third floor in the hospital elevator.

"You don't even know him, Trey. He's my father."

The elevator dinged when it reached the third floor. Trey allowed Baylee to precede him out of the car. The doors slid closed with a swoosh behind them. The nurse's station was positioned directly across from them with a deserted waiting area nearby. Trey maneuvered her to the waiting area out of earshot of the nurses at the desk who hadn't even acknowledged their presence.

"Do you want your father to get help for his alcoholism?"

Baylee lifted her chin. "Yes."

"How's your relationship with him? Does he listen to you? Pay any attention to what you need? To what's important to you?"

Baylee's chin wobbled. "No."

"Oh, sweetheart." Trey gathered her in his arms and stroked her hair. This is what it's like, she thought, to have someone to lean on. This is what it's like to not have to do everything alone.

"Come here," he said. He walked her to a row of chairs set up along the wall.

"I've been where your dad is," Trey informed her. "I know what he's thinking. He'll offer you ten excuses why he doesn't need treatment. If that doesn't work, he'll put a guilt trip on you, he'll get mad and try to make you feel bad and make you think his drinking is your fault.

"I know every trick, because I used them all, until somebody I had no connection with who wouldn't put up with my bullshit forced me to get help. Let me talk to him."

"Okay."

A few minutes later, Trey tapped on Dan Westring's hospital room door and opened it. Baylee's father was awake and looking belligerent. The remnants of his breakfast sat on a rolling tray table and had been pushed to the far side of the bed. He wore a hospital gown and his left arm was encased in a foam brace and held over his chest by sling. His face showed the damage he'd suffered from whatever had occurred last night. He had a black eye, a split lip and a cut above his left eyebrow.

He watched Trey's approach with apprehension. "Who are you?"

"Trey Christopher." He reached out a hand and Dan begrudgingly shook it and introduced himself.

"I'm a friend of your daughter's," Trey said. "Baylee," he added to eliminate any confusion.

"Yeah. Okay. Where is she? I thought she'd come to pick me up."

"She's here. I wanted to talk to you first"

"About what?"

"Treatment for your alcoholism."

Dan snorted. "Just because I like a few beers now and then doesn't mean I'm an alcoholic."

"Bullshit," Trey said calmly. Dan glared at him. "Want to know how I know it's bullshit? Because I've been there. Right where you are. Trying to deny it, trying to convince everyone I didn't have a problem and most importantly trying to convince myself. It won't work. If you want me to get you a mirror so you can take a good hard look at yourself and what you're doing and what you've done not only to yourself, but to your family and anyone else who gives a damn about you, I will. But I don't think I need to. You don't like yourself much right now. You probably haven't for a long time. But that's neither here nor there. You've got a family and I'm going to assume they love you and want what's best for you, even though the only one I know for sure that feels that way is Baylee."

"You've got a lot of nerve—"

"You better believe it. I've also got two Super Bowl rings and believe me when I tell you my nerve's got more value right now than they do. I don't care about much of anything except how what you do affects Baylee. You've spent a lifetime making her feel badly about herself, making her feel unimportant and lately, causing her to worry about you. It stops today, or I swear to God, I'll encourage her to stay away from you because you're like poison to her and everyone else when you're drinking."

Trey ignored Dan's glare and attempt to interrupt.

"This isn't just me talking. The doctor who admitted you suggested treatment. They'll transfer you directly. You don't have to go home. Admit you've got a problem and you get help starting today. If you don't, say good-bye to your daughter. After that you can probably say good-bye to your other daughter. Your son and grandsons. You've got a lot to live for, it looks to me like, but if you don't wise up, you'll lose it all, just like I did. You'll wake up one morning and everything and everyone you loved or cared about will be gone." Trey snapped his fingers. "It slips through your fingers, and you can't get it back. So, what's it going to be?"

Some of Dan's defiance had left him during Trey's speech. Trey saw a man twice his age who was afraid. Afraid to commit to treatment. Afraid to give up the crutch he'd depended on for so long.

Sensing he was close to Dan capitulating, he pulled up one of the visitors' chairs and sat. "I won't lie to you. It isn't easy. At first, I hated rehab. I was pissed at the whole damn world, but when it came down to it, mostly I was pissed at myself. I screwed up everything and it was my own damn fault. I stuck it out in treatment because being under the influence is how I got where I was.

"I'm going to make this one-time offer to you. You go into treatment right now, transfer in from the hospital when they release you today and I'll be there to help you every step of the way. I'll help you in whatever way I can. What do you say?"

"Why? You don't know me. Why would you bother?"

Trey held Dan's gaze. "Because I know Baylee cares about you. I care about her."

"There you are."

Baylee looked up from her seat in the waiting area to see that Lisa stepping off the elevator and charging toward her.

"Thanks for leaving me a note. I've been trying to call you all morning and all I get is your voice mail."

"Sorry. I guess I turned my phone off last night when I was here, and I forgot to turn it back on."

Lisa took the seat next to here. "I saw Dad as soon as I got here."

"How is he?"

"Not happy. Dr. Barber is under the impression that Dad's planning to transfer to the rehab clinic once he's released."

Baylee bit her lip.

Lisa stared at her. "You know he won't go."

"He might."

"When pigs fly," Lisa snorted.

"Okay, we're all set." Trey materialized in front of them. Baylee stood and so did Lisa. Baylee let Trey wrap his hand around hers.

"Trey, this is my sister, Lisa. Lisa, Trey Christopher."

Lisa's hard gaze went from Baylee to Trey and back. "You're kidding, right?"

"I talked to him," Trey informed them. "Your dad agreed to in-patient rehab. It's all set."

Lisa's gaze narrowed. She gave both Baylee and Trey a look filled skepticism. "I'll believe it when I see it. I have to get back to work. Trey, your reputation precedes you, but it was lovely to meet you in person." She poked Baylee's chest. "I'll talk to you later."

Trey watched Lisa walk away. "Kind of a hardass, isn't she?"

Chapter Twenty-three

♥

Matty was missing something really important to be here today. The whole family was supposed to be at the rehab clinic for a family therapy session. His dad had stopped drinking and sought treatment. The least the rest of them could do was show up today and try to be supportive. That's what Lisa had told him yesterday. Even the twins would be there. And Baylee, of course. Matty had been torn. He never stopped wanting his dad to get better, to lay off the booze and be a dad. Be a man. Now that his dad was giving it a shot, Matty had bailed on him.

He'd consider all the options last night. He didn't want to do whatever it was Spoley wanted him to do. But he didn't think he had a choice. He'd laid it all out in his head. There wasn't anyone in his family he could go to.

There hadn't been since his mom had died. Now with them all rallying around his dad, Matty's problems were even less important.

He could go to Jack Frost. Explain everything about Mamacita and Des. How he was trying to help them and that's why he often broke his curfew. But Jack Frost was a by-the-book kind of guy. Matty didn't think his probation officer would care what his reasons were. Probation was probation and Matty needed to toe the line and follow the rules. Jack would likely make sure somehow that he couldn't help Mamacita any longer. Maybe he'd even go to her and explain how Matty had gotten into trouble and about probation. Matty didn't think he could stand disappointing Mama. Maybe she wouldn't love him anymore or want him around.

If that happened, he'd lose Mama and Jasmine, too. In her eyes he wouldn't be the kid who was helping Mama. He'd be a loser who couldn't stay out of trouble. She'd want nothing more to do with him. He had no idea how he'd gotten together with her to begin with, but he knew he didn't want to lose her and this, whatever this was that had started between them.

Matty swallowed down his fear and wiped his sweaty palms on his pants. That sick feeling of dread he always got when he was anywhere near that cop washed over him once again as Spoley approached on foot.

They were at the far end of a deserted soccer field in the county park. Matty planned to make it clear to Spoley that he wouldn't be blackmailed a second time. He had his reasons for going along with it once and they were good reasons. But he wouldn't do Spoley's dirty work in the future. If Spoley tried something else, Matty had made up his mind he'd tell everything to anyone who would listen and take whatever came.

"Right on time. I appreciate that," Spoley greeted him. He offered his hand, but Matty just stared at him.

Spoley gave Matty a look and then he glanced around the area. There wasn't much to see except more fields, a small concrete block building that housed restrooms, and a closed concession stand.

"I'm not sure I care for your attitude, son. You need to show some respect."

"I'm not your son." *I'm not anyone's son.* "Let's get this over with."

"I could call your probation officer right now," Spoley said.

"Go ahead. As a matter of fact, I thought about calling him myself."

"But you didn't." Spoley offered up one of his self-satisfied grins.

"Not this time." It occurred to Matty that he had something on Spoley now. A cop blackmailing a kid instead of turning him in. Spoley was breaking the rules. "But if you try and pull this shit on me again, I will make that call." It felt good to call Spoley's bluff. Matty relaxed a degree.

"I doubt it will be necessary. You do this for me, and we're done."

"Good."

"Your sister works for Trey Christopher."

"Yeah."

"I heard you been out there doing some work for him, too."

"Yeah, so?"

"Arrogant son of a bitch, isn't he?"

Matty shrugged not feeling as relaxed now. He wished Spoley would get to the point. Truth was he liked Trey.

The guy had been decent to him. He'd overheard Lisa and Baylee talking so he knew Trey had something to do with getting his dad into rehab. Plus, even though Baylee was typically clueless, he was pretty sure Trey was in love with her.

"Thing is, he screwed me over a long time ago. Now it's payback time. That's where you come in."

Matty stared at Spoley some more. What did the guy expect? That he'd jump up and down in excitement to be part of whatever the payback scheme was?

"I want you to plant something in Christopher's car for me."

"What?"

"Just some drugs."

Drugs? "Okay, now wait a minute—"

"Not real ones. They're fake prescription drugs," Spoley went on. "Nothing will happen to him. This is more like a practical joke I've been dying to play on him."

"I don't know—"

Now it was Spoley's turn to stare. They had a deal. Matty had already agreed to it. It was too late for him to back out and they both knew it.

Matty knew Trey had money. Even if Spoley was trying to trick him by telling him the drugs were fakes when they weren't, Trey could hire a good lawyer and probably get off with a fine or something. That's how the world worked.

"Fine."

Spoley smiled his creepy smile. "Good. Now here's how it's going to go down."

Chapter Twenty-four

♥

Baylee stared at Trey over the hood of the Cayenne, barely aware that she'd been handcuffed. *Handcuffed!* He stared back at her, his head moving back and forth in denial, but denial of what? There were drugs in his car. Illegal prescription drugs. Painkillers. Surely the kind he'd once been addicted to. He was trying to communicate with her without saying anything. He wanted her to believe he was innocent. *She* wanted to believe he was innocent. More than anything she wanted to believe it, but she couldn't quite get herself there.

One of the sheriff's deputies was reading her rights but she barely heard him. Not like she hadn't heard the Miranda warning recited on television shows often enough that like every other red-blooded American she practically had it memorized.

"Do you understand these rights?" the officer asked for the second time.

"I understand," Baylee replied, knowing it was a lie even as the words left her mouth. She didn't understand anything. About herself. About Trey. About their *relationship*.

Had she been fooling herself all this time? She'd allowed herself to believe Trey was a changed man because that's what he wanted her to believe. He was trying hard to be. Wasn't he? Or had it all been an act? Another man who'd lied to her and pretended to be something he was not, and she'd fallen for it. Fallen hard.

Damn Trey. He'd made her start to believe in that fairy tale, made her want her own happily ever after. With him. *Idiot!* She silently screamed at herself. What was wrong with her that the men she cared about easily fooled her?

"Baylee." Trey said softly.

She wanted to cover her ears because the sound of her name coming from his lips was like torture to her. She wasn't going to listen to him anymore. She willed back the tears that threatened to blur her vision and glared at him. "Liar," she spat at him as the deputy led her to the patrol car.

"Baylee!" Trey called again.

She didn't turn around. She couldn't look at him. He was now just one more in a long line of mistakes and foolish choices.

She obediently ducked her head as the deputy helped her into the back of the patrol car. Several of the concerned citizens of Henderson had stopped to watch the proceedings from their front stoops. Baylee wanted to sink down below the window she already felt so small and humiliated, but she refused.

Instead, she straightened her spine and stared back at anyone whose eye she caught until they looked away. *There but for the grace of God go I.* That had been one of her grandmother's favorite sayings and for some reason the thought comforted her. *This could be you,* Baylee informed her gawking audience. *If you made the wrong choice, hung out with a former drug addict whose track record was littered with rebellious behavior and broken hearts. If you gave someone a second chance—*

Her thoughts slammed to a halt when the other passenger door opened and Trey ducked awkwardly, nearly folding himself in two to get his large frame into the back seat. Baylee squeezed herself against the door and pretended to find the curiosity on the other side of it fascinating.

"Hey," Trey whispered. Baylee ignored him.

The deputy got in behind the wheel and started the engine. He put the car in gear and eased out onto the street.

This was for real. He was taking them to the Henderson County Jail. Where they'd be fingerprinted and booked. There'd be a trial; a conviction. No one would listen to her protestations of innocence. She'd been warned and she hadn't listened. She'd foolishly believed she could for once throw caution to the wind, do what she wanted simply because she wanted to and because it felt good. Being good had got her nowhere. Now she'd pay the price for being bad.

"Baylee," Trey tried again more insistently.

She felt sick inside, like a big rock had been dropped into the pit of her stomach and it'd be there forever. Panic and fear of the unknown along with a deep-seated disappointment, in herself and in Trey coated her like a layer of thick gooey paint.

"Don't even bother," she said without looking him, shocked at how disgusted she sounded.

"Baylee, come on. This is a set up."

She continued to stare out the window as downtown Henderson swept by. "Of course, it is."

"Baylee—"

"Poor Trey Christopher. Hometown boy comes home all reformed to make good. Let's all give Trey a second chance. He screwed up but look how he's changed." She turned to look at him, sure her eyes would burn a hole in him if they could. "Save it for the judge, Trey. I don't want to hear it."

Something faded out of Trey's eyes. The laser blue clouded over and turned dark and murky. He set his jaw and shifted in the seat, turned to look out of his own window.

Baylee bit down hard on her lip. She knew she'd hurt him. But wasn't that how Trey had gone through life? Charming his way along, captivating everyone with his smile and his winning ways, knowing they'd be honored to be part of his golden circle. Hadn't she? Twice. The experience had somehow scarred her the first time, like a small burn on a pinky finger that leaves a mark forever. Whether it was part of her conscious thought she knew it was there.

But like a child who touches a hot stove for the second time, she hadn't learned her lesson. No wonder she got burned again.

By the time Baylee had been photographed and processed, stripped of her purse, her jewelry, and her shoelaces and placed in a holding cell she was numb. Her entire life seemed to have exploded right before her eyes. She thought this might be how NASA scientists felt when a rocket they'd spent ages planning and building blew up on the first launch. They'd have to go back to the drawing board and figure out what they'd done wrong. Baylee didn't even want to do that.

She looked with distaste at the narrow, vinyl-covered cot which jutted out from the wall, but then decided she could care less. She laid down on it, curled into the fetal position and tried not to think.

If only it were that easy. Her eyes hurt from holding back tears. Her throat was raw from swallowing the sobs begging for release. Her stomach was in a knot. Overlying it all was a sort of dreary exhaustion. She hadn't called anyone. Not Lisa or Jenny. Certainly not her father. An arrest on drug possession would simply be one more thing the fine citizens of Henderson, North Carolina could add to the long list of what had happened to poor Baylee Westring.

Her sister the high school slut.

Her mother passing so young.

Her father a drunk.

Her husband gay.

Her adopted trouble-making brother on eternal probation.

Her bank failed.

Her job lost.

Her home foreclosed.

Her near declaration of bankruptcy.

Then she took up with that Trey Christopher. Why everyone knew he was a drug addict. No wonder she went and got herself in trouble with him.

Oh, God, Baylee pleaded silently, *make it stop.* She squeezed her eyes shut hoping to turn the gray cinderblock walls into her own private fortress and the scuffed vinyl beneath her into a canopy bed fit for a princess.

All I wanted was to be happy. Just a little bit of happiness. Was that too much to ask? To hope for?

When she got out of jail, she would leave. Even if she couldn't *be* happy she'd get as close as she could to the happiest place on earth. She'd get in her car and drive until she reached Orlando. She'd build a magical kingdom of her very own and no one would take it away from her.

She escaped into her fantasy so she wouldn't have to deal with reality right at this moment. She'd had enough of reality to last her a lifetime. Somehow, eventually, comforted by her fairy plum visions of the future, she must have dozed off.

Baylee shoved the hair out of her eyes and blinked at the female guard who'd opened the door to her cell. Slowly she sat up.

"You got a visitor," the guard informed her.

"Who?" Baylee asked warily. She couldn't think of anyone she wanted to see at the moment.

"Lawyer." The guard was nothing if not succinct. She hadn't called a lawyer. The only one she knew was Ryan and he was Trey's attorney. Surely it would be a conflict of interest for him to represent her as well. Besides, if Ryan was now in Trey's camp, she didn't want him to help her anyway.

Baylee shuffled along in front of the guard through a few more locked doors which buzzed open as they approached until the guard said, "Right here." Baylee stopped and the guard opened a metal door with a glass window checkered with metal lines. She stepped inside and the guard closed the door behind her. Baylee heard a lock click.

A woman maybe a few years older than her stood at a table. Her head had been bent as she looked at a file in front of her, but when Baylee entered she smiled and came toward her with her hand outstretched. "Baylee? I'm Danica Hawthorne. I'm here to help you."

Baylee shook hands with the woman who had cool slender fingers and a firm grip. She was professionally dressed in a well-fitted navy blue suit and white blouse. Tasteful jewelry peeked out from her earlobes and neckline. She had chin-length wavy dark hair and brown eyes that looked like they didn't miss a trick.

She indicated the chair on the other side of the table and Baylee sank into it. "Where'd you come from?" she asked. "I didn't call anyone."

"Ryan Reagle asked me to handle your case if you're amenable. If you'd prefer to retain another attorney, you're certainly free to do so."

Baylee considered her options. Her current savings were earmarked for travel and finding a place to live once she reached Orlando. She had no intention of spending money she didn't have on legal fees. If they threw the book at her for something she'd had no part in, she'd do her jail time and take off when she got out. What difference would a conviction or a jail term make on her already dismal resume? "I don't have money for an attorney."

"My fees have already been taken care of," Danica informed her.

"By whom?" Baylee asked suspiciously.

"Is that important?"

"I'd like to know."

"Mr. Christopher."

As it should be, Baylee thought. She waited for Danica to continue. The woman took a seat and leafed through the pages in the file in front of her. "Tell me what happened."

Baylee did, sticking to the facts. Danica asked a few questions about the manner in which they'd been pulled over, the way the search was conducted. "Did the pills in your purse belong to you?"

"No."

"Do you have any idea how they came to be in your purse?"

"Not really."

"What does that mean?"

"It means I don't keep an eye on my purse twenty-four/seven. When I'm working sometimes I leave it in my car or I hang it on a hook in the mudroom or on the kitchen counter. I don't carry it around with me all day."

"What about when you're at home?"

"I keep it in my room most of the time. Sometimes I leave it on the entry table by the front door."

Danica asked other questions, sometimes the same questions in different ways about who had access to Baylee's purse. Danica seemed to be implying that she'd been set up. *Why? Who?* If she'd been set up, Trey had also. *I called him a liar.* What if he wasn't? What if Trey was as innocent as she was? A victim of some crazy plot to ruin both their reputations?

Who would want to hurt both her and Trey?

She didn't think she had any enemies. Although Trey had disappointed a lot of the locals, she doubted any of them would go to such lengths out of sheer spite or some misguided sense of seeing him get what they thought he deserved. Except one. Maybe.

Justin Spoley?

He'd had it in for Trey for years and he'd seized the first opportunity he had to pull Trey over his first night back. Justin wasn't her biggest fan either. He'd made no secret of his disappointment when she'd rebuffed his advances. He didn't like the fact that she much preferred his twin brother's company to his. It would only reason he also resented her relationship with Trey, assuming he knew about it. After the Fourth of July party at his parents, he'd likely heard about the two of them through the local grapevine.

Baylee drummed her fingers on the table while her mind whirred and clicked putting puzzle pieces into place. *If* Spoley was responsible, he had help.

"Baylee." Danica patted her wrist to get her attention. Baylee realized she'd asked the same question twice.

"You might want to talk to Justin Spoley. He's a deputy with the county sheriff's department."

"Why? You think he'd know something about this?"

Baylee hesitated. Dusty was one of her best friends. Tossing unvalidated accusations at his brother might irrevocably damage their relationship. "He and Trey have had a few differences in the past. Justin's not my biggest fan, either," she said carefully.

"It's a pretty big leap from having differences with someone and seeing them arrested on narcotics charges," Danica said.

"I know. I was just trying to think of anyone who'd want to make trouble for Trey."

"And you."

"Maybe he had nothing to do with it. I probably shouldn't have said anything."

Danica nodded. "I'll talk to him anyway." She stood and gathered her file together. "Your arraignment's in a couple of hours. The judge will set bail."

"I don't have any money," Baylee reminded her.

Danica held up a hand. "Mr. Christopher will pay your bail. Just for the record, he made it clear to me he wants the charges against you dropped because they're entirely bogus."

Baylee stared at her. She'd already blown it with Trey and if she thought about what she'd done, what she'd said, she'd be reduced to a mass of blubbering emotion. She'd grabbed the first opportunity she had to destroy the happily ever after she wanted. She'd hurt Trey deeply with her lack of trust before he could trample on her heart and walk away from her.

Second chances were important to Trey. He'd given her one with him and she'd blown it.

In her mind's eye Baylee kept seeing Matty hand Trey a small plastic bag. Was Matty selling drugs? To Trey? She didn't want to believe it. But she couldn't discount what she'd seen, either. Flower seeds? Seriously?

"You might want to talk to my brother, Matty, also," she told Danica.

"Is there some reason you think he's involved?"

"Honestly, I don't know. I don't want to think so. I don't want to think any of this is happening. If he's innocent, it won't do any harm to ask him, though, will it?"

"We'll get to the bottom of this," Danica reassured her. "Don't worry."

She pressed a button near the door and the guard appeared to escort Baylee back to her cell.

Trey had counted to a thousand, done his deep breathing, searched for a modicum of Zen-like peace the entire time he'd been in the back of the patrol car. He knew enough to keep his mouth shut, even if it sent his blood pressure skyrocketing along with his temper and caused his head to explode.

He had the worst case of pissed off he'd ever had in his life. He'd known as the entire scene played itself out, the two patrol cars pulling him over, the search and seizure of those planted drugs, that Spoley was somehow behind it. He'd watched Baylee's belief in him shatter before his eyes and he'd been powerless to stop it. What was he going to say in that moment? *I didn't do it?* She'd called him a liar. She might as well have stabbed him in the gut. Maybe he hadn't been one hundred percent entirely honest with her, but she was the first woman in his life he'd never lied to.

Spoley had wanted to mess with him from the moment he'd blown back into town, and he'd found the perfect way to do it. He'd brought back Trey's past, thrown it in his face, and in Baylee's, too. He'd messed with the reputation Trey was trying to rebuild, with the relationship he was trying to forge with Baylee, the fences he wanted to mend with everyone else, including his parents.

Damn him! Trey could have torn the guy from limb to limb given the opportunity, but he'd settle for seeing the guy humiliated and stripped of his badge and fired from the Henderson County Sheriff's Department.

The first thing Trey did was call Ryan. He paced and waited in a small meeting room which held a table, a couple of uncomfortable chairs and nothing else.

He tried not to think about Baylee or what they might have done with her. Locked her up, he supposed. How had those pills come to be in her *purse?* There were pills everywhere all of a sudden. It was one thing for a cop to plant drugs in a vehicle during a search when the owner was otherwise occupied. But Trey had kept an eye on the deputy doing the search. Either he was a magician or the small plastic bags containing those pills were already in the Cayenne before they'd left the house this morning. *How though? And who?*

Dan walked into his house and looked around at it with fresh eyes. He'd been out of rehab for two days and had just returned from an AA meeting at the church hall. He'd been surprised to discover a couple of guys he knew as well as an old friend of Diana's. He vaguely remembered Diana mentioning that they'd drifted apart after the woman's husband left her for another woman and she'd begun drinking heavily.

Over a Styrofoam cup of coffee after the meeting, she told Dan she'd been sober for two years and was getting her life back together. She'd squeezed his hand and told him how sorry she was about Diana's death. Then she'd given him her phone number and told him if he ever needed to talk to call her.

Dan hadn't felt hopeful in, well, he couldn't remember when. Certainly, before Diana's death. He'd been lost these past few years. She'd kept him steady and without her, he hadn't known quite what to do. All he'd wanted to do was numb himself to the loss and loneliness and the fear that he hadn't deserved her in the first place. He hadn't valued her enough and that's why she'd been taken away from him.

The living room looked sad. The furniture Diana had chosen years ago and lovingly cared for was sagging and worn, the coffee and end tables bore scratches from the twins' rambunctious behavior. The walls need a fresh coat of paint. Hell, the whole house needed a major over-haul.

A project like that would be good for him. It'd keep him occupied. He'd start with the living room. Between meetings he'd patch and paint and maybe even shop for a new sofa. He fingered the piece of paper in his pocket. Maybe Paula would like to go furniture shopping with him.

He started toward the kitchen, aware now of a foreign sound coming from that direction. He proceeded cautiously until he stood in the arched entrance. Matty was hunched over the kitchen table, his face buried in his folded arms, shoulders heaving.

"Matty?"

Matty raised a tear-streaked face to stare at him. Snot dripped from his nose, but he made no move to wipe it away. "What?" he said almost defiantly. But Dan could see his tone was meant to mask despair.

Dan took a step closer. Fear clutched at his heart. He couldn't remember the last time he'd seen Matty cry. Maybe at Diana's funeral. But then, Dan reminded himself, he hadn't been seeing much of anything or anyone very clearly since then. "What's wrong, son?"

Matty gave a bark of laughter. "Oh, great. Now I'm your son?" He swiped his hand across his face and rubbed it on his pants leg. His eyes dared Dan to answer the question, but underneath the disgusted tone, Dan sensed Matty's vulnerability.

He'd been warned about this in rehab. He had amends to make. The people closest to him would be angry at him. They might not believe he'd changed or that they could trust him again. He would have to prove himself to them and it wouldn't be easy. The Serenity Prayer raced through his head. He couldn't change what he'd done in the past. He could only move forward and try to be better and do better. Starting with his son.

He took another step closer willing himself not to be as afraid of this moment as Matty apparently was. "You've always been my son. I just haven't been much of a father to you."

Matty stared at him. More tears welled in his eyes.

Dan inched closer. "I can be, though, if you give me a chance."

Matty shook his head, his gaze sliding away from Dan's. "You'll hate me."

"Never."

At his adamant tone, Matty's gaze snapped back. "I screwed up again. Big time."

Dan took the remaining steps it took to get next to Matty and laid a hand on his shoulder. "Then we'll figure it out together. We'll fix it."

"I don't think it can be fixed," Matty muttered.

Dan hugged his son awkwardly against his side. "Oh, son, there's very little in life that can't be fixed."

Surely it had been more than the couple of hours Danica had said it would be, yet Baylee had not seen a judge. The female guard who'd brought a meal on a tray had shrugged when Baylee asked if she knew what was going on. Baylee stared at the food which looked decidedly unappealing, even if she'd been able to muster any appetite. She drank the small carton of milk and nibbled on a sandwich of white bread spread with a thin layer of margarine.

Shortly after she'd finished eating, the guard returned and motioned her out of the cell.

She was led to a small conference room crowded with people. Ryan, Trey, Danica, Matty, and her father and were there. For some reason, Jack Frost was there as well, along with a couple of other individuals she didn't recognize.

Trey was wearing the same clothes he'd had on earlier just as she was. He looked up when she entered then looked away, focusing his attention anywhere but on her. Ryan whispered something to him, and he nodded.

"Miss Westring, if you'd take a seat," said one of the men she didn't recognize. "I'm Detective Sommers with the sheriff's department. This is Assistant District Attorney James Canfield. I believe you're acquainted with everyone else present."

Baylee sat.

"Hi, honey," her father said. He gave her a look that was encouraging and apologetic at the same time. She couldn't help but stare at him. He looked like the father she vaguely remembered from childhood. His clothes were clean, his shirt tucked in. He'd gotten a haircut recently. He looked healthier than he ever had. She nodded at him and gave him a weak smile. Matty, on the other hand, looked horrible. His eyes were puffy, his clear complexion mottled. He sat stiffly on the chair next to her father, his hands tucked beneath his legs.

She glanced at Ryan, but he was here in an official capacity as Trey's attorney. His expression was stoic, although he inclined his head in her direction.

"Miss Westring," Detective Sommers began. "Mr. Christopher. It appears we have an unusual situation on our hands involving one of our own members of the sheriff's department. We're still gathering evidence, but based on what your brother has told us, and after discussions with Mr. Canfield, we're in agreement that all of the charges against both of you will be dropped."

"Matty?" Baylee asked turning to look at him. Her gaze moved from Matty who wouldn't meet her eyes, to her father to Jack Frost and the detective.

"Apparently, one of our officers coerced your brother into planting the drugs that were found in your purse and in Mr. Christopher's car. Matty has come forward and confessed. There are...extenuating circumstances surrounding his involvement. We've decided to allow Mr. Frost to determine what should be done considering Matty is a juvenile and already on probation."

If her brain had been filled with quicksand, Baylee didn't think she'd be any more confused. "I'm sorry, I don't understand. Matty? You set us up? Why? After everything Trey did to help you—"

"I'm sorry!" Matty's eyes welled. He looked Baylee in the eye. "I'm sorry." He looked at Trey. "I'm sorry. It was dumb. I know. But I didn't know what else to do."

"It's okay, Matty," Trey said softly. "We all screw up."

Baylee could deal with Matty later. She looked back at the detective. "You said something about extenuating circumstances?"

Detective Sommers looked at Jack Frost. He addressed Baylee's question. "As I'm sure you're aware, Matty repeatedly violated his curfew without consequences. Officer Sp—er the officer in question caught him but didn't report him. After a few incidents he threatened Matty with arrest for crimes he had nothing to do with, unless Matty cooperated. Matty's after-curfew activities were important enough to him that he made a difficult choice. The wrong choice, as it turns out. But with help from Matty's family, I'm confident we're going to work our way through this. Aren't we, Matty?"

Matty lifted his head. "Yes, sir."

"I still don't understand, though. What were you doing that was so important, Matty?"

"I was helping this lady I know. She's old and sick. Her grandson's in the army and she's alone..."

"She took care of Matty when he was a baby, isn't that right, Matty?" Her father put in.

"I just wanted to help her," Matty said stubbornly, his gaze on the table in front of him.

"We understand that now, son," Dan said, patting Matty's shoulder.

Baylee slumped back in her seat. "Justin caught you. Threatened to lock you up unless you helped him."

Matty nodded.

She looked at Trey again, but he was also staring at the table in front of him. She willed him to look at her, but he didn't.

"The drugs we found are actually imitation," Detective Sommers said. "I'm sure the officer in question thought nothing would come of this except to make a bit of trouble for the two of you. He apparently was unaware that it's recently become illegal in the state of North Carolina to possess an imitation controlled substance."

"We will be bringing charges against the officer. He's been suspended pending an investigation," James Canfield said. "We may need more formal affidavits from you, Mr. Christopher and from Miss Westring. Matty, we'll expect you to testify against the officer if we go to trial. Until then, Mr. Frost will be overseeing your probation and sending me regular reports." He turned to Dan. "Mr. Westring, I expect you to keep a close watch over your son as well."

Again, Dan clasped Matty's shoulder. "Yes, sir. I will, sir."

Canfield pushed his chair back and stood. "I'm sure Detective Sommers will take care of the formalities, but I do believe you are all free to go."

"There's a bit of paperwork to be done," Danica told Baylee as they all stood and began to move out of the room. "You can wait in the lobby if you want. I'll meet you there in a few minutes and they'll release your belongings."

Baylee nodded and followed Danica out. Trey and Ryan were deep in conversation several feet away. Dan approached her with Matty trailing reluctantly behind him.

"Honey, I'm sorry about all of this. I'm to blame. If I'd been there for Matty, been paying attention..." he lifted a hand and let it fall.

Baylee didn't know what to say to her father. Everything he said was true. She wasn't feeling very forgiving at the moment of either him or Matty. Out of the corner of her eye she saw Trey still talking to Ryan. She had an apology of her own to make. If she wanted Trey's forgiveness, she would have to be forgiving.

"It's all right, Dad. You're here now. So is Matty." She shifted her gaze to her brother.

"I'm sorry, Baylee." He opened his mouth to say something else, but he didn't, as if the scope of what he'd done was too massive for words. He looked so miserable, Baylee knew she could forgive him.

"We should have been looking out for you," she told him. "We let you down. All of us," she said, looking at her father. She'd been as much out of her element in helping Matty as he had. The kid had nowhere to turn.

"We'll see you at home?" Dan asked.

"Yes. I'll be there in a little while." Ryan and Trey were approaching.

"C'mon, son." Dan put a hand on Matty's shoulder.

"Wait." Matty took the few steps necessary to meet Trey. He and Ryan halted.

"I know it isn't enough to say I'm sorry, but I am."

Trey held Matty's gaze with his own for a few seconds before he nodded in acknowledgment. "I appreciate the apology."

Matty may have hoped for more from Trey, but apparently, he wasn't in a forgiving mood at the moment, either. Her father and Matty left. Trey and Ryan made to walk past her. Baylee put her hand on Trey's sleeve. "Can I talk to you for a minute?"

Ryan's steps slowed but he continued on.

Trey stopped but he didn't look happy about it. Baylee dropped her hand. She looked into his eyes, shuttered now against her. "I'm sorry," she said so softly she wasn't sure he could hear her. "I shouldn't have assumed—"

"No. You shouldn't have," Trey agreed. "I thought you—and I—hell, I don't know what I thought." He glanced away at the sound of a throat clearing at the end of the corridor. Baylee looked that way to see Ryan, pointing at his watch.

"I can't talk about this right now."

Trey walked away from her.

She'd lost him. The only man she'd ever truly wanted. That's all she could think. She'd screwed everything up, been so ready to lay blame at Trey's door. *What* was wrong with her? Why hadn't she been able to trust him? Had she been waiting for something to ruin things between them, so sure that happily ever after she'd been dreaming of was never going to happen that she jumped on the first opportunity to speed things along in that direction?

She watched as Trey joined Ryan. Without a backward glance they disappeared through the double doors at the end of the corridor. She sank down on a nearby bench. Her insides were hollow. The enormity of what she'd done seemed almost too big to absorb. It was easy to identify with Matty now. No apology was going to change what she'd done. She hadn't trusted Trey when she should have. She'd been all too ready to believe the worst of him because of his past mistakes.

Maybe, surely there was a way they could salvage this. Except she remembered the look in Trey's eyes a moment ago. That look that always made her feel like she was in his spotlight was gone.

"Baylee." Danica signaled to her from the double doors at the end of the corridor. She dragged herself in that direction. If she could just hold it together until she was officially released, then she could go home, curl up and die.

Danica dropped Baylee at Trey's house so she could pick up her car. The first thing Baylee did when her belongings were returned to her was check her cell phone. There were several missed calls, but none were from Trey. She sat in her car half hoping and half dreading that Trey would return, and she could talk to him privately. After half an hour, when his Cayenne did not make an appearance, she drove home. Her father and Matty were in the kitchen putting a meal together. Baylee went to her room and dialed her voice mailbox. A couple of the messages were from her clients asking if she was still available for pet sitting or cleaning. A couple were telemarketers. The last one, however, began, "This is James Falcon. I'm the operations officer at First Bank of Orlando. Larry Sellers sent me your resume along with a letter of recommendation." Good old Larry. He'd felt horrible when the bank had failed and many of his staff were thrown out of work. He'd insisted Baylee send him her resume and he'd send it along if he heard of any openings. She'd updated it after she started working for Trey and e-mailed it to Larry. "I have a position I'd like to speak to you about if you're interested. I look forward to hearing from you."

Baylee disconnected after she'd copied the number. Was this, finally, the answer to her prayers for a real job?

Chapter Twenty-five

♥

When Trey finally left the police station it was almost dusk. Henderson didn't have an impound lot. The Cayenne was parked behind the station's vehicle maintenance building at the far end of the lot. His keys and wallet had been returned to him and he was more than ready to go home. He unlocked the driver's door with the remote and opened it. He slid into the seat and reached for his cell phone, but it wasn't there. He stared at the space in the console where he normally left the phone when he was driving. Could this day possibly get any worse?

He was almost a hundred percent certain the phone had been there when he and Baylee had been pulled over. But like one of those normal, every day routines, he supposed it was possible that he hadn't had the phone with him when they'd left the house that morning. On rare occasions in the past he had forgotten it and came home to discover it on his desk or the nightstand.

If the phone had been in the car, would the police have left it there? He had no idea.

He didn't bother with the breathing routine, but instead let loose with a healthy dose of profanity and a temper tantrum that any two-year-old would be proud of, punctuating it by using all of his strength to slam the driver's side door shut.

He retraced his steps to the police station.

By the time Trey pulled into his driveway he was so disgusted he didn't know what to do. The officer on duty seemed unconcerned that his cell phone had gone missing while his vehicle was technically in police custody. Trey couldn't file a report about a stolen phone unless he was sure it had been stolen.

He searched the house, looking in all the logical places he might have left his phone, becoming more and more convinced that he'd had it with him that morning, that it had been in the car when it had been towed and had since disappeared.

He'd thought about driving to his parents' to make some calls, but he didn't feel up to explaining the day's events to them either. Briefly, he thought of calling Baylee and letting her help him out. She was, after all, his assistant. But he wasn't ready to see her or talk to her, either. That surprised him a little, because he was crazy about her. He was pretty sure he was in love with her. But he was also majorly pissed at her. He couldn't get over the way she'd turned on him, believed the worst about him without giving him a chance to say anything.

Although she had tried to apologize earlier, it hadn't seemed the time or the place and besides, he hadn't been ready to hear it. If he had a phone he'd probably call her and tell her not to come to work tomorrow. He needed another day or two to cool off and get his thoughts and feelings together before they had a conversation. Since he couldn't call her, he'd simply arrange not to be here when she arrived. Tomorrow he'd stop by his parents and use their phone to call the insurance company and the cell phone company. Maybe he'd take his mom out to lunch. He'd stay away from the house until he was good and ready to come home. If Baylee had left for the day by then, so much the better.

Plan in place, he rummaged around in the refrigerator for a quick meal. He flipped through the channels on the television while he ate, but he couldn't concentrate on anything he saw. He took a long hot shower and downed a couple of ibuprofen. Tomorrow, he assured himself, everything would look brighter.

"Hi, Jenny."

"Baylee, are you all right? Seth, give me that. Oh, no you don't. Seth! One. Two. Good boy. Thank you. Sorry." From her end of the phone Jenny sounded out of breath.

"Hey, look, I'm fine." For the first time in she couldn't remember how long, Baylee really didn't want to rehash details of her life with her best friend. "I just called to tell you I'm leaving town for a while."

"Leaving? What do you mean? Where are you going? When are you coming back?"

"Jen, I'm not sure about anything right now. I've got a lead on a job, but I'll be in touch, okay. Don't worry if you don't hear from me for a bit, though."

"Baylee. What are you talking about? You can't just leave. What about Trey?"

"What about him?"

"Well, I don't know. Is he going with you?"

"No. That's over."

"What do you mean it's over? Baylee—Seth! What did mommy just tell you? Leave the kitty alone."

"Jenny, I'll call you. Don't worry, okay?"

"Baylee—"

Baylee pressed the end button on her cell phone.

For Trey the following day proved no less frustrating than the one before.

His mother had generously offered the use of her cell phone but declined his offer of lunch in Asheville. She had a morning appointment scheduled with her hair stylist and an afternoon Apple Festival planning meeting. Trey spent the day alone, with only his mom's cell phone for company, which, he realized, was entirely useless to him. At the police station he reported the phone stolen and waited for them to write up an official report. From his parents' land line, he'd called his insurance company and his cell phone carrier. The numbers of anyone and everyone else he might have called, including Baylee, were in his missing phone.

A duplicate of his state-of-the-art cell phone would have to be ordered and shipped to him. He'd considered throwing another fit when the clerk told him they didn't have any in stock. Instead, he'd thanked her, climbed into the Cayenne and did his breathing routine until he felt calm enough to drive.

It would have been a good idea, he realized now, to have a list of all those contact numbers somewhere besides inside the cell phone itself. He should have told Baylee to create a file for that in his laptop and print out a copy so it would be readily available should he ever lose his phone. Live and learn.

He knew almost the moment he walked in the door of his house that Baylee had not been there. He didn't have to check any further. The house felt as empty as it had this morning. If she'd been here and left, he'd have known it. Somehow, she left a spark of energy behind each time she departed, something he could sense even after she was gone.

He grabbed a soda from the refrigerator and took it out to the porch. Lowering himself into one of the chairs he sipped and silently contemplated the fact that he missed her. If she had called him, he wouldn't know it. He couldn't call her. He could, however, stop by her house. Find out why she hadn't come to work today. Find out if everything he'd thought about her, about *them* was wrong. If it was, he knew he really didn't want to know. His relationship with Baylee had seemed right in a way nothing had in a long time. Fresh. New. Without too much baggage to weigh it down despite their past history which Trey barely remembered anyway.

Tomorrow, he decided as he drained the last of the soda. If she didn't show up for work, he'd track her down and they'd have that conversation.

"Dad, I'm leaving." Baylee entered the kitchen where Dan was poring over the newspaper. A mug of black coffee sat steaming nearby.

"You're sure about this?" Dan asked.

"I need a job, Dad. This is the first nibble I've had in months of sending out resumes. If this doesn't work out, I'll look for something else, but I feel like I have to go."

Dan's gaze searched her face. "What about...?"

"What?"

"Well, Trey. Aren't you even going to tell him you're leaving?"

"I tried. I called him. I left a message. I told him how sorry I was. He hasn't called back. I haven't heard from him at all." Baylee bit her lip, shifting her gaze away from her father and blinking rapidly. "I think it's over."

"Are you sure? Because he sure seemed to care an awful lot about you. He told me that day he came to see me in the hospital."

"I said such hurtful things to him. I can't take them back. I don't think he'll ever forgive me."

"Maybe. Maybe not." Dan pushed a chair out. "Sit down for a minute."

When Baylee didn't immediately take the seat he'd indicated, he said, "Just for a minute."

Baylee complied, wary of what her father might say. They hadn't really talked since the family sessions during his stay in rehab.

Dan contemplated his cup of coffee as if he might find an opening there. He'd never been much of a communicator. That had been her mother's department. Just as she was about to rise, to tell him it was okay, they didn't need to talk, he spoke.

"When I came home the other day and Matty was here I told him there was very little in life that couldn't be fixed." He gave a self-deprecating laugh and glanced at Baylee. "Words of wisdom from the old man, huh?"

"Dad, you really don't have to—"

"I'm going to tell you the same thing I told Matty. The only time you lose your chance to fix things is when someone dies. I found that out the hard way when I lost your mother. Matty didn't believe me. Didn't think there was anything he could do to make up for what he did wrong. It'll take some time and some effort on his part, but he'll move past it. He'll find a way to repair the damage he did, as long as he doesn't give up. I think Trey will forgive him. I hope you will, too."

"I have. I did."

Dan looked at her again. "Maybe in your head you have. Your heart might take a little longer. But that's what I'm saying. You're both still here, so there's a chance to fix things, to make them right again. For you and Matty and for you and Trey."

Baylee had to look away from her father's knowing eyes. She blinked rapidly and gazed out the window at the wildly overgrown wisteria bush outside the kitchen window. If Trey wouldn't talk to her, wouldn't return her call, wouldn't listen to her, how could she fix anything between them? Already a part of her dreaded ever speaking to him again, of hearing his voice tell her they were done. That it was officially over.

"That's it," Dan said, his voice breaking into her thoughts. "Dad's words of wisdom. Long overdue and probably not worth much."

"I appreciate it, though," Baylee said. At least Dan was trying to help, even if it was hopeless. "

She stood and so did he. "Bye, Dad. Thanks."

"Bye, honey. At least think about what I said."

"I will."

Trey could feel the black hole he'd crawled out of almost two years ago oozing up behind him, threatening to envelope him again. He remembered that crash and burn feeling, knowing he'd hit rock bottom, he'd lost everything, and he had nowhere to go but up if he wanted to survive. He'd hated every second of the climb back out of the dark hole he'd created for himself with drugs and booze to mask the physical and emotional pain he was in.

Somehow, right now, the lure of the black hole beckoned, called to him. In its comfort of oblivion, he wouldn't have to care, wouldn't have to think, wouldn't have to hurt. Wouldn't have to acknowledge that Baylee was gone. She'd taken off at the first sign of trouble, the first crack in his armor. The first time his past came back to haunt him in a serious way she bailed on him.

Although Dan had willingly given him Baylee's cell phone number when he explained why he didn't have it, he claimed not to know where she was. Neither did Ryan, nor Ryan swore, did his wife. She had a possible job offer somewhere in Florida, and she'd be in touch. That's all anyone seemed to know, including Matty. Trey had leaned on him at the animal shelter and reminded Matty that he owed him. He'd been certain Matty was telling the truth when he said he didn't know where Baylee was.

Damn her! He drove his fist into the kitchen wall. The old plaster cracked but whatever was behind it, a two by four or a brick wall held and Trey cradled his hand while his knuckles began to swell.

He stared at the coffee maker and knew coffee wasn't going to cut it this time. He needed a drink. A nice strong drink. Whiskey. Bourbon. Scotch. He didn't really care. Something, anything, to take the edge off. He didn't have to drive. He had nowhere to go, nowhere to be. He had no one. He also had nothing to drink.

Unless Grandpa Mike or Grandma J had left something behind. Trey began opening cabinets in the kitchen. He'd been through most of them and knew there wasn't much there. His grandparents hadn't been drinkers, although occasionally he'd seen Grandpa Mike share a beer with his dad. Grandma J had liked those sweet fruity frozen drinks and occasionally ordered one if they were out to dinner for a special family event. She'd get mildly tipsy and giggle like a little girl. Trey had thought it was funny.

But it gave him something to do, rummaging through the cabinets, searching high and low for a bottle of something. The kitchen turned up nothing unless he counted a bottle of red wine vinegar.

He turned on the light in the mud room and looked around at the shelves where Grandma J had stored old jelly jars and flowerpots. The gardening miscellany was a jumbled mess. Grandpa Mike had a shelving unit of his own which held jars of screws and nails and other hardware. Old doorknobs, an ancient drill, machinery parts and a few dusty tools.

Trey opened the cabinet beneath the big laundry sink and began removing half-full bottles of cleaning supplies, insect repellant and bug killer. Something dusty and dark brown glinted from the furthest corner. Trey shoved aside moth-eaten cleaning rags and a disintegrating sponge and reached for the bottle.

He had no idea how many years of dust coated the outside, he only cared about the contents. He stared at the label which was a brand of whiskey he'd never heard of. He unscrewed the sticky cap and sniffed the stale aroma of well-aged booze.

I don't give a damn, he reminded himself. He took the bottle out to the porch, settled himself in his favorite chair, propped his leg up and took a swig straight from the bottle.

It burned down his throat and hit his stomach in a most unpleasant manner, but he reminded himself once more that he didn't give a damn. After a minute or so, he swallowed another mouthful of the disgusting brew. Then another, and another, until he lost count. But who was counting anyway? He'd quit drinking as soon as he didn't hurt any more.

"Hey, Trey. You in there?"

Trey woke face down on his pillow with a blinding headache, a stomach threatening to pitch into the back of his throat and a gauzy-like blur around everything else.

Someone was tapping his shoulder and talking to him, but he couldn't quite discern who it was or what they wanted. He turned his head one degree and opened one eye to see his father bent over him.

He saw concern not condemnation in Andy Christopher's blue eyes and for some reason Trey suddenly felt close to tears. Before he could process the feeling, however, he leapt out of bed and made for the bathroom nearly knocking his father over in the process.

He dropped to his knees in front of the toilet, for once ignoring the protest from his right one because he had more important business to take care of. He heaved violently and repeatedly, vaguely wondering if everything inside of his body, not just the contents of his stomach, might end up in the toilet bowl.

Grandpa Mike's old whiskey hadn't tasted very good going down and it was massively disgusting coming back up. Trey vomited, flushed, gagged, threw up some more and dry heaved himself into exhaustion. He gave the toilet handle a final push and sat on the floor with his back to the tub berating himself for such a stupid moment of weakness. Hadn't rehab and AA taught him anything? Hadn't he learned to call his sponsor when he felt tempted to drink or start popping pills again?

He hadn't felt tempted, though, not for over a year. He'd lulled himself into a false sense of security, believing he was so strong he didn't need help from anyone.

He could hear his dad moving around in the kitchen. He wasn't ready to face him just yet. He hauled himself up from the floor and stripped off his clothes. He turned on the shower and stared at himself in the mirror until the steam obscured his reflection.

The hot water pouring down on him helped minimally. His head pounded and his throat was raw. He had a God-awful taste in his mouth that gulping water had no effect on. Truth was he felt shaky and weak as a newborn kitten and he didn't like the feeling. He also didn't like knowing he had no one to blame for his current state except himself.

Eventually he turned the water off and toweled dry. He brushed his teeth and his tongue which helped a little.

In the bedroom he donned clean boxers and a tee shirt and sank down on the bed, his mind a big ball of fuzz. Now what? He had no answer to that question.

His father appeared holding a bottle of water in one hand and a steaming mug in the other.

He had the same expression of concern he'd worn before, but Trey could see no judgment or disappointment beneath it. His dad didn't seem angry with him. He'd waited an awful long time for his dad not to be mad at him anymore and now that it was here, he didn't know how to react.

Andy handed him the bottle of water and set the mug on the nightstand. "I made coffee, but if you tell your mother I know how, I'll deny it."

A weak chuckle escaped Trey.

"Bad night?" Andy asked. The empathy in his tone pushed Trey further toward the edge. He was seriously in danger of completely losing it in front of his father.

He sat there on the bed, holding the bottle of water with both his hands. He twirled it around, peeling at the label with his thumbnails, blinking furiously.

"What can I do to help?" Andy asked. Trey lost it. No amount of blinking was going to hold the tears inside.

He shook his head. He didn't know how to answer his father's question. What was he going to say? *Just be my dad. Love me even though I screwed up. Don't be mad at me anymore.*

His shoulders heaved. His nose started to run, and the tears kept coming. He didn't bother trying to wipe anything away and it started to drip onto the floor along with the condensation from the water bottle and the little bits of the label he'd peeled away.

"Oh, now, son." Andy sat down next to him. As soon as Trey felt the weight of his father's arm across his shoulders, the floodgates opened completely. He was five years old again, in pain and afraid, and he needed his dad. He had no idea how long it was before he got hold of himself. Long enough for Andy to take a clean handkerchief from his pocket, wipe his face with it and pass it to Trey. Trey set the water bottle on the floor and buried his face in the slightly damp cotton. Calm washed over him along with a hundred memories of his childhood, brought home by the faint scent of the laundry detergent his mother always used.

He wiped his face, afraid it was going to take more than his dad's handkerchief to clean up the mess he'd made of himself. He grabbed tissues from the box on the nightstand to complete the job. His dad kept his arm around him, his hand on his shoulder.

"Couple of tough guys, aren't we?" Andy finally ventured.

Trey glanced at him sideways. Traces of tears glistened in his dad's eyelashes.

"Suck it up, walk it off," Trey agreed with a watery chuckle.

"Rub some dirt on it," Andy finished softly.

"Wow. Sorry about that." Now that it was over, Trey was embarrassed.

"Nothing to be sorry about."

Trey looked at his father directly. "I am sorry, though, Dad. About everything. I know I disappointed you."

"Hardest thing about having a kid. Watching them screw up. I hated every damn minute of it. Couldn't do a damn thing about it."

"Yeah." Trey picked up his water bottle and studied it some more. "I was trying—"

"I know you were—"

"But I screwed it up again."

"Maybe not."

Trey looked at his father again, afraid to hope.

"I've got a lot to be sorry for, too, son. Your mother says I've been behaving like an ass where you're concerned. I believe she might be right because she usually is. But if you tell her I said that, I'll deny it."

Trey almost smiled. "Seems like there might be a lot of things Mom doesn't know about you."

Andy grinned. "Maybe."

They sat in companionable silence for a minute before Andy said, "Think that stomach of yours can handle some food? If you tell your mother, I'll deny it, but—"

"Don't tell me. You're a gourmet chef."

Andy clapped him on the back. "Nah. But I can fry up bacon and scramble an egg every now and again." He stood. "Bring that mug of overpriced coffee out to the kitchen and let your old man teach you a thing or two."

Trey followed Andy to the kitchen. His coffee was lukewarm, but he drank half of it before refilling it from the carafe. Andy had bacon sizzling in a skillet and was cracking eggs in a bowl, tossing the shells in the sink. He threw a dishtowel over his shoulder and starting beating the eggs with a fork on his way back to the stove. He used the same fork to rearrange the bacon in the pan.

"Need any help?" Trey asked. "I don't guess your culinary talents extend to grits and home fries."

"Nope," Andy replied. "Tell you the truth we'll be in luck if any of this is edible."

"I'm pretty good with the toaster," Trey offered.

"Go for it."

A few minutes later they loaded their plates and went out to the porch. The sun was up, and while it was cool under cover, the day held the promise of heat.

Trey had given up the fight and downed a couple of Advil. The headache hovered around and behind his eyes, but it looked like he was going to survive. He'd noticed the empty whiskey bottle in the garbage can.

The breakfast was edible, but eating it reminded him of Baylee. After a couple of bites he pushed the food around on his plate before he gave up.

"Thanks, Dad," he said, pushing his plate away.

Andy glanced up from his own meal. "Seems like you've got more going on than just a hangover."

"She left."

"Baylee?"

Trey nodded.

Andy grunted. "Where'd she go?"

"Went to see about a job in Florida is all I know."

"Small town like this. You could find out. If you want-ed to."

When Trey didn't say anything, Andy pushed his plate away and sat back. "Do you want to?"

"I miss her."

"You know why she left?"

"When we got pulled over, she looked at me like she'd been waiting for something like that to happen. Like she knew I was too good to be true or something. She called me a liar."

"Did you lie to her?"

"No."

Andy ruminated for a minute. "You know what they say. When you point a finger at someone and accuse them of something, there's three fingers pointing back at you."

"What are you saying? She was lying to me?"

"Maybe she's been lying to herself."

"Wow, Dad. That's deep."

Andy flashed a smile. "Told you I could teach you a thing or two. I learned most of it from your mother, but if you tell her I said so—"

"You'll deny it."

"Right. Woman knows more about human nature than the two of us put together. I'll tell you what thirty-five years of marriage has taught me. People say things in the heat of the moment they wish later they hadn't. You can't take them back and sometimes you don't know how to apologize or you're afraid your apology won't be accepted. Sometimes you're so scared you're going to lose the thing you want the most you don't know how to deal with it. You willing to leave things between you and her the way they are?"

Trey hadn't really thought about it. He could barely get past the fact that Baylee was gone. But now that his dad had asked the question, he knew he wasn't going to let it go. He wanted to have it out with her. If she was going to dump him, she could damn well do it to his face.

"No. No, I don't think I am."

"Well, then, sounds like you've got some work to do." Andy pushed his chair back and stood. "I cooked. You can clean up."

Trey smiled. "Sure thing, Dad. Thanks."

Andy braced his hands on the back of the chair. "You know, you're not the only one who screwed up."

Trey looked at his father. Something passed between them that couldn't be put into words. "So are we good here?" Andy asked.

"Yeah, Dad. We're good."

As soon as his father left, Trey put in a call to Ryan.

"She shouldn't be that hard to track down," Ryan told him over lunch at the Mountainside Diner. I have an investigator I can call. It will probably take him a day or so to check into it and get back to us. If she's employed, it won't take long.

"Your wife's her best friend. You sure she doesn't know where she is?" Trey pressed.

"Jenny's as put out with her as you are. Can't believe she just up and left. She hasn't returned calls or texts, except she told Jenny to knock it off and she'd be in touch soon."

"This is all a bit out of character for her, wouldn't you say?"

"I'd say it's more than a bit out of character. According to Jenny, Baylee's barely set foot outside of Henderson or Asheville her entire life. The two of them have been closer than sisters since they were kids. For Baylee to take off and not tell anyone exactly where she is? It's definitely out of character."

As much out of character as it was for me to run to a bottle after all this time? Trey wondered.

"Call your investigator. Tell him it's worth it to me for him to make it a top priority."

Baylee walked out of the restaurant into warmth and dampness. What she hadn't remembered about Orlando, which apparently was the norm for most of the state of Florida, were the almost daily summer deluges of rain. She'd been caught in it a couple of times and had discovered her portable umbrella was not much of a shield against it.

Oddly the downpour never lasted long and when it was over the temperature had dropped from the mid-nineties to somewhere in the high eighties. During the day steam rose off the pavement, but in the evenings there was a soft, lush quality to the air. She breathed in the heat and moisture, so different from the crisp coolness of a North Carolina summer evening.

She'd landed the job James Falcon had discussed with her plus she hostessed a couple of nights a week at this steak and seafood restaurant. Three days after she'd arrived in Orlando, Trey had finally called her. When she saw his name on the list of missed calls panic set in. Although she wanted more than anything to hear his voice, she was afraid of what he might say. It had taken him so long to call, to acknowledge her apology, she'd had the thought that his belated effort was too little and too late. She'd listened to his voice mail message but she hadn't called him back. Not then and not after the other two times he'd called. She'd ignored his text messages in which he also asked her to call him. Maybe she'd waited too long because he hadn't called or texted in two days.

She approached her car with her keys in her hand, to see a male silhouette leaning against the hood, arms crossed over his chest. She wisely made sure to park as close to one of the light poles as possible and she could see the glints of gold in his hair. *Trey.*

Her steps slowed as she approached. His stance didn't change, but she knew he knew she was there. She stopped a couple of feet away. She wanted to run to him, throw herself in his arms, hope he'd forgive her, give her a second chance, but she was afraid he wouldn't. She was afraid she'd lost him forever. But if that were true, why was he here?

Though only a few feet separated them, it felt like a much wider gulf neither of them knew how to cross.

Was Trey waiting for her to say something? She didn't know what to say. But she couldn't stand the silence between them. "What are you doing here?"

"I came to see you."

Duh. "Why?"

"You promised you'd give me two weeks notice before you quit."

Baylee stared at him. Her leaving without notice couldn't possibly be the reason for his presence here now.

"I'm sorry now that I gave you a decent job reference since you left without telling me," he said.

Baylee didn't know what to say. She had the sense that Trey was toying with her, but she didn't know why. Why would he bother?

"Why didn't you return my calls?"

Shame washed through Baylee. She claimed to want a real, adult relationship with Trey, but she'd been acting like a sulking teenager, unwilling to acknowledge her own part in creating this distance between them. "I should have called you back. I'm sorry I didn't."

"Why didn't you?"

Out of the corner of her eye, Baylee saw the first sparkles of the Magic Kingdom's fireworks display. From her bedroom window she could view a different fireworks display put on nightly at one of the other amusement parks as well. She thought of that long ago wish of hers to live in Cinderella's castle, to create her own magic kingdom.

"Baylee?"

She took a deep shuddering breath. The very least she owed Trey was the truth, even if it was a truth she didn't want to acknowledge to herself. "I didn't call you back because I didn't want to talk to you."

"Oh."

"I was afraid you'd tell me it was over. Even though I knew it was—if I didn't talk to you, it wasn't official. I could still—hope."

"Oh."

Baylee wished Trey would put her out of her misery and get it over with. Instead, he said, "I've always thought that if you're going to dump someone you should do it in person."

Baylee stared at him. She licked her lips. Her mouth went dry. "I understand."

Trey inclined his head and locked his gaze on her even tighter. "Are you sure?"

Baylee nodded. "I'm sure." Uncertainty made her voice tremble. "It's really decent of you to come and do this in person."

"Do what in person?"

"Dump me."

"That's why you think I'm here?"

"I said such horrible things to you."

"You were upset."

Baylee lifted her chin. "I was scared."

"Of what?"

"You. Myself. Afraid I'd never get what I really wanted."

"What is it you want, Baylee?"

"You. Just you. You're all I ever wanted."

"Well, darlin', I'm yours."

She didn't consciously cover the space between them, but the next thing she knew she was in his arms. "I'm sorry, Trey. I'm so sorry."

"Me, too."

"You don't have any furniture," Trey noted when they arrived at the one-bedroom apartment she'd rented.

"I have a bed, which in some cultures is considered the most important piece of furniture in the home." She took his hand, and he followed her into the tiny bedroom. The queen-sized mattress and box spring set took up most of the space. An open suitcase held an assortment of clothing and toiletry items as did a couple of boxes pushed against the wall next to it.

Baylee started to unbutton her shirt. "Want to take a shower? After an evening at the restaurant, I always feel like I smell like food when I get home."

"Yeah, sure, but just, could you hang on a sec?" He looked around somewhat uncomfortably before his gaze came back to hers. "This isn't exactly how I planned to do this, but..."

Baylee's brow furrowed. "Do what?"

"Could you sit down here a minute?" Without waiting for a reply, he maneuvered her to the end of the bed. He tried to keep his focus on her face instead of the distraction of the unbuttoned shirt which offered him a glimpse of a lacy white bra.

"Trey..."

He pressed a finger against her lips.

He braced himself with both hands on either side of her and awkwardly dropped his left knee to the floor. An unwilling "Ouch" escaped his lips.

"Trey, you don't have to—"

The look in his eyes quelled her interruption.

"I do have to. Because the truth is, I don't think I can live without you. I found that out the hard way, which is the same way I seem to find out everything important in life. Usually, I don't figure it out until it's too late. But I'm trying to change that. Hang on."

He dug in the right pocket of his jeans and withdrew a ring. He held it out to her. Baylee gasped. Trey grinned. "Apparently I did something right."

He sobered quickly, though. He picked up her left hand and held it in his, rubbing his thumb along the back of it. "Baylee, will you marry me?"

"Really?" Her eyes filled with tears.

"Really. Forever," he assured her softly.

She swiped a knuckle under her eyes to brush away the tears and gave him a watery chuckle. "I think I know how Cinderella felt when Prince Charming finally tracked her down."

"Is that your way of saying yes?"

"Yes."

"Good, can I put this ring on you now? My knee is killing me."

He slid the ring onto her finger then braced himself once again on either side of her until he was in her space forcing her back on the bed.

"Shower," she suggested as he undid the rest of the buttons on her shirt and kissed her tummy. "I'm pretty sure I smell like fried shrimp and filet mignon.

He unzipped her pants and dragged them off. "What do you know? Two of my favorite things.

Hours later, after a reunion that had blown Baylee's socks off followed by a steamy shower, they were lying in

Baylee's bed. She stretched out against the length of him, and his hand played idly through her damp hair. "Why Orlando?" Trey asked. "What made you come here?"

"Besides the only decent job offer I've had in months, you mean? I was trying to get as close as I could to the happiest place on earth."

"Did you?"

She poked him. "Yeah. About twenty minutes ago."

"Ow." He grabbed her hand and turned on his side so he could look into her eyes. "You want to know where the happiest place on earth is for me?"

"Where?"

"Wherever you are."

The end

Epilogue

♥

The horse-drawn carriage drew up to the formal gardens of the Grand Floridian Hotel. Baylee flashed her father a quick smile. He in turn, squeezed her hand. As the carriage drew to a stop, a string quartet began to play *I Can Only Imagine*.

Baylee's grin widened, her heart ready to burst with happiness when she saw Lisa and Jenny. Her sister and best friend were wearing simple silk dresses in a sunny shade of yellow. Both clutched bouquets featuring a sunflower surrounded by yellow roses and greenery trimmed with navy blue ribbon.

Dan exited the carriage first and helped Baylee down the steps. Her gown was simple and strapless in a pearly shade of white trimmed with a navy blue band. Her bouquet mixed yellow mums with white roses surrounding a sunflower.

Jenny reached for her hand. "I can't believe this is happening."   Baylee understood what Jenny was trying to say only too well. Ever since Trey had arrived in Orlando she'd been pinching herself. She'd stopped waiting for something to ruin her happiness. Today was going to be perfect.

Even Lisa was smiling. Trey had insisted she take advantage of the hotel's spa along with Baylee and Jenny, and Lisa hadn't argued. The three of them had spent two days being massaged and waxed, buffed and polished, and generally spoilt by the luxury surrounding them. This morning they'd had their hair done and make-up professionally applied while they'd enjoyed a room-service champagne brunch.

Baylee looked beyond the entrance to see white chairs arranged in neat rows on either side of a brick walkway which led to a gazebo adorned with more flowers and greenery intertwined with ribbon in sunny shades of yellow and navy blue.

She stepped back behind a large hibiscus bush as Trey and his groomsmen approached the arched gazebo entrance where a podium was set up. Ryan and Andy wore dark blue suits. Trey in a black tuxedo nearly took Baylee's breath away. She couldn't help but sneak peeks at him from her hiding place.

"You've got the rest of your life to look at him," Lisa drawled. "Get a grip."

"Are you ready, ladies? It looks like everyone else is," Dan said.

The musicians had paused after the end of the tune. An expectant hush descended on the small group of guests. Josh and Jonah were there, Baylee knew, and could only hope they were behaving themselves. Matty, Trey's mother, as well as several of his aunts, uncles and cousins. Her father had invited a woman he'd met through AA to be his companion.

Lisa and Jenny took their places as the musicians began the traditional wedding march.

Baylee tucked her arm beneath Dan's. He patted her hand. "Are you sure about this, honey?" he whispered as they prepared to take the first step along the walkway.

Baylee's gaze caught Trey's at that moment. Her answer was there, in his smile, the look in his eyes, and the way he said, "Wow," out loud and made all the guests chuckle.

Her answer when it came, came from her heart. "I'm sure."

Acknowledgments

♥

As always, I thank God for every bit of writing talent and ability He gave me, and for the daily inspiration and assistance He sends me.

To Bill for everything he has done for me for the past 40+ years.

To Cathy, Sandy, and Danielle. They know why.

To my beta reader/editor, Alison Nissen.

To my cover artist, Steven Novak, Novak Illustration.

To my Facebook, Twitter, Instagram, TikTok, LinkedIn and newsletter followers for their support and feedback on everything from research to covers.

To all the members of Lakeland Writers as well as Novelists, Inc., and Florida Writers Association friends for their assistance and support.

Many thanks to Samhain Publishing, Ltd., who first published *The First Time Again* in 2013.

About Author

❤

Dear Readers,

Here's a little bit about me:

I am originally from Southwest Missouri and currently reside in Central Florida with my hubs and our rescue pup, Winner. The kids are grown and grandkids are arriving. I started writing fiction a very long time ago and for 18 years I worked for Starbucks. If I'm not writing I'm probably reading.

If you enjoyed Trey and Baylee's journey in *The First Time Again,* I hope you will leave a brief review on the site where you purchased it, and/or on Goodreads. Reviews are so helpful to authors, especially indie authors. I also hope you will tell others about the book. *The First Time Again* is the third in the stand-alone connected series, The Braddocks. The stories started with Rick and

Kaylee in *A Month From Miami* and continued with Ray and Haylee in *A Forever Kind of Guy*. Book four features Niko and Lesley in *What A Rich Woman Wants*.

I love hearing from readers. You can contact me, follow my blog, and sign up for my monthly newsletter at www.barbarameyers.com.

Wishing you all the best,

—*Barbara Meyers*

Also By Barbara Meyers

♥

Scattered Moments

Not Quite Heaven

Misconceive

Cleo's Web

White Roses in Winter

Training Tommy

Phantom (Manuscripts Under the Bed)

The Color of Nothing (Manuscripts Under the Bed)

A Family for St. Nick (Christmas Novella)

<u>The Braddocks Series (Connected, Stand Alone)</u>

A Month From Miami (Book One)

A Forever Kind of Guy (Book Two)

The First Time Again (Book Three)

What A Rich Woman Wants (Book Four)

<u>The Red Bud, Iowa Series (Connected, Stand Alone)</u>

If You Knew (Red Bud, Iowa, Series Book One)

If You Dare (Red Bud, Iowa, Series Book Two)

If You Stay (Red Bud, Iowa, Series Book Three)

Works in Progress/Coming Soon:

If You Touch (Red Bud, Iowa, Series Book Four)

Those Who Can, Date

Animal

<u>Barbara Meyers writing as AJ Tillock</u>

The Grinding Reality Series

The Forbidden Bean (Book One)

Cool Beans (Book Two)

www.ingramcontent.com/pod-product-compliance
Lightning Source LLC
Chambersburg PA
CBHW050949210726
48287CB00004B/1198